Praise for

Without Jenny

"*Without Jenny* is a heartbreaking journey of love and loss, of mourning and memory, of faith and doubt. Mark Gunther offers his readers a meditation on strength, courage and the healing power of family."

—RABBI NAOMI LEVY, author of *Einstein and the Rabbi*

"*Without Jenny* tells the story of Joy, who must find some way to remake a life and a sense of meaning in the wake of her young daughter's death, Anyone who has ever experienced a devastating loss will recognize the wisdom and honesty of this novel. Gunther vividly dramatizes how grief grants a horrible exceptional status that isolates us from others *and* makes us long to retreat from the petty concerns of the living. He also movingly depicts the loving embrace of family and friends, even when it can't be felt by the grieving person, and the courage it takes simply to go on surviving. There are no palliative proverbs here—no reassurance that suffering strengthens us, no sense that time heals all wounds. Yet we witness Joy fight valiantly with and for her husband and surviving child to be a family again, without Jenny but with the memory of her. This novel draws us intimately close to the mysteries of imperfect love and of human resilience."

—CATHERINE BRADY, winner of the Flannery O'Connor Award for Short Fiction

"A fatal tragedy can rip a family apart. *Without Jenny* immerses the reader in the unbearable pain and sorrow of child loss, yet love and compassion guide this family through the darkness to a place of hope, faith and healing. An absorbing read, *Without Jenny* shares the experience of all bereaved parents and can help inform the people who support them."

—JANET ROBERTS, editor, Grief Digest magazine

"*Without Jenny* is the page-turning story of a family who lose their ten-year-old in a tragic accident, and as such, it is a novel about grief. Grief is revealed in all its chaotic manifestations with realistic, unsentimental detail. First we see the family reel in shock and then we see them begin to navigate a no-man's land littered with landmines. Everything is now called into question.

"If we have ever grieved, this is our story, and we watch with sober clarity as the family constricts painfully from four into three. We watch, and our compassion is aroused not simply for the characters in this story, but for ourselves as well, struggling not to feel and also struggling to feel. Where do the dead go, this story asks, and Joy hears the voice of her dead daughter speaking inside of her.

"So the dead may live on in those who have loved them, and yet, can love ever really be stronger than death? Most marriages fail with the death of a child, each spouse endlessly reflecting the loss back at the other. What is the calculus, the magic formula that can make everything add up once again? The answer this breathtaking novel offers is going to surprise you."

—SHERRIL JAFFE, author of *You Are Not alone and Other Stories.*

"If there is nothing as whole as a broken heart, then Gunther's novel about the broken-heartedness that emerges for all who grieve offers readers a window into a paradox—how can so much luminosity emerge from such deep darkness? Protagonist Joy is our *psychopomp*, daring to guide us through the valley of death's dark abode, encountering so many layers of experiences in this mourning process—rabbi, synagogue, home and more, so as to emerge more whole and open to the holy within this devastating moment. Gunther's debut novel is part *Kaddish*, part *Cuckoo's Nest*—something every seeker yearning for the presence of the empty fullness of reality must read and reflect upon. Joy is the key to the wholeness that might emerge for every one of us broken human beings."

—RABBI AUBREY L. GLAZER, PH.D., Director of *Panui*; Research Fellow at *Katz Center for Advanced Jewish Studies*

Without Jenny

by Mark Gunther

© Copyright 2018 Mark Gunther

ISBN 978-1-63393-544-0

This is a work of fiction. The characters may be both actual and fictitious. With the exception of verified historical events and persons, all incidents, descriptions, dialogue, and opinions expressed are the products of the author's imagination and are not to be construed as real.

Lyrics in Chapter 11 from "Both Sides Now" by Joni Mitchell

Published by

210 60th Street
Virginia Beach, VA 23451
800-435-4811
www.koehlerbooks.com

WITHOUT JENNY

MARK GUNTHER

VIRGINIA BEACH
CAPE CHARLES

FOR ALL WHO GRIEVE

1.

MOMENTS LIKE THIS, Joy thought, *were dangerously close to perfect.*

Cozy inside her windbreaker, body wet and hot with the sweat of her workout, Joy rode her bike back across the Golden Gate Bridge, the early morning postcard view of San Francisco spread out before her. Black bay water slowly turned blue as bright swords of light sliced open a featureless gray sky, highlighting serrated blocks of pastel houses climbing the hill.

Ignoring her thighs' objections, she maintained an aggressive cadence against eight thousand miles of stiff Pacific wind. Dropping away from the bridge, Joy tilted her bike into the hard-right turn at the bottom of the hill, stood on the pedals, and pushed toward home. Joggers and dog walkers were randomly scattered on the shoreline pathway. Joy cut sharply right and stayed on the road, spinning quickly down the false flat, bouncing over the crummy pavement at the Mason Street warehouses. The day loomed—work and two school meetings and taking Jenny downtown and making dinner and putting Jake to bed. *I'll have to work tonight*, she thought. *Maybe not too late if Danny can get home early.*

She unlocked the basement door and pushed it open with the bike's front wheel. The basement was a riot of bikes and bike equipment, rusty garden tools and half-used bags of fertilizer, no-longer-needed-but-not-yet-discarded baby equipment and clothing, boxes of old college textbooks still waiting to be sold back to the bookstore, pieces of lumber emplaced for some theoretical future use, and dirty laundry piled high on the washer and dryer against the back wall. *I really need some furniture,* Joy thought. She balanced her gloves, helmet, and jacket on top of a pile of similar items already overwhelming a too-small bin, put on her cleat covers, took her water bottle, and went up to the kitchen to report in.

"Mommy!" Jake grabbed her leg. She dropped her arm to pat his head and her hand reached his shoulder. *Six years old. So tall already,* she thought. *My sweet boy.* She sat on a stool and reached down for her shoes.

"I wanna do it!" he said. Joy stuck out her feet. Jake found the clicklock on her cycling shoe fascinating. When he figured it out he had to show his dad and his sister and all of his dolls and everyone who came to their house for the next two weeks exactly how it worked. He still liked to do it, so Joy wore her shoes upstairs instead of leaving them in the basement where they belonged. *He wants to be with me,* she thought, *on the bike. This is as close as he can come.*

Jake took her shoes off and unzipped the ankle-high closures on her legwarmers. She peeled them off, revealing tanned, muscular legs in thigh-baring cycling shorts. Jake headed out of the kitchen to leave shoes and warmers at the top of the basement stairs.

"Nice legs," Danny said.

"You always say that."

"It's always true."

Danny stood on the other side of the island counter, silhouetted by the morning sun, a halo surrounding his close-cropped curly black hair, arms and shoulders thrown into strong relief. He was making sandwiches and serving breakfast. The counter was strewn with bags of bread and cheese, bottles of mustard and milk, boxes of cereal and cookies, a half-opened melon, two dirty white coffee cups and various pieces of newspaper. Danny's loosened tie was bunching up above the "I only look like a lawyer" apron Jenny had picked out for his last birthday. He had been a lawyer once, but was much happier now that he ran his own business.

Jenny sat on a stool next to Joy, still in her pajamas. Her head was in her hands, elbows on the counter, stubby fingers entwined in her curly back hair. Jenny looked worried, making Joy want to comfort, engage, direct, reassure, and snap her out of it. *Calm down,* Joy told herself, *she's fine, but something is up.* Joy waited for it, remembering how she had played for her own mother's sympathy.

"I don't want to go to school today, Mom."

"How come?"

"I don't feel good."

"Are you sick?" Joy put her hand on Jenny's forehead. "You don't have a temperature."

"No. It just feels like I should stay home today." Jenny focused her eyes on the comics page in front of her. Joy gently moved her hand to her daughter's shoulder.

"Did something happen?" Joy asked.

"I don't want to talk about it," Jenny said.

"Give me a clue?"

"Janie."

Ah, Joy thought. *Janie can be kind of bossy.* But normally she and Jenny were good friends. She wrapped a companionable arm around her daughter.

"Do you remember, I'm picking you up and we're going downtown? You need some boots."

Jenny brightened. "Girls day out!"

"If you go to school. Why don't you go get dressed?"

Jenny went upstairs.

"What do you think is up?" Danny said.

"Who knows? She's ten. It'll probably be forgotten by the end of the day." Joy got chips from the cabinet behind her, apples from the fruit bowl, and went to wrap the sandwiches.

"I'll get that," Danny said. "Have your coffee!"

It was one of his mornings with the kids, dressing, feeding, and transporting them before heading off to his Sausalito office.

"I'm here, I'll help. Good marital politics," Joy said.

"I'll put a point for you on the scorecard."

"I wish," she said. "I have to redeem it tonight already."

He grimaced. "I have a dinner."

She grimaced. "Well, try to keep it short, please."

It was one of their standard arguments. "Even though you bring in more money these days," she had said, "and my work is more flexible, it can't always be about you."

"Absolutely," he had agreed, but she still was the one who stepped up when he scheduled dinner meetings she only found out about at the last minute.

Jake came back into the kitchen and let Joy lift him onto his stool at the counter. His light brown hair brushed the top of his collar. He was growing it out. "Like Thor," he said. His hair was thin enough that the tangles weren't too bad. Jenny, on the other hand, would have dreadlocks if they weren't careful. Danny set Jake's toast in front of him. Joy poured herself coffee. Danny finished packing the lunches. He took off the apron and left it on the counter—*for me to put away later,* Joy thought. Jenny returned and sat next to Jake.

"Do you want jam, Jakey?" she asked him.

"I'll do it!" Jake said, but Jenny was already spreading the jam. She held the toast out to him. Jake grabbed it from her and shoved the whole thing into his mouth, bugging his eyes out. Joy and Jenny both said, "Yuck, Jake!"

Jenny shouted, "Jinx!"

Joy presented her arm to Jenny, who socked it lightly.

"Chew that up, Jake," Joy said in her best mother voice. "And don't do it again; you could choke."

Jenny bent down to tie her shoes; her socks showed through the holes along the seams.

"Jenny, those shoes are falling apart."

"I'm keeping these shoes, Mom." Jenny had painstakingly decorated her sneakers with little curlicues and paisleys and infinite box doodles in blue, brown, and black. They were beautiful, but completely broken down. *My mom never would have let it get that far,* Joy thought, but her argument with Jenny had been going on for weeks. *I have to make her replace them today.*

From behind Jenny's back Danny made a wide theatrical gesture and blew Joy a kiss. She remembered that very hot day in Berkeley at a 10K race in Tilden Park when the obviously Jewish guy in her start group could barely stop gazing at her hip-hugging spandex running briefs and midriff-baring singlet. He had blushed when she caught his eye, looking away, but after the start he found a way to get next to her. They had found a lot to talk about, when they had breath to spare. She was twenty-two and graduating, he was twenty-four and heading to law school at Berkeley. They had both grown up Jewish in San Francisco, gone to Lowell and to Cal, shared some of the same teachers, knew some of the same families. He had kept eyeing her body, kind of sideways, as if he wasn't really doing it, but he was, and she knew it, and she felt even warmer than the run and like maybe something important was happening. By the time they got to the finish they were so deep in conversation he didn't look at her body at all. She accepted a ride down the hill with him and they had coffee for hours on Telegraph Avenue. Now they had been married fourteen years.

"Time to go, children," Danny announced.

Jenny wiped Jake's mouth, cleared his plate, picked up his lunch, and stuffed it in his backpack. She helped Jake into his jacket and held out the pack. He thrust an arm through a strap and it settled on his shoulder. Jenny had the same jacket and the same backpack, something she had insisted on when they went back-to-school shopping in the summer. Jake had been incredibly happy about that.

Joy bent down and kissed her son.

"Mommy," he said, "can I come with you and Jenny today?"

Joy felt Jenny's eyes boring into the back of her head. Joy had promised her. "No, I'm sorry, honey, Jenny and I need to do girl stuff today. You need to stay in after school."

Jake looked at Jenny. "Will you say hi to me when you come?"

"Okay, but it'll be fast. Daddy will pick you up later, okay?"

He just wants more time with me. I'll make it up to him, she thought, *when Jenny gets older, but now I'm just the imperfect mom I am, I guess.* Joy wrapped Jake up in a goodbye hug. Jenny joined in, wrapping her arms around her mom and her brother.

"Jenny, wait your turn," Danny said.

Joy slung her other arm around Jenny. "It's okay, Danny, I have two arms."

Danny shook his head and turned away. He had told Joy more than once that Jenny was too jealous of any attention Jake received and that he should have more alone time with his mom. Joy didn't think Jenny was jealous, just that she was full of love and had to share it. Danny thought that was a recipe for difficulty later in Jenny's life, but Joy defended her daughter. She leaned against the doorway watching the circus make its way down the stairs and into Danny's Camry, then cleaned up the kitchen and went up to shower and change.

Crisp wool pants, a simple silk blouse, light gold chain. Dressing for the office made working at home much more palatable. Her only concession to home was bare feet, but shoes were in place at the foot of the stairs. Passing through the kitchen, she refilled her coffee cup and went to work. Her office had been added to the back of the house when they redid the kitchen, a year before Jacob was born. The décor was diplomas and family photos. A glass wall with a sliding door looked south into the yard, where natural light would touch the classic antique drafting desk she had found up in Amador City. Joy had painted the long wall in a durable, washable paint to allow the kids to write on it when they were with her while she was working. It currently held Jake's drawings of silly dinosaurs and the set design Jenny had done for her fantasy tap dance play of "Beauty and the Beast." Joy's workstation with its two monitors occupied the opposite wall.

On the drafting desk were sketches of three versions of a poster she was designing for Rachel, a new client who taught yoga at the gym. The stretched sweeping lines suggested the figure of a woman in *anjaneyasana*, lunge pose, against a blue and brown background hinting of earth and air. Joy knew the one she liked the best, but popped Rachel an email to set a time to review them together.

Joy had a new job to start this morning, a package design plan for an East Bay chocolate company. She started at the table with some quick sketching, then switched to the computer, scanning the sketches, trying out ideas, seeing how they would work on different shapes of packages, printing the better ones and sticking them to the corkboard above the desk. Soon it was 1:30. The time counter showed she'd be able to charge three and a half hours. *A good morning's work. Time for mothering!*

* * *

Jenny climbed into the car gripping her cell phone, immersed in a game. She dropped her backpack on the floor and buckled her seatbelt. Her phone chirped the end of her game.

"How was your day, sweetheart?" Joy asked.

"Fine. I had a math test. I got an eighty-five; we graded them in class."

"Did you see Janie?"

"Yes. She apologized."

"That's good." Joy remembered her teenage years of hormones and heartbreak, and for a moment wished she could save Jenny from all of that. They stopped at a traffic light. Joy looked over at her daughter and saw a woman, curly black hair cascading around her shoulders, her eyes alive; thoughtful, vital. *So fast,* Joy thought. *So fast.*

"I'm thirsty, Mom."

"We'll be downtown in ten minutes, honey. Can you wait?"

"If I have to." A large sigh and small cough accompanied the exclamation.

Down the street Joy saw the apartment building with the tall scaffolding that had been up for months. There was a place to park in the construction zone, empty of cars and trucks at this time of the afternoon. *Good parking karma,* she thought. A liquor store was across the street. She pulled her car to the curb; the scaffold came right to the edge of the sidewalk and blocked Jenny's door.

"You're in luck, Jenny. Let's go."

"I can't get my door open." She waved her phone at her mother. "Can I keep playing?"

Joy usually wouldn't leave her alone on the street, but it would only take a minute. Jenny was hardly a child anymore, and she knew about being safe in the big city.

"Okay. Just keep the car door locked."

She opened the door and the wind ripped it from her hand. She forced it closed and ran across the street and into the store. *I really should have made her wait for the water,* she thought. *I spoil her. But she'll have a long time to take care of herself. I like doing things for her. And there was that parking space.*

Suddenly there was a tremendous noise, an echoing, crashing, terrifying sound. The door of the store blew open and banged against the ATM machine; dust billowed in the suddenly stabbing sunlight. Joy ran to the door, and through the billowing dust and the sound of her own screaming saw a giant pile of wood and steel and tile where her car had been parked.

Oh god; oh no Jenny; oh Jenny oh Jenny, and her feet were taking her across the street and she grabbed a piece of wood that was sticking out and it didn't move and the next one she yanked didn't move either and the steel scraped her arm and she tried to crawl inside the pile to where she thought the car was and she threw off the hand that was pulling her away.

"Jenny, I'm coming! My daughter is under there! Help me. Help me get this off!" The dust made her cough. The blare of sirens approached as she fell against the pile, grabbing at anything, but two strong arms encircled hers and pulled her away.

"Ma'am, ma'am, get away from there."

A police officer. A woman.

"No, no, help me! My daughter is under there I have to get her! I have to get her!"

"Ma'am, we can't do anything right now. Help is coming."

Joy twisted and pushed, but the arms held her like iron. She ground her feet into the pavement but was lifted into the air and carried away.

Jenny must be dead; she has to be dead; she can't be dead; maybe the car protected her, but how can anyone be alive under there? The officer sat with Joy in the back of a police car.

"I can't sit here I have to get to her!" She tried to get out of the car but the hand was implacable.

"Help is coming. What's your daughter's name, ma'am?"

"Jenny. Jenny Rosenberg. Danny. I have to call my husband."

Joy fumbled with her phone and pushed the speed dial button showing Danny's picture. He picked up.

"Danny, Danny oh my god Danny! Jenny, Jenny, she's in the car and it's buried and she might be dead. Oh god Danny."

"Where's Jake? Where's Jake?" Danny screamed.

She remembered Jake. "At school. Go get him, go get him, take him home."

"No, I'm coming. I'll help. I'm coming."

"No, no don't! Don't bring Jake here. I'll see you at home. I have to go!"

But there was nowhere to go. The air was too thick to breathe. She dropped her phone on the seat and grabbed the door handle, but the hands restrained her. Outside the car a big machine and some men were working on the pile.

"I have to get out! I have to help!"

"No, ma'am, it's too dangerous. Let the men work."

O'Reilly, her badge read. She started asking Joy questions about her name and address and where she was going and what she was doing and why the car was there and had she seen or heard anything at all. Joy must have been answering because she heard the scratching of the officer's pencil, but the horrible crashing echoed over and over in her ears and everything else was in slow motion and happening outside her body. *This is the end of my life,* she thought.

She watched the backhoe extend its shovel and two men took a chain that drooped below the bucket and slid it under a collapsed section of the scaffolding. As it slowly lifted away, the debris pile shifted.

Joy screamed. Bile rose in her throat and she threw up out the window.

The men moved another section and she saw a huge piece of wood sticking straight up into the air. The ambulance crew crawled over the pile and they disappeared behind it and then soon, too soon—Joy knew it was too soon—they reappeared and climbed back out and walked slowly away.

"What are they doing? Why aren't they helping her? Oh my god they can't help her!"

O'Reilly wrapped her arms around Joy as she sobbed and screamed and just thought over and over, *Jenny's dead, Jenny's dead.* A paramedic came over to the car with Jenny's backpack and phone; Joy took them.

"Can I go say goodbye to her?" she asked. "Please?"

O'Reilly exchanged a glance with the EMT.

"I'm sorry, Mrs. Rosenberg," O'Reilly said. "Let me take you home."

* * *

"Is this my house?" Joy wanted to know.

"Yes, ma'am," said O'Reilly. "Let's go inside."

She offered Joy her hand; when Joy didn't move she reached down under her arm and lifted her out of the patrol car. O'Reilly kept hold as

Joy moved woodenly up the stairs. She fumbled for her keys; O'Reilly took them and opened the door.

Joy didn't want to touch anything, in this house where Jenny lived.

O'Reilly led her into the hall, past the stairs, past the wall covered with family pictures, into the living room. She sat with Joy on the couch under the window. A car door slammed.

Joy's body rose up and her feet took her to the hall and when the front door opened she threw herself at him. "Ah Danny, Danny. Oh my god. Jenny Jenny!" She wrapped her arms and legs around him and squeezed with all of her athlete's strength.

"What's wrong, Mommy, Mommy, what's wrong, why are you all dirty?" Jake was crying and pulling at her leg. Joy fell to her knees and held her son, sheltering him for one last second.

"Oh Jake," she said. "There's been a terrible accident. Jenny isn't coming home."

"Where is she?"

Danny fell to the floor with them and they huddled in the hallway, by the open door.

"She died, honey," Joy said. "She died."

"Can I ever see her again?"

"No, Jakey," said Danny. "We can't. No one can."

Jake's face crumpled.

"Ma'am. Folks." O'Reilly's voice cut through the moaning. "I'll need to be going, and you've got some visitors. I'm so, so sorry for your loss."

Joy's friend Carly was running up the walk, mouth open, face tear-streaked. Joy's father Hiram had left his car sitting in the middle of the street with its door open and he was close behind Carly. Joy screamed again, and they were wailing and huddling. Joy held on to Jake like she could actually protect him, and Danny had both of them wrapped in his arms. Carly's body pressed into hers and Hiram got in behind Jake with one arm around Danny and one around Carly. They all cried and moaned and screamed until things quieted enough for Carly to take them into the living room. She vanished and reappeared a few times and soon there were pillows and blankets and tea and cut-up fruit and cheese and chips and crackers in bowls with salsa and hummus, and meanwhile Hiram took Danny's keys and Carly's keys and moved all the cars around for legal parking. And Joy told Jake and Danny how it had happened.

* * *

Later that night, after Danny's parents, Jerry and Elaine, arrived from Calistoga, the doorbell rang. Hiram went to answer it and returned with a round-shouldered, clean-shaven man with a slight paunch and a kind depth in his eyes. He had a small *kippah*, skullcap, bobby-pinned to his hair.

"Rabbi Abravanel," Hiram said.

Rabbi said, "I'm so, so sorry."

Joy had only seen him from a distance before, from their seats at the back of the sanctuary on the High Holidays. "What do we do now?" she asked.

"I can help you," he said. "What do you want?"

Joy looked at Danny.

"I don't want to cremate her," he said.

Joy didn't like the idea of having an urn on the mantle or going to visit a set of ashes in a columbarium either.

"Okay," she said. "Okay."

Rabbi asked if they had cemetery plots, and when he found out they didn't he telephoned the cemetery and left a message to expect Joy and Danny tomorrow. He said it was likely the coroner would release the body to the mortuary in the morning, and they would have to go there to buy a casket and plan the funeral. He said the funeral should be on Wednesday, "because we Jews always bury our dead promptly," and with no embalming. The body belonged to the earth after the spirit was gone. He talked about the order of Jewish grieving practice: Seven days to be shattered, thirty days to be broken, a year to accommodate, and a day every year for Judaism to remember your dead. He talked about what they would have to do on each day and what kind of help they should have.

"It will be very, very hard for you," Rabbi said. "But the *shul,* the synagogue, is here to help, however we can."

Rabbi got his phone out again and left some more messages. He left, then, and eventually Hiram went home and Jerry and Elaine went to a hotel, but Carly insisted on sleeping on the couch. "Anything you need," she said. "Wake me up."

Joy and Danny and Jake went upstairs and lay down together in their clothes on Joy and Danny's bed. No teeth got brushed. No stories got read.

After Jake fell asleep, Danny wanted Joy to tell him every little detail. He made her describe exactly what happened, what she had seen and heard, what everyone had said. Where was the pile? What was she wearing? Did she see any of the car at all? Who helped her?

"I'm going there tomorrow," he said. "I will not leave you on that street alone."

But she always would be.

* * *

In the morning, Joy, Danny, and Jake still were heaped on the bed. Joy couldn't feel anything at all. Danny made her take off her dusty clothes and take a shower. Carly had made coffee and put out breakfast. Jake was eating cereal, and Joy thought it was good for him to do that.

"I called your mother," Hiram told Joy. "She got a flight and should be here tonight." He and Rose had been divorced for twenty years.

"I should have called her," Joy said.

"No, she's okay," Hiram said. "Ready to go?"

Carly stayed with Jake. Joy made her promise that she wouldn't take him anywhere except into the backyard, but only if he wanted to.

Joy and Danny sat together in the back seat as Hiram drove to the cemetery. They shopped for a gravesite and found the spot they liked. The director offered a "pre-need" discount and they bought six sites for the price of five because now they knew that you never know. Deeds were issued. Joy had never thought about a gravesite as owned property. Danny asked if there were property taxes and assessments, but the director said gravesites were exempt.

Then they met Rabbi at the mortuary. He had told them the night before to bring an outfit to bury Jenny in, and they both thought of the new dress they had bought for her tap dance recital. Which was weird, because real-life Jenny preferred big T-shirts and leggings and hardly ever wore girly dresses. Danny wanted Jenny to wear his Bar Mitzvah prayer shawl, and Joy agreed. She had put the dress on a hanger with the *tallis* draped over it and put it in an old suit bag from Macy's. In a separate bag were some panties and socks and old black leather shoes. Not her tap shoes. Joy wanted to keep those, and Danny agreed.

Mothers used to do this themselves, wash and dress their dead children for burial. Now someone else does it.

Rabbi had gently suggested Joy not view the body until the mortuary finished the preparations. *The repairs. Maybe it's better to remember her alive than dead.* But right now she couldn't remember anything.

They picked a plain, unadorned pine casket, sanded smooth, with gently knurled edges and a triple beveled top. Rabbi left them to go sit with the body and pray, relieving the man from the *chevra kadisha*, the volunteer burial society, keeping the Jewish custom of constant prayer and vigilance between death and burial so her spirit wouldn't get hijacked by a *golem* or become a *dybbuk,* or whatever else could happen to an uninhabited, untended body before it was buried.

Joy and Danny sat at the walnut conference table in the mortuary's quiet upstairs room. Together, they selected the appropriate mortuary services. She watched Danny approve the estimate and sign the credit card receipt; an unexpected chunk of frequent flier miles accrued. Joy accepted a little velvet bag holding the jewelry Jenny had been wearing and things from her pockets; she opened it and onto the table trickled her rings, earrings, necklace, some change, a hard candy, and two gum wrappers. She also was given a one-gallon Ziploc bag with Jenny's hand-decorated sneakers; the air had been sucked out of the bag and the shoes were grotesque. The man at the table with them said the rest of her clothes, unfortunately, were "unable to be preserved." *At least my daughter died wearing her favorite shoes.*

When they got home, Danny's brother Joey, his wife Leah and their eight-year-old daughter Sarah had arrived from L.A., and they did more crying and screaming, and soon after that Joy's childhood best friend Lizzie came in from Seattle with eleven-year-old Amanda, Joy's goddaughter, and they did even more crying and screaming. When Joy wasn't crying and screaming she was rooted in the doorway of the minimart with the crashing sound and stabbing light and billowing dust.

Later in the day, Rabbi came by the house to sit with the family and lead them in a discussion of Jenny's life, to help him compose a eulogy. You can't know someone's life until it's over, he said.

Her life is over. Mine, too.

2.

ON MONDAY, JOY was going to buy Jenny some new shoes. Today she was going to bury her. From beneath the weight of the covers Joy reached out her left hand and Danny was there.

"Oh, Danny." Her voice rose like smoke from her burning throat.

"I don't believe it." He paused. "Did you sleep?"

"I can't tell."

"Me neither."

They lay there. After a while he said, "I'll get Jake ready."

Danny had carried Jake into his own room after he fell asleep on their bed the night before. It had taken the focused effort of both of them to get him out of the clothes he had been wearing for two days and into his pajamas. The bedding rustled over Joy as Danny got up. She knew she had to get up, too. She forced her feet to the floor and lifted her hips, stacking them precariously on her legs, her body a set of unrelated parts only coincidentally connected. She wobbled to her closet, but it confounded her. So many things, so many wrong things, memories that belonged to someone else.

A shadow crossed behind her. In the closet's mirror she saw Danny, unshaven, in an old ugly suit. He mumbled something she couldn't hear and shuffled out the door.

He did it. I can do it.

She pushed through all the nice things she would never have any reason ever to wear again and found a drab black suit of washed-out cotton, a decades old hand-me-down of Mom's. It felt heavy as chain mail. The habit of hands and feet dressed her. Across the room on the vanity, bottles stood in an ordered row: face cream, hand cream, cleanser, sunscreen, moisturizer. She would sweep them all into the trash if she could lift her arm that high. A shrew stared back from the mirror, the mirror that Monday could barely contain her happiness. She had called out to Danny and he had come and embraced her and the mirror had shown her just what she imagined them to be.

Danny and Jake's footsteps echoed in the stairwell. Joy slipped on the staid old-lady pumps that had been Mom's too, and turned back to the mirror. The shrew had no comment. She put a thousand tissues in her pockets.

The door to Jenny's room stood open, the bed still unmade. Joy shook her head and thought, *Jenny, you can be so lazy!* And she turned toward the top of the stairs to yell at Jenny to "Get up here and make your bed now!" But dust clogged her throat and she had to hold the wall to keep from falling. She stepped into the room and it was full of her daughter.

Maybe she's not really dead; maybe if we don't bury her she's not really dead.

But sound and dust said no, Joy, she is, you saw it, you came home without her, she's dead. Joy closed Jenny's door. The little block *J* hanging on its outside rattled into stillness.

Joy went downstairs to wait with the family—brother, mother, father, grandfather. They sat, staring at nothing in particular, black clothes on white couches. Jake sat gravely next to Danny, his shoes bouncing arhythmically off the front rail. *How can he possibly understand this? It will break him forever!* But all Joy could do was straighten his little red tie and kiss his forehead. She sat. Her hands, unsupervised, ground another wet tissue to pieces.

Rabbi arrived, wheeling a large suitcase that had three stubby-legged chairs strapped to it. It was the synagogue's funeral kit, he explained, the things needed for the *shiva* services in their house this week.

"Shiva means seven," he said, "and in the first week we bring the *shul* to you, until the next Shabbat."

He unzipped one of the small side pockets and took out several small, round black pins with two inches of black silk ribbon hanging down.

"Pin these to your lapel," he said. Danny and Hiram each took one. "Tear it like this, from the bottom," and the ribbon separated. "Tearing shows how you have been torn."

Joy leaned toward her son. She barely had the strength to resist the gravity draining her soul toward the center of the earth.

"Do you want to tear this, Jakey?"

She took the thumb and fingers of each of his hands, covered them with her own, and together they pulled the two sides of the ribbon in opposite directions. She stabbed her thumb twice trying to get the pin through his lapel into the hook. A drop of blood formed. She fumbled her own pin to the ground. Trembling, Joy grabbed the lapel of her jacket and ripped it. She shook and radiated a low agonized sound. She stood in the minimart doorway, the noise, the dust-filled air surrounding her, the car buried, screaming echoing in her head, arms reaching out, scrabbling at the immovable steel, pulled away, puking out the back of the patrol car, going home alone. Calling Danny, saying for the first time, "Jenny's dead." The empty house, opened by O'Reilly with Joy's keys, waiting for Jake and Danny, falling to her knees, hugging the frightened little boy, indelible physical memory of that moment, the dark knowing she had changed his life forever. And again, the noise, the dust, the empty air, the quick violence, the fear, the . . .

"Joy. Joy!"

Rabbi was in front of her, firmly holding her hands. Everyone was staring at her. Jake nestled tightly against his father, his face a welter of fear and incomprehension. She had torn her clothes and groaned with pain and clawed at her own face in front of her little son.

"Jakey, I'm so sorry. I didn't mean to scare you."

She reached out to touch him. He turned his eyes away from her and leaned into his father's side. She touched his leg, tentatively. He pulled it away, solidly in Danny's embrace, his only living child. Danny fixed his eyes on her, demanding: Keep. It. Together. She looked away and sat, hands folded in her lap, close enough to Jake that he could touch her. He didn't.

Rabbi reviewed the week's schedule with them. "Be prepared," he said. "Many congregants will come. Everyone who ever knew you or your parents will come. Here, to your house, until Friday. You can come to the shul on Saturday to say *kaddish*, the memorial prayer, if you wish, but it's not expected in the first week. After the first week, mourners can come to the daily service at the shul to say kaddish in the first year. Or you could come weekly, on Saturday morning or Friday night. Find what works, but don't be alone."

That's what I'll be forever.

* * *

The mortuary chapel, painted in a timeworn institutional beige, had a twenty-foot ceiling and undecorated walls. Every seat was taken. People stood in the rear and crowded the side aisles, leaning against the wall. School families, shul families, their parents' lifelong friends, high school and college classmates, Danny's staff, their neighbors, the drycleaner and the shoemaker, people from their favorite restaurant, from the grocery store, people Joy had worked with over the years, from Danny's early law office, and even some of the neighbor families from where they first lived before their kids were born. Joy walked woodenly down the center aisle, holding Jake's hand, Hiram and Danny behind her. Hands reached up, lightly touched her arms; murmured words of condolence emanated from unidentified faces.

The small stage had a seating section for the family off to the side. She took the two steps up the stage and turned to the family section. Rose, Joy's mother, was there. They brushed cheeks.

Even as a child Joy thought her Mom had lived a desiccated existence. Attentive, competent—and lonely. Instead, Rose had studied. As a result, she gradually increased the Jewishness of their home until she met active resistance. The teenage Joy had no patience for that and even less for her parents' constant bickering. Hiram refused, as he said, to turn his house into some kind of a cultic museum, and after twenty-four years of marriage Rose stepped away. Hiram soon had a steady supply of girlfriends. And Rose was so happy and relaxed when she invited Joy over to her little apartment inside the *eruv* in Berkeley that Joy had to forgive her. The match with the widowed Rabbi Pinchas Gelberman in New York came four years later.

"Mom. I'm glad you came. I didn't know if you could."

Joy reached, awkwardly, to embrace her; Rose took Joy's hands.

"Joy, please. She was my granddaughter. You are always my daughter. You don't deserve such pain. I'm so sorry."

"Are you alone?"

"Yes, Reb Pinchas couldn't get away." She always referred to her husband as *Reb,* even in private conversations.

"Or he won't eat in my house." He was strictly kosher.

"Please, Joy, not today. I love you, and I loved her. I'm so sorry. *Zichrono livracha,* may her memory be a blessing. It's a terrible thing, but she's with God now."

"How do you know that, Mom?"

Rose patted her on the shoulder. Joy wanted to believe that Jenny was in a better place. But what could be better than living with your mother and father and brother and getting everything you needed while life carried you forward? Who made this future for Jenny? How could Mom even think that? *Of course,* Joy thought, *Mom's daughter is alive. Jenny wouldn't be dead if she hadn't had me. Maybe this is her fault, too.*

Arm-in-arm, Joy and her mother walked three steps to the front row. Joy sat Rose next to Hiram. He patted Rose on the knee and kissed her cheek. Joy liked that. Jake sat between his grandfather and his father. It was hard to look at them all at once, all these people that Jenny had been made of.

A lectern banked by flowers stood to one side of the stage and a large photo of a happy Jenny decorated the other. Joy wondered vaguely how the picture got made. She was the one who usually did that sort of thing. The casket sat stage center, quietly minding its own business, unfazed by all the people. Joy wondered if Jenny actually was inside it and she tried to picture her lying there.

"I can't remember what she looked like, Danny," she whispered to her husband.

"You still could go look at her now," he said.

"Come with me?"

"No. I don't want to see it."

A lifeless body in a strange, brand-new dress and black shoes, Danny's tallis draped over its shoulders. *It,* Joy noticed. *There is no her.*

Rabbi came to the podium. The whispering crowd quieted.

"With any death, the element of the incomplete is always present, but with a child it is overwhelming. So much of her life was not yet lived, her accomplishments forever unaccomplished. However, Jenny did not regard her life as incomplete, and so neither can we. We have only one reality, and in this one Jenny lived a life that was perfect, whole, and graceful. Her death is inexplicable, yet it occurred at the end of a chain of causes, as does every moment of each of our lives. The death of a child cannot be justified, or explained. Jenny was and will remain our leader by example, challenging us to live joyfully, lovingly, and with the kind of focus she brought to all her activities. Jennifer Hannah Rosenberg was born . . ."

Joy could never accept Jenny's life as complete. Sighs and chuckles emanating from the crowd showed the eulogy was masterful—clearly Jenny was recognized in his words.

What did Jenny look like? What does she look like now?

Danny squeezed Joy's hand, and she came back to the moment. He got up and approached the lectern. He embraced Rabbi.

I didn't hear what he said about her.

Danny began speaking. Joy shrank from the disrupted cadence of his voice. She knew his words, he had read them to her last night, but she could hear only total incomprehension as her man spoke of love betrayed by disaster.

She had tried to prepare something. She fumbled in her pocket for the piece of paper, held it in her hand while Danny talked, twisting it around, making little tears in the corners. Joy stood as Danny finished, seeing his tears through hers, his hand lightly caressing the casket as he moved toward her. They embraced briefly, avoiding each other's eyes, cheeks softly touching. Joy stood at the podium looking out at the crowd. She looked over at her family, her mother's face impassive, Dad with a half-smile, Danny's arm around Jake, all of them watching her. She turned to the front, notes forgotten as she crushed the paper in her hand, her voice quivering.

"Never in a million years would I have imagined standing here. We were doing so well! We were happy! I loved Jenny more than anything. I couldn't wait to see her every morning. She loved me." Tears streamed. She stopped, looking up. "The world deserved her. She deserved a whole life. I just don't understand this."

Abruptly, she turned away. Danny came to get her. Rabbi read the stanzas of the 23rd psalm in Hebrew and the crowd read each back, responsively, in English. Everyone stood. He chanted the ghostly *el ma'le rachamim*. He began the kaddish, haltingly, so the family could join: *Yisgadal v'yisgadash sh'meh rabba . . .* The congregation voiced the rhythmic responses. Joy stumbled over the transliteration. The prayer soon would be drilled into her memory.

The pallbearers, the men of her family, surrounded the casket. It rolled quietly on its gurney, industrial smoothness contrasting harshly with the jagged world it rolled through. Joy, holding Jake's hand, followed behind the casket, no longer of the community that was estranged by the living of their own children. Her torn lapel bounced off her ribs. She took refuge in the limo, with Danny and Jake and Hiram and Rose. Jake lay down on the wide back seat.

Hiram said, "Amazing he could write that after just a couple of hours with us."

"That's his job," Danny said.

Joy said, "I don't know how to do this."

"You will, honey," Hiram replied. "You'll have to."

"Oh, Hiram," Rose said, tiredly. "Give it a rest. Now is not the time."

It was a familiar argument to Joy, his willfulness, the deprivations of his Depression-shaped youth pushing, always pushing against the gentle nature of her mother.

"Will I, Daddy?" she said, for once taking Rose's side. "Can you make it okay for me?"

Hiram looked at her and held his tongue. Rose said nothing more.

"Let's just get through today first," Danny said. "I didn't know we knew so many people. Are they all coming over later?"

No one knew. Jake fell asleep. Joy watched weekday street life move slowly by as the procession wound through her city.

* * *

The cemetery was on a shallow slope with a western exposure, facing the ridge of green hills that were an inadequate barrier to the ocean fog that today rose in bilious gray clouds high above their crest. The limo drove up the hill slowly, past the older gravesites with their large, complicated sandstone monuments softened by a hundred years of aging, past the small family mausoleums of last century's rich, past the Russian section garish with a photo of the deceased on each brightly polished granite headstone, to the synagogue's small section where Jenny was to be buried. They had chosen—*Was it just yesterday?*—a site near the top, isolated, a place to be undisturbed. Joy imagined a little bench where she could sit each day and stare at the headstone, spending forever with her daughter.

The procession rolled to a stop. The funeral director took Joy gently by the elbow. Danny carried the just-waking Jake. Joy was gratified to see Hiram offer Rose his arm. They were led to a set of linked canvas chairs under a blue temporary awning. They all sat. Joy felt her family next to her, but the grave demanded her attention.

Jenny's grave. How do I have more tears?

The hole was dug with exacting precision, corners squared off cleanly. Four wide boards surrounded it, placed tightly to the edges. Two two-by-fours, about three feet apart, spanned the grave. The dirt was piled on a blue tarpaulin next to the hole, along with the neat stack of grass strips that would return lawn to the grave after the hole was filled.

The line of cars grew longer as the mourners arrived, silently gathering at the grave, their funereal black offsetting the bright green lawn and brilliant blue sky. They all turned toward the hearse. The casket moved efficiently onto its gurney and the assemblage rolled to the grass. The director placed a white bouquet on top. The casket was held for the last time as the pallbearers guided it.

High production values, Joy absently noted. Things proceeded on cue. Jenny would have appreciated that. The gurney stopped at the head of the grave. The pallbearers moved away and the casket had a brief moment alone, preparing. When finished, the Rabbi nodded and the casket was gently lowered into the ground.

Joy wailed. Tears came in rivers. Danny pulled away and took Jake into his lap. Rabbi came to Joy and took her hand.

"Come," he said. "We have something to do."

"Okay," Joy said. She stood.

Danny put Jake on the ground, and the trio approached the hole. They had each brought a token to leave with Jenny forever. Jake had a little toy truck. Danny had the flyer from the tap performance she would never dance. His tallis already was with her, in the casket. Joy had the first candle she and Jenny had ever bought together at the Japanese Tea Garden when Jenny was not quite two.

Then they each took a handful of earth and, one by one, dropped it onto the casket.

It can't be helped. This is what happens. I have to leave her here.

Hiram and Rose were next. Then Danny's parents and his brother. Handful by handful, into the grave. After the family, the friends, in a long, dark line led by Carly and Lizzie, each dispensed a shovel full of earth. Some held the shovel upside down, another Jewish custom unknown to Joy. Each spadeful undid the days of Jenny's life, one by one, back to the day of her birth. They came then, each one of them, to Joy and Danny and Jake, and to Hiram and Rose, gripping hands, wordless kisses, then melting back into the crowd. Joy and Danny stood near the grave's edge and watched the casket disappear.

The workers placed the vault. Danny's brother Joey and some of the other men took the shovels and put their backs into it, jackets flying, ties dangling. Carly, Lizzie, and a couple of the other women left to prepare the house for visitors. People began to drift away. Soon the grave was full. There was leftover dirt. *That makes sense,* she thought. *The casket gave itself to the grave and left some dirt behind.* She thought briefly she should take some home, but she had no way to carry it.

"Can we go now?" Joy asked.

3.

HOME DID NOT resemble the place she lived. People were packed in, shoulder to shoulder. The din was enormous. Joy fought suffocation on her own couch, defended by her women, Lizzie and Carly, stalwart on each side of her. Excruciating seconds ticked by.

"What time is it? Do I have to stay here?" she asked repeatedly. Like a concussion victim.

"You're home, honey," one of her girls would say. "Nowhere else to go. We have you." But Joy wanted only to go, to go where Jenny was.

One by one the guests came to her, and some part of her would think *Oh, this is a nice thing, I should remember this person was nice to me, maybe they'd like a drink, maybe Danny can get a drink for our guest.*

She remembered a husband, her lover. She wondered if he was home from work yet, and the crowd asynchronously parted to reveal him surrounded by his men, his brother, their fathers, others, his head in his hands. Looking in his eyes ripped her open. Rose sat in an easy chair, in the corner, with Lizzie's mom and a couple of other old friends. Joy would hear a small piece of a conversation and lift her head, try to understand it, and her shepherds would take it as a sign.

"Here, honey," the girls would murmur softly in her ear, "drink this, just a little water, eat this, just an orange slice, close your eyes, just for a minute, we'll be right here."

Once she heard the sound of the men talking. Someone laughed. "What could possibly be funny?" she asked her girlfriends.

"I can go find out," said Carly, but Lizzie put a hand on her arm.

"Let them be." she said.

Danny's brother Joey was on the phone in her office, behind the closed door, slowly cancelling Jenny out of their future. Danny had needed her help to find all the phone numbers. She could imagine the conversation: "Jenny won't be coming to camp next summer, can you please send the refund?" "Oh yes, we saw it on the news, so terrible." Getting an authorization to return the box with the new clothes; invoking the tuition insurance to make the payments to the school; cancelling the next hair appointment; cancelling the evaluation with the orthodontist. *No braces now, I can at least be grateful Jenny won't have to suffer that.* All the minutiae that made up the life of a ten-year-old girl taking time and thought and effort to end.

When Jake came to Joy, her heart would gladden and her face soften in the moment before his loss crushed her, but still she could take him into her lap hold him close with wooden arms, maybe say "I love you," but too often saying nothing at all. After a while, Sarah or Amanda would come looking for him and they would go off. She wondered what they were saying to him when she didn't know what to say. Some brave parents brought their kids, Jenny's friends, the little girls from the sleepovers, not so little any more, but still hesitant and afraid, mumbling something about how they liked Jenny, staying glued to their mothers. Allie was different. She held out her hand to Joy.

"I'm sorry, Mrs. Rosenberg," she said. "I asked my grandma to find Jenny and take care of her in heaven. I know they are both in heaven."

Joy reached past the barricades, taking the proffered hand with both of hers, saying "Thank you, honey, thank you so much. Thank you for coming. Thank you for remembering her. I'm sure your grandma heard you and is looking forward to playing with Jenny, too."

Allie slipped back against her mother.

"We just lost Mom a few months ago. Jenny was her favorite of Allie's friends," said Allie's mom, arm protectively around her. "She liked how forthright she was."

"Yes," Joy said wistfully. "She certainly was that."

"We all will miss her, Joy. I'm so sorry. Whatever we can do . . ."

Joy thanked Allie's mom for bringing her. She would never know them like this again, these vibrant girls she eavesdropped on when they inhabited the backseat of her car, sweet girls soon enough to be women with men and breasts and children of their own to lose, growing up with the ever-shrinking memory of someone they knew in grade school who got killed when a building fell on her (what was her name?), going on to full lives, their parents filled with joy and pride at their accomplishments, the Bat Mitzvahs or confirmations or *quinceaneras*, the graduations, the weddings, grandchildren coming, everyone's perfect happy life going on and on while Joy stayed glued to her couch, shrinking, cadaverous, clutching the ever-more-distant memory of the daughter she once had, the forever dead ten-year-old, the most consequential thing ever to happen to her.

* * *

Wednesday. Thursday. Friday. Danny's staff closed the office down at 2 PM each day. Only his secretary was Jewish, but all eleven of them came each day. Danny showed her the sales guys furtively checking their smartphones. *I might lose him to these people*, she thought. He would go back, business would flower, they would need him and love him and crave his presence while she still would be couch-bound and bereft.

Each afternoon the house inhaled strangers and their food, and exhaled them in the early evening. They came in a constant parade, these mourners, by the dozens. Joy received them all. The honest ones looked at her, simple looks, held her hands and ventured a kiss with closed eyes, a whispered condolence. The dishonest ones chattered on gratingly about death, life, purpose, reason. Joy wondered about the ones who didn't come at all, didn't want to know, couldn't tell their children, paralyzed by the fear. Who has the courage to stay with the wizened witch, the shrew? Who walks that road with her? Only those who need no invitation.

As the sun approached the horizon each day, Rabbi would clear his throat and everyone would stand. *Mincha*, the afternoon service, was recited quietly, often in silent meditation, the spirit of fifty people lifting the house against the pressing weight of grief. The family said kaddish at the end, in call and response with the congregation, a prayer for the dead without a mention of death. It took a certain kind of genius for the medieval rabbis to make that choice for the prayer of remembrance, Rabbi had said, life's divine prevalence a counterweight to the pernicious backdrop of death.

People shared memories of Jenny, of Joy and Jenny, Jenny and Jake, and when the room fell quiet, after the stories, *Ma'ariv* was said, the evening service, another kaddish. The house would empty.

Joy and Danny sat, immobile, until someone told them to go to bed.

4.

THERE WAS EVENING and there was morning on the sixth day, the first of a lifetime of transformed Shabbats. She hardly had eaten since Monday. Everything was ugly on her caved-in body, grief denying her even the simple act of standing erect.

Lizzie and Amanda came to stay with Jake while Joy and Danny went to the synagogue. Back when they had joined, in the self-directed confidence of their young family life, Danny had wondered if they really needed to become members. "Couldn't we just do fee-for-service?" he asked her, but to Joy it was the civic-minded thing to do. Take her place, preserve the institution, stand up and be counted on the High Holidays. Today, the memory of that arrogance burned as Judaism, in its patience, held her. Her disaster was not survivable; she was neither strong nor solid, just one more Jew living one more disaster in a history laced with them.

They parked in front of the synagogue's tired old building in a residential Richmond district block. The sanctuary was on the second floor. The rumpled man at the top of the stairs wore a comfortable suit without a tie, jacket unbuttoned, his tallis draped around his shoulders, a pin reading *Host* prominent on his lapel.

"I'm so sorry for your loss," he said. "May her memory be a blessing."

He knew them. It couldn't be helped. *Who would have thought I would need this?* Joy thought. He handed them their prayer book and *Chumash*, the Torah with commentaries, and opened the sanctuary door.

The service was already underway. Joy led Danny to seats in the front where she could see no one. She had no Hebrew, only rote memories of certain prayers and the rhythm of certain chants, so she used the transliterations when they were there, or read the English, or just sat and tried to be touched by the vibe of the place, to let it be whatever it was, or could end up becoming, to her.

Can I pray? Where, Oh Lord, where is my Jenny?

Singing, some of it familiar. Standing as the Torah scroll was paraded by, Joy touched it with her prayer book, kissed the book, waited, and sat when the scroll was opened. One by one the seven sections of *Vayera*, the day's *parasha*, Torah portion, were chanted in Hebrew. She read the English commentaries, newly vulnerable to the power of the story. Today's *parasha* had a lot of well-known action— the birth of Isaac, the exiling of Hagar, and the almost-sacrifice of Isaac, the *Akedah*.

Joy never had thought of Torah as living literature, as something she actually could hear, could feel and have a response to as she might to a bestselling novel. She was jealous of Sarah's happiness over the birth of Isaac, and angry at Sarah's jealousy, forcing Abraham to exile Hagar, mother of his own son Ishmael. She despaired with Hagar, sitting in the desert, sure her child would soon be dead. Joy had been unable to hold her dying child. No angel interceded; no one came to delay the scaffold's crash so Joy could slip in underneath and pull her daughter out.

Joy was shocked at the insanity of the *Akedah*—Abraham lying to his family, traveling for days, and then binding his only son, lifting the knife, ready to kill him to prove—what, exactly? Faith? Obedience? Obsession? Her child had been sacrificed for nothing. A bottle of water. Abraham will never forgive himself, she thought, when he comes down from his frenzy. How could any parent? At least God sent him a ram to sacrifice instead, but God couldn't send Joy anything to keep her from leaving the car there at that time, anything to make Jenny come into the store with her mother. Anything.

In the quiet moments it seemed that her sobs filled the sanctuary. She calmed as the last reader lifted the Torah, spreading the scrolls wide and turning so all could see the hand-scribed text.

Torah: law, story, idea. But what is prayer? *I want an impossible miracle. Does God change the world? For me? Did God kill Jenny? Call Jenny? How? Why?*

The mourners' Kaddish came at the end of the service. Everyone knew. Rabbi named the long-established dead whose *yartzeit*, annual remembrance, was in the coming week. He named the recent dead of the past year. And the newly dead? Only one. Rabbi compared the death of Jenny to the binding of Isaac. Joy didn't get it. Joy knew they were supposed to stand up but she wasn't sure when exactly, and she couldn't see anyone else, so she asked Danny, and he said he was new at it too, but it was obvious and they stood with the others who remembered.

Fifty-one more weeks. Fifty-one more years. Forever.

"How do you survive it?" She could hear the unspoken question asked from the shallows, as she and Danny fled. He found their car.

"How do we do this every week?" Joy asked.

"We don't have to," he started.

"I want to." She wondered why and didn't know.

"Okay," he said.

"Let's go," she said. "Jake is waiting." The authority in her voice surprised her.

"Just another minute." Danny was breathing deeply. White-knuckled hands gripped the steering wheel in the ten and two position. She put her hand on his arm; it landed like a butterfly, softly. He didn't react at all.

She felt a disconcerting kindness emerge. "You don't have to come every week with me, Danny."

"I can't let you come here by yourself." He was still looking ahead.

"I won't break."

"No, Joy, I will. Sitting there by yourself with everyone looking at you, and me sitting at home by myself, looking at nothing? I couldn't stand it."

She loved him. It hurt a lot.

He started the car, but they didn't go anywhere. The fan blew warming air as they sat.

"My Dad said he'd watch Jake every Shabbat," she said.

"We're lucky he lives here. After a while Jake's friends' parents can take him."

"Maybe after a while. Maybe he should come."

"Maybe."

Another moment passed.

"Danny, we can't lose track of Jake, he isn't going to know what he needs. God, he's only six; he's going to have a dead sister his entire life."

"Terrible," he said. "Just terrible."

He put the car into gear. Joy stared straight ahead. Another wet tissue disintegrated in her hand.

At the front door, Jake came to her. She dropped to her knees and hugged him. He studied her face.

"Are you sad, Mommy?"

"Yes, honey, I'm so sad."

"Is Daddy sad, too?"

"Yes, sweetheart. We're both sad, but we love you and we won't be sad all the time. Did you have fun this morning?"

"Mandy and Sarah went to Chestnut Street," he announced. "Can we play a game?"

Joy's body went rigid. Her knees ached. Tears streamed down. She couldn't stand. She couldn't lift her arms.

Carly came into the hall, rescuing her. "I'll play with you, Jakey," she said.

"Can we juggle?" he asked. Carly, who had studied clowning before law school, knew how.

"Good idea. I'll teach you. C'mon."

Carly touched Joy softly on the cheek, brushing a hair from her forehead. She put two fingers to Joy's lips, brought them to her own mouth and kissed. She swept Jake into her arms and hustled him up the stairs. He looked back at Joy. From her knees she watched them go. She was alone in the hallway. Everything was so high. So far away. Was this what the world had looked like to little girl Jenny?

Lizzie came in, reached down, and took Joy's hand. Sweet, sweet Lizzie, frizzy blond hair, piercing blue eyes, wide face, black dress draping her breasts, nipped in at the waist above her wide hips and sturdy legs. Joy and Lizzie. Best friends always, through grade school, high school, college, inseparable, always finding their way together. When they were teenagers they would meet before school in one of their secret places and talk about homework and movies and rock stars and the mean girls and which boys were cute, and which were bad and which girls they thought were doing what with which boy, and whose mom should learn what from the other's, and thousands of other things. But when they were little they built worlds. One time they played hospital when Joy the mommy and Lizzie the doctor had a baby. Cradling the doll, they named her Jenny. Sweet Jenny, Charming Jenny, Wild Jenny.

Dead Jenny. Is it lonely, Jenny, where you are?

Joy held tightly to Lizzie's arm.

Lizzie said, "I've got you, Joy. Let's go sit down." She sat Joy down on the couch. "Let me get you something."

Joy could see the dining room table filled with platters of cookies, muffins, bread. It was the first time the room had been empty all week.

Lizzie returned with a plate of fruit. "Here, honey."

Joy took the plate and put it down. She gestured at the dining room. "Why did people bring all that stuff? We'll never eat it all."

"Most of it is getting donated. Your dad already filled the freezer."

"He would," Joy said.

Hiram's parents had lost their tailoring business in the Great Depression. They moved to a tiny flat in West Oakland. His mom took in washing, and his dad picked up work loading gypsy trucks outside the Port of Oakland, one eye always open for the Teamster goon squads. Later on, his mom had a bookkeeping job with the WPA, but Hiram's dad never really recovered. He died of a heart attack at fifty-four. Joy never knew him.

Lizzie picked up the plate again. "Here, sweetie, let's eat something."

"I'm not really hungry."

"Joy, you have to start eating again, you're just skin and bones. Try please, for me?" Lizzie batted her eyelids coquettishly, her face a catalog of feeling, concern, care, maybe even a little anger.

Joy took a piece of pineapple, put it in her mouth, chewed, swallowed. "There, I did it."

"That's great, Barbie. Now finish the plate."

"You haven't called me that for a long time."

"You never had the boobs, but you always had the clothes."

"Then Mom would get upset when I got dirty."

Jenny's final set of dirty clothes was in the undone laundry downstairs. One more thing to cry about. Lizzie handed her a piece of cantaloupe. Jenny had been wearing a San Francisco Giants Orange Friday T-shirt on Monday. One more thing to cry about. Joy settled into the crook of Lizzie's arm. Lizzie picked up a strawberry and put it in Joy's mouth. It tasted good.

"This is getting way too maudlin," Joy said. "Give me the goddam plate."

Danny came in. Stacked on his plate was a sandwich, a pile of fruit, and two cookies. He looked at her plate, then at her.

"That's a little ascetic, Joy, isn't it?"

They looked at each other and giggled.

"That is a welcome sound, you guys," Lizzie said.

"Here, Joy, take a bite." Danny held the sandwich out to her. "Rye bread, turkey, cranberry, lettuce."

It was good! The Common World was knocking on her door and she was too weak to resist.

"Maybe I will have one."

Lizzie gave a happy little clap and bustled out. Joy watched Danny eat. Lizzie came back in with a sandwich and a glass of wine. Joy raised her eyebrow.

"The wine's for me. Thank God you at least want a sandwich."

Joy was overcome with love for her. "Lizzie, you can go home. You've been here all week."

"A few more days. I don't want to be anywhere else. If you want to get rid of me, start eating more! You should know, Carly is taking care of your dinners for the next month. When people ask what they can do, she assigns them a day. You'll find Tupperware on your front porch every afternoon."

Joy began to protest, but Lizzie didn't let her get a word out.

"No, Joy. You will accept this. Your friends want to give you something. And you are in no shape to go to the grocery store tomorrow. It's good for everyone."

Joy shut up. They ate. They finished. They looked at each other. Lizzie cleared the plates. It was too quiet. Danny took the plunge.

"You want to go for a walk?"

"Okay. Jakey too."

"Of course. Everyone."

They went upstairs to change and heard laughter coming from the juggling lesson.

"Thank God for Carly," Danny said.

"For everyone," she said.

"I know," he said. "Joey was on the phone for hours. I'm so glad I didn't have to do it."

They stopped and held each other. It was the first time they could. He was warm and strong and big and comfortable. She recognized him. Joy thought that perhaps she wouldn't die today.

Danny whispered to her. "I don't know how to think about it. It's so horrible but life itself is so ordinary. He was making these calls and we were making these stupid jokes and she was barely gone. I just don't know."

Joy didn't know either.

The door flew open.

"Aunt Lizzie says we're going for a walk. Can I get ice cream?"

They looked at each other. It begins.

Joy hated it, but she said, "We'll see, honey. We're going to the water first. Do you want to bring your ball and glove?"

5.

JOY REMEMBERED SEEING the moon. Now, grey light was peeking around the edges of the bedroom blinds. It must be the next day. She rolled over and sat up. The bedroom was cool. Her feet found her pajamas on the hardwood floor. She couldn't remember taking them off. She put them on. Danny had bought them for her. They had little bicycles all over them. She liked bicycles. She had thought that was sweet, before.

Eight steps usually took her across the bedroom. It did today. She wondered why she remembered that. When finished in the bathroom she walked quietly on the runner in the hallway, and padded down the stairs.

Coffee's aroma permeated the kitchen. A return to routine. Danny always set the auto timer for her before he went to bed, especially on her training mornings, so she could save the minutes it took to brew. She liked that he took care of her, and he liked that. She sheltered briefly, there, but then the crash echoed, the dust billowed, the sunlight stabbed, the scream locked in her throat. She had to brace against the counter to keep from falling. When she was sure of her footing she filled a mug and fumbled her way to a chair.

She heard Danny come downstairs. The front door opened and closed. He must have picked up the newspapers. She watched him come into the kitchen and take some coffee, then disappear into the den. That was where he liked to drink his weekend coffee. She went in and sat next to him on the couch. They held each other's hand for while. Then they didn't. She leafed through the *San Francisco Chronicle.* She put the paper down and stared for a while at the blank flat screen TV on the wall. Danny took their cups to get some more coffee. Then he came back. She leafed through the *New York Times.*

"Mommy!" Jake was calling her. Joy remembered that he was her son and she of course had to take care of him. She went upstairs. He was curled up under the covers, hugging Jenny's favorite stuffed bear, Teddy, and sucking his thumb. Joy lay on the bed next to him and rolled close. She gently pulled his thumb out of his mouth. He opened his eyes.

"Do I go to school today?"

"No, honey. It's Sunday."

"Is Daddy here?"

"Yes, honey. It's Sunday."

"Can we have breakfast?"

Joy thought to herself, *That's a good idea.* She asked him, "What do you want?"

"What would Jenny want?"

Joy turned to ask her. The dust billowed. She controlled her tears and turned back to Jake.

"What do you think, honey?"

"Jenny liked waffles. Can Daddy make waffles?"

"I think so. Let's go see."

Neither of them moved. Maybe they fell asleep again.

"Can we make a waffle for Teddy?"

Joy didn't know if that was a good idea or not. It might be a bad idea. It might not matter at all. Maybe Teddy would eat the waffle. Maybe Jenny would reach down from wherever she was and take the waffle. Maybe a waffle was too sticky. Maybe it would be easier for her to deal with a pancake. A silver dollar pancake would be good; smaller would be easier for her to take. But Jenny liked waffles better. Maybe if the syrup was warm she would come and eat a waffle. Maybe if we just imagine waffles she'll have a waffle wherever she is and we don't have to make one here. But maybe we have to make one here so the possibility of her having one there exists. Maybe she doesn't like waffles anymore, where she is. Except they probably have a lot of waffles there.

"Mommy?"

Joy looked up.

Jake was standing by the door, Teddy dangling from his left hand. "I'm hungry."

How did she miss him getting up? Joy levered herself out of Jake's bed. She took his right hand, and they went downstairs. Jake went to Danny and hugged his leg. Danny patted him on the head. Jake had flour on his head. Danny was making waffles. Joy wasn't surprised at all, but she remembered that a couple of weeks ago they had run out of syrup and Jenny had to put honey on her third waffle.

Joy cried for a while.

Danny looked at her. "Tissues are over there. I didn't know what to do. I thought I'd make waffles."

"Okay," Joy said.

The front door opened and Lizzie came in with a shopping bag. She had gone home to Seattle for three days and come right back again. She unpacked a bottle of pure Vermont maple syrup. It was the most marvelous thing.

Joy sat at the counter with Jake in her lap and they watched Danny work. Joy remembered Jenny, at age four, watching her dad separate eggs for waffles. "It's dumb, Daddy! Both parts of the egg go in the batter, right?" Then he whipped the whites to their rigid frothiness and Jenny was enthralled, pestering him so much that after breakfast he baked a poppyseed cake with her because it used four separated eggs. Poppyseed cake became her go-to kitchen activity. She had baked one recently. The cake was in the freezer, behind the bags of leftover muffins, challahs, and cookies. Joy remembered, and started to wilt.

Jake jumped down off her lap and went into the den with Lizzie. He must have felt it. He was leaving her too. *Makes sense,* Joy thought. *I lost his sister.* She heard Lizzie reading him *The Lion, the Witch and the Wardrobe.* She stood. Her hands were itchy, pulsing, clutching and opening.

Danny said, "I can't believe I just did this with her."

"You didn't need to do anything. We still have so much food."

"Right. Thank you."

He kept at it. *Of course he did,* she thought. *That's what he does.*

He poured the first batch into the waffle iron.

She tried again. "Amazing that Lizzie brought syrup."

"I called her."

Of course he did. She sat down.

She stood up. "Maybe I'll set the places." It was nice to be busy. Jake and Lizzie came in. The four of them took their seats. Joy had set five places.

Danny made a gentle joke. Lizzie said "Look, Jake, there's a place for Teddy!" She put two pillows from the den on the chair. Teddy's head just appeared above the countertop. When they finished, Lizzie washed the dishes. Joy watched Danny clean the waffle iron. The entire arc of waffle-making was clear to Joy: resources, construction, fulfillment, caring for his tools—his cleaning was scientific, and the waffles were always good.

This is the way he will conduct his grief.

Strange that she had never really noticed how he cleaned the waffle iron before. She must always have been on to the next thing already: Who she was. There wasn't a next thing at ten AM on this second Sunday of her bereavement. Probably no one would stop by today. No one had stopped by yesterday. A Tupperware dinner should appear on the porch later.

Sitting alone in the clean and empty kitchen, Joy wondered if the boys had taken Jenny to tap. Danny and Jake would do that Sundays, so Joy could ride her bike. Why wasn't she on her bike? Then she felt the dust in her eyes and the weight of the pile and the rawness of her throat. The wound was not cauterized.

She found her boys in the den with Lizzie. Now Danny was reading *The Lion, the Witch and the Wardrobe* to Jake, and Lizzie was reading the *New York Times*.

Lizzie looked up and threw her arm across the back of the couch. "Sweetie, come in and sit down over here next to me." Joy thought she could do that.

Joy curled softly up against Lizzie and pulled the afghan over her legs. Lizzie stroked her hair. She looked at Danny and Jake, reading the book, and loved them. Her heart broke.

Later on they took a walk.

Eventually the day passed.

6.

IT WAS THE third Shabbat after. Joy and Danny sat alone in the front row. The Hebrew she had given up trying to follow washed over her; it felt reassuringly ancient, a language of rhythm and image, stirring feeling and memory from somewhere deep within. Today's Torah portion was *To'le'dot*, beginning with the birth of Jacob and Esau and ending with Jacob's terrified flight to Haran, where he eventually wed the sisters Leah and Rachel. Joy was surprised at Jacob's venality, forcing a starving Esau to trade his birthright for a bowl of soup. An indefensible crime of opportunity. But even that wasn't enough for him. Jacob hid away in Haran for fourteen years and then, despite being welcomed home by his brother, connived with his mother to steal Esau's blessing at their blind father's deathbed. Creepy. Power, duty, honor, lies . . . Joy was glad she wasn't a man. Joy remembered the death of Sarah from the previous week. Such a long life, and at the end of it both generosity and fear. Abraham built her a shrine and she had many descendants. Her Jacob had no competition for his father's blessing. Joy was the matriarch of an infinite line of forever-unborn women.

Rabbi smiled at her. Their family was a symbol to him too, she realized, a part of his teaching, a pseudo-Biblical tragedy in his own congregation, to teach compassion and mindfulness through the power of his metaphor. What would his teaching be when wisdom's currency was modeled by some other happening?

Are you that capricious, God, that you involve yourself in my family's affairs like some jealous Olympian? Did you really inscribe this sweet child in the book of not-life? Did Jake earn the punishment of a life without his sister?

Joy stood as the Torah was carried past, touching with her prayer book, bringing the book to her lips. All of the words, the ideas, the stories, the love, the brutality of God's victories and punishments—all here in my broken little family. Maybe it's true our life is only metaphor now, purpose found only in roles cast on us by others.

Afterward, at the car, she and Danny changed their shoes and rolled up the cuffs of their nice wool pants. They exchanged their sports jackets for quilted Cal Bears warmup jackets and walked through the Presidio down to Baker Beach. The day was cold but sunny, filled with that sparkly, cleansing beach air. They sat on the sand, close together, but not touching. Joy took off her shoes and socks. She buried her feet, seeking absent warmth in the sand; her attention drifted in the still of sun and waves. The teenagers that Jenny never would be played hacky sack in front of them, laughing, most of the boys shirtless, one brave girl in a bikini. Joy wondered why she wasn't freezing, but she probably was. A large freighter weighted with empty containers sailed west, the world of commerce rushing forward without Joy's participation. She couldn't imagine working.

Joy saw her lifetime unfolding in tiny monochromatic steps, forever backed up against the Moment When Everything Changed. Danny had been busy—a small pile of tiny red stones lay in front of him, sifted from handfuls of sand. She put an arm around her husband, squeezing his shoulder, pulling him from his engineering into her reverie. He rested his hand on her knee. They each watched the water. A sailboarder whipped by in front of them—a brave man far from the safety of the harbor.

Hagar didn't want to watch Ishmael die, so she left her boy sitting alone under a sheltering tree. He minded her. Such a good boy. Sarah couldn't cooperate, so she used her power over Abraham to get what she wanted. And Abraham, clueless, obedient, died a contented death after traumatizing both his sons. Jacob stole his brother's place. Esau got turned out for being incredulous. Yet they all lived. Trauma resolved with reunification and faith, and there were awesome booby prizes for the losers.

When it seemed time, Joy and Danny helped each other up. Joy wanted to walk home alone. Danny wanted to stay with her and pick up the car later. "Please, let me," she said. She was embarrassed, but she said there just wasn't enough space right now. He shook his head at her, bemused, sad, and probably hurt. She watched him trudge through the sand and disappear; another fraying of the Rosenberg Commons, the shared belief in their communal perfectibility in an otherwise indifferent world. Her suffering was no more bearable because or in spite of his. Still, she smelled the water and tasted the salt air and saw the sand and the beached shoals of rock and abandoned pieces of driftwood, and the constant weight of time's fingers pressed her down into it all.

She carried that weight down the beach and up the sand ladder, a spy in the manufactured world, stealthy on the Crissy Field promenade, her burden invisible to the joggers, walkers, bicycles, dogs, strollers, and wheelchairs that surrounded her. Wind and wave and sun and green grass, and the chatter of hundreds of living beings, and suddenly a powerful wind blew up from a giant chasm that opened within, beneath her. It was vast and kneaded with black and gray and dark blue and white clouds with bright silver highlights like Hubble star factories and she wanted it, oh God she wanted it. She saw the path and the people and she saw this other world. She saw them both and they were moving in and out of her and each other and they both were real.

Sound reverberated upward, deep rhythmic grinding as if huge gears enmeshed, straining to move the massive fossilized casts of all the grief and all the glory felt by all humans from the beginning of time. She saw herself from a distance, dressed in a sturdy green linen riding gown and knee-high boots. Light armor covered her torso; a sword hung at her side. As the clouds boiled high above her she stood at an altar at the bottom of the chasm, invited to stride into a vast, treacherous landscape. The Other World—a world without artifice, where motives were clear, where choices had predictable consequences, where honor was respected. Where the dead may be alive. A sensuous flush of terrified pleasure rippled through her body, from spine through ligament and muscle, to caress the tiniest nerve endings in the tips of fingers and ears and toes . . .

"On your left, lady!"

She jumped right. A row of tourists on Segways slipped by her.

Slowly lengthening shadows of afternoon played across the city. Absurdly, she was excited.

Maybe that's where Jenny is.

7.

WHEN JOY ANSWERED the front door she expected to see Hiram. Instead, a tempest swept past her.

"Hello, hello, here's your dinner for tonight! Where's the kitchen? Back here? Oh, good!"

Joy wasn't quite sure who it was at first. Gail. Her son was in Jake's class. Joy followed the sound of whistling back to the kitchen, where Gail was taking out pots and pans.

"Gail. What are you doing?"

"Don't you worry, hon, I'll do it all, no problem!"

"Can you just leave it here and we'll tend to it later?"

"Oh, no, honey. This meal takes some real cooking. Jeffy and Bob will be over later to help us eat it."

"Gail, we're not really having guests these days."

"That's all right! You'll be the guests!"

Instead of strangling her, Joy retreated up the stairs. She wanted to keep going up, up to the hidden place in the Other World, the place Jenny might be, the room at the top of the stairs, tantalizingly close—but when she reached the landing there were no more stairs. Jacob's ladder had not been lowered for her. The only way to go was to turn left, into Jake's room. Her boys were sitting on his bed reading Disney's

Beauty and the Beast. What would they do when they finished? Read another book, probably.

"Danny," she said. "Invaders."

"*Sacrè bleu!* Call the forks and candlesticks!"

Jake fell on the floor laughing. That was good to see. She looked into Danny's eyes, pleading, sharing, resolving, handing off the pain. Didn't work.

He made to get up. "Do you want me to deal with it?"

"No," she said, "I'll do it. Just needed a recharge."

"We love you, Mommy," Jake said.

That worked.

Downstairs, Gail had almost every pot in the kitchen out on the stove.

"Honey, do you have a Dutch Oven?"

"Gail, please listen to me. It isn't time for us to have people in the house. Please just leave the food or take it back. We can't have you here all afternoon. We're in no position to host your family."

Gail gaped at her askance. "I'm just cooking. You don't need to be here."

"I hardly know you. I can't have you in my house for four hours. I can't have anyone in my house for four hours. Please go."

Joy watched Gail's face work through anger and pity to settle on incomprehension.

Gail said, "I've been planning this meal for two days. I bought all this food, but if you don't want it, fine."

She picked up her grocery bags and flounced out, slamming the door behind her.

Joy dropped onto a stool. Stared out the window. Shook her head. Cried for a bit. Banged her fists on her thighs. Stood. Banged her fists on the counter. Dried her eyes on her shirtsleeves. Went back upstairs.

Danny looked up at her over Jake's head. Flipping the double bird felt great. She said, "I practically had to throw her out. Bridges are burned. She took her food."

"We have way too many leftovers anyhow," Danny said.

No one knows how to cook for three.

Jake got up and hugged her leg. "Mommy, did Lumière help you, and all the dishes too?"

Joy laughed and hugged him back. "Oh Jake, you're my Lumière! Yes, the drawers flew open and everyone jumped out!"

To Danny she said, "I think she took out every pan in the house."

He shrugged and held out his hand to her. "We'll put them away later."

She cuddled up with them while Danny finished reading the book. It really was a great story. Hiram did come around later, just to show up, as he said. They all ate leftovers for dinner. The next day, Joy found food sitting on the doorstep. There wasn't even a note.

8.

DANNY'S MOTHER ELAINE had claimed Thanksgiving for her Tupperware night. The family gathered at Joy and Danny's this year, instead of going to Elaine and Jerry's in Calistoga as usual. Joy couldn't imagine feeling thankful after only three weeks and three days and resisted enforcement of family custom until Danny pointed out that the others had suffered Jenny's loss too. Being together was important to everyone. "We all somehow have to get used to it," he said.

Joy dawdled in her bedroom. Going downstairs she heard Sarah and Jacob's voices through his closed door. Joy's proprietary motherly impulse kicked in and she felt her ears enlarging, but she kept walking.

Jake gets to have his own relationship with his cousin. They both deserve that.

At the bottom of the stairs she heard the whispered sibilance of the Other World and turned right to find it, away from the familiar voices in the kitchen. She fell onto the couch.

Are you there, somewhere, Jenny? Are you scared? Did you get scared on the street, right at the end? Did you know you were dying? Do you know you're dead now?

She heard Elaine ask for her, and recognized Hiram's footsteps coming down the hall.

The clouds subsided. She prepared to rise.

"There you are," Hiram said. "I thought you were still upstairs."

"No," Joy said, "I've been down here for a while."

"Well, come on, then." He stretched out his hand.

Hiram came by Joy's house, usually unannounced, almost every day. When he found her there he always was getting her to do something. One day they washed the car. Weeded the backyard. He helped her organize the basement. The day they washed the windows he wouldn't let her climb the tall ladder to the second story. He thought they could paint Jenny's room, he had told Danny, evidently thinking that the male conspiracy to protect women from their own feelings was a stronger bond than marriage. It wasn't; but when Danny told her, she said that Hiram just wanted to fix it. "You do too," she told Danny, but Danny said, "Not me. It's unfixable."

Hiram pulled her up off the couch and pushed her toward the dining room. Joy had set the table earlier in the day, and it turned out to be one place short this time. No one said anything. Elaine got herself a chair and a setting. Joy thought that Jenny would be happy to see them all sitting together like this, everybody she loved in one place.

After eating, Danny stood. Joy loved the improvised eloquence of his Thanksgiving toasts. "I don't know how to do this without her. I was remembering those twisted cliché jokes she liked."

He tried to mimic her voice. "Don't hatchet your counts before they chicken!"

"People who live in grass houses shouldn't stow thrones!" Joey said.

"If the *fu* shits, wear it!" Jake said. The table erupted.

Joy felt her lips curl upward and her face became warm. *I'm smiling,* she thought. *Huh.*

"Remember her picking up my rum and Coke and taking a big swig?" Jerry said.

Joy remembered. Jenny had spit it out and thrown the glass and it had crashed into a million pieces on the kitchen floor. Joy had gotten mad at her for breaking the glass, but Jenny got mad at her grandpa for fooling her.

She was right and I was wrong.

"I thought I was watching my little girl growing up," Danny said. "Now . . ."

Joy saw his eyes recede and his face twitch in the way that it did when something just got to be too much. He wiped at his left eye while blinking his right eye rapidly and looking away at something that seemed to have appeared over the top of Joy's left shoulder. Joy thought she should try to help him, but she didn't know what to do.

Elaine reached out and held her firstborn's hand. "We'll never be the same," she said.

"Maybe not," Hiram said, "but we still have what we have." He raised his glass, and they all drank to Jenny. These people wanted Joy to stay here. She really needed them, each one, if that was going to happen, but it felt equally reasonable to imagine that it may not. She sat on the sidelines of her mystery while the winds of the Other World echoed unendingly in her ear.

* * *

Hiram returned the next morning. They sat in the kitchen with coffee; Joy could hear Danny upstairs with Jake. Joy stared out the window at their brown autumn lawn.

"That was nice last night, Joy," Hiram said.

"I guess."

"Well," he said, "it was. Everyone you love was here."

"Not everyone," she said.

"No. But you can't control that."

"I should have."

"No, you shouldn't have. You did everything right."

"I didn't. She's dead."

"You didn't do it, Joy." He spoke in his all-knowing lawyer voice. Joy wondered if he really was going to be like this, even now, so soon after. But he always was Hiram. Blunt and to the point. What's good about that was instilled in her one memorable night when she was seventeen. She had a date. She wore a short black skirt over bare legs, black work boots, and a sheer white shirt over a black bra with a black leather vest. Hiram and Rose came home earlier than she had expected. They walked in on her in the living room with a boy, their hands in R-rated places. Her skirt was at her waist, her shirt mostly unbuttoned, her bare leg wrapped around the boy. A bottle of vodka was open on the table. Rose got angry at the boy, but Joy screamed at her that she had unbuttoned her own shirt. "Mom, I did it!" Hiram gave his wife's shoulder a little squeeze as she stormed off to their bedroom. He took the boy's keys and called his parents. Joy ran up the stairs into her room, ashamed and embarrassed and so, so angry.

After a time, Hiram came up. He knocked and entered. She was loaded for bear, but he came upstairs with two glasses full of ice and the bottle of vodka. He poured. "*Nasdrovya,*" he said, and drank. Then he told her a long, adjective-heavy story about how much he loved to drink when he was younger and how he had gotten away with it, pretty much. Nothing bad had ever happened and he believed all the girls had been willing. He said that he didn't presume to know Joy's thoughts, but he did know boys can get really stupid and selfish sometimes and mostly he didn't want her to get so drunk that she would find herself having done something she otherwise may not want to have done. She said with anger, "It's my choice. You have nothing to say about it." She wanted him to get mad, too.

But he didn't. He pointed to her still-full glass and asked if she was going to drink it. She said no. "*Nasdrovya,*" he said, downing the glass, "I hope that's true. That doesn't excuse the boys, no, and it is your body, yes, but sex is too cool a thing to take casually. You are going to have a lot of it in your life, and it's easy to screw it up. Be deliberate," he said. "Don't get swept away until you're able to go there and come back. Know what I mean?"

She actually didn't know what he meant but something in that moment was just so amazing anyway. She smiled and hugged him and said, "Daddy, I promise you can trust me even if I don't tell you anything."

"Okay, Honey. Fair enough." And they drank to it. That was the beginning of their adult relationship. Joy loved him. She appreciated him. But he still could be pretty single-minded sometimes.

Like now.

"It was an accident, Honey," Hiram said. "Please accept that."

"No. There's no accepting this."

She could see him getting that look in his eye and she knew he was thinking about their family crossing Siberia to get to America the long way, on and off the train for weeks, and how many people died. She was relieved when Danny came in.

"Hey, Hiram." He gave his father-in-law's shoulder a squeeze.

"Where's Jake?" she asked.

"In the bathtub with his boats. I'll go back up in a minute."

"While I've got you both here," Hiram said, "did you have life insurance for Jenny?"

"For a ten-year-old?" Danny said.

"It's possible," Hiram said carefully, "to file a claim with the insurance companies for the construction and scaffolding firms. With insurance, your company would do it for you."

"We haven't thought about it yet," Danny said.

"Why?" asked Joy.

"Money, Joy," Hiram said. "Maybe a lot of money."

"Daddy, I can't get paid enough to make up for this."

"Of course not. But you could ensure Jake's future. And his kids even."

"We don't need insurance money to do that," Danny said.

"I don't mean to insult you, Danny," said Hiram. "You don't need to decide this right away. But it should be done."

"Grandpa!" Jake was calling from upstairs. Hiram looked to Danny.

"Go on. He must have heard you come in," Danny said.

Hiram went up.

Maybe he can fill some of Jake's Jenny-space.

"How much money, do you think?"

"Maybe a couple million," Danny said.

"That's a lot. But fuck me for thinking it." She paused. "Is it just some paperwork?"

"You'd probably get deposed. If it went to trial, you'd testify."

"I don't want to," she said.

Parade my shame in a courtroom in front of everyone?

"Unlikely it would go to trial. You know your dad, though. He won't let it go."

"I'm his daughter," she said.

"The irresistible force and the immovable object. Jake and I'll hide in the basement."

She smiled at that, and felt something like sweetness before the billowing dust and silent screaming took her attention again.

9.

SHLOSHIM MEANS THIRTY in Hebrew. Ritually Shloshim, thirty days, marks the time the bereaved once again take up the yoke of the world. Joy sat with Danny on their bed cross-legged, facing him.

"What do we do now?" she asked.

Danny said, "Life goes on, I guess. I need to get back to work or go to the asylum. I can try to make some days shorter. . . ."

"Do what you need to do. Jake is home until January. That'll keep me busy for a while."

"You could go back to work now."

Her voice quavered, like the high strings on a prepared piano. "Not yet."

"Why not?"

"I don't think I can be very creative," she said. "That's what I get paid for."

But what she was worried about was being out—dressing, gabbing, appointment-making, and presenting and invoicing and hassling with printers who couldn't match a color to save their life—out, in public, bereaved. *How?* Joy pulled her knees to her chest. Her husband lay on his back, arms clasped together hard across his chest, legs reflexively kicking, as if he could force their disaster away from them. They lay there for a long time, she a rock, he a stick, flotsam thrown haphazardly against the ruined banks of their once peaceful life. Danny fell asleep. Joy let go of her knees, eventually. And lay there, staring at the ceiling, until it was time to do something else.

* * *

Some number of days later, Joy toted three bags full of Tupperware, finely stacked, with every matching top, to the Goodwill truck in the Marina Safeway parking lot. They wouldn't take it, so she lugged it to the back of the store and threw it in the dumpster.

The grocery store used to be a social experience. She'd always see someone she knew. When she went back for the first time she went at five in the morning. Gary the produce man wasn't even there yet, just Joy and the homeless guys with their few dollars that bought them a license to be inside for a while. Her selection had been haphazard at first, but recently she'd gotten better at it. This morning she asked Danny and Jake what they wanted and she told them she would get it and wrote it on a list. She remembered to bring the list to the store. All the things on the list were in her cart. *Pretty damned competent,* she thought.

Joy was comparing cauliflowers, and thinking she just might have preserved her anonymity, when she felt a hand on her shoulder. Lila was a taut bundle of seemingly fat-free muscle wrapped around a tiny frame, packaged neatly in fully coordinated size zero workout clothes. Joy had never seen her wear anything else. Her shopping cart overflowed with leafy green vegetables. She and Joy had sweated together in the gym, been naked in the sauna. Before, Joy would have said they were friends, but Lila hadn't been to the house, or sent a note. When Joy looked at her today all she saw was a big empty hole with a nonstop mouth. The conversation was over quickly.

The cauliflower, on the other hand, wasn't demanding anything. Very empathetic. She decided to take it home. On the way to the cash register she saw a fresh mozzarella. She put it in her cart because it made her think of *caprese*. She went back for some basil.

Huh, a spontaneous creative idea. Maybe I can think about going back to work now.

Joy rolled her cart to the front of the store and scanned the checkout lines, picking one where she was hidden from the rest of the store by a portable product display. Joy's food went up on the conveyor and through the scanner. The cashier treated her just like everyone else. Joy felt as if she was concealing a great secret.

* * *

"Mommy, Mommy, look what I won!" Jake was laughing and talking loudly, exactly like a normal boy.

"Wow, Jakcy, look at that!" Joy said. *He is normal. I'm not normal.* "What did you play?"

Lizzie had flown down yet again and brought Amanda back with her. Jake needs me, Mandy told her mother, just like Aunt Joy needs you. Lizzie had taken Jake and Amanda to Pier 39, to play in the arcade and eat crappy food.

"I played Pac-Man and Star Wars and Skeeball and then Mandy helped me play pinball and then she won a huge amount of tickets at Skeeball, more than Aunt Lizzie, and then she gave them all to me, and Aunt Lizzie gave me hers too, and then I got this car that was a thousand tickets! Look!"

The car was a flywheel-driven Monster Truck. He spun it up and it leaped across the kitchen floor, heading out the door toward parts unknown. Jake went racing after it, and she could hear him spinning it up again. Amanda followed him. Jenny and Amanda had bonded as babies, as if the lifelong love of their mothers had been transferred through some kind of spiritual Lamarckism. Amanda seemed to be transferring it, in turn, to Jake. Joy heard them run up the stairs.

"I don't think Jake's laughed like that since the last time you were here," Joy said. She couldn't deny the life that came pouring out of him.

"We had fun. Mandy really loves him. Maybe she'll wait for him. Wouldn't that be a kick?"

"Kind of weird, I think."

"I guess. Almost like incest," Lizzie said. "Where's Danny?"

"Reading." She pointed upstairs.

"How was the morning?"

"Okay, I guess. Danny's ramping it up at work now. Then Jake goes back to school and I'll be alone."

Lizzie didn't say anything. Joy's hands were clasped on the table. Her eyes dropped from Lizzie's and her forehead followed the eyes, settling on her hands.

"I can't believe it's only been thirty days. Danny's doing what he does. What do I do?"

"Wait. At least you have each other."

Do I? Will I?

"I hope so," Joy said. "Can I tell you something really secret?"

"Of course."

"I've been having these visions. Danny isn't a part of them."

Joy told Lizzie about the Other World, about how surprising it was, how it felt true, how Jenny might be there, and how she felt called by its power. "Why would I be seeing this if there wasn't a reason? Am I supposed to do something?"

"Like what?" Lizzie asked. "Go on a vision quest? Sit in a cave? It's only been a month, Joy. I see what you mean about not telling Danny, though. He'd worry. Take some time."

"All I have is time. One second at a time."

Joy heard the scraping as Lizzie pulled her chair close. She wrapped both arms around Joy's shoulders.

"Oh honey, I get it. It's just so unbelievable she's gone."

Joy burst into tears. Lizzie kissed her ears, her forehead, rubbed her back, whispering words Joy couldn't hear and didn't need to know. She lost her bones, melting into Lizzie's lap and the hard kitchen chairs.

Danny appeared, pixilated through crosshatched eyelashes. He lifted her. Joy found her feet and the three of them went to the den, huddling on the couch, Danny's head on Lizzie's shoulder and Joy curled in both of their laps: a *pièta*. She wished she could stay that way forever, but the children came downstairs so they got up and Lizzie made everyone dinner instead.

10.

"ARE YOU SURE you want to do this today?" Danny asked her.

"A field trip to the Academy of Sciences? I've done it every year. I don't have to drive with them. Getting there can be my walk today."

"Lot of people," he said. "Lot of sympathy. Lot of eyeballs."

Joy shrugged. "How hard can it be? I'm a freak already."

"I wish you wouldn't think about yourself like that."

She took his hand. "Why don't you come with me?"

"Sorry. I'm going to work. Only predictable surprises for me."

The sun shone in the south-facing window and lit his profile, elongating his nose and shortening his forehead like a goblin.

Couldn't you give me today, just today?

But instead of making a scene she said, "Jenny liked it there. Maybe I'll remember something."

"Just what I'm afraid of," Danny said. "Good luck." He went upstairs.

She checked the clock and started to make Jake's lunch.

Jake came downstairs still wearing his Star Wars pajamas. Teddy was dangling from his left hand. He leaned against her side, tentatively touching her.

"Jake, you need to get dressed. Time for school."

"Help me," he said. She wrapped the curve of his shoulder with her palm. Jenny used to be there to help, right in the room next door.

"Okay," she said. She kept her hand on his shoulder. The stairs seemed to go on forever. She was sure they were running late and she kept glancing at her watch. *No hurry at all. He's such a little boy,* she thought, and her heart broke. She cried for the third time that morning. She picked out his clothes. He got dressed. When he went to the bathroom she went downstairs again.

Quick Danny footsteps echoed down the stairwell, followed by squeals and giggles and running and bouncing noises. They were playing.

Maybe this was normal, on Danny's mornings, before, back when Joy used to ride her bike. Or maybe Jenny got him up. But did she on my mornings, before?

She was still trying to remember when the boys came downstairs and they all had breakfast. Then she said goodbye to Danny and kissed Jake, telling him that she would see him later, at the museum. Then she cleaned up and then she put on her fleece and her sneakers and ran a brush through her hair and started to walk.

She got to the Academy early and wandered downstairs to the aquariums, which Jenny had loved. Under muted lighting each aquarium reflected the Other World in the clouds of fish and bubbles of water and waving fronds of seaweed. *Not now,* she prayed, *can't I just be here now, the kids aren't even here yet.* She remembered when time was rich and compliant.

Upstairs there were hundreds of kids and lots of noise. The barely controlled vigor of their living frightened her, but she found Jake's group and formed a rictus of a smile. The other moms were uniformly glad to see her, but when they talked about all the things she used to talk about with them, the crush descended on her heart and she grew silent. That life was no longer hers.

Time pressed down, thickening the air around her. *Danny was right,* she thought, *I'm going to lose it.* But Jake grabbed her hand and said, "Look at this, Mommy." *God bless him,* Joy thought, *and damn me for making him keep me in this world.*

The morning was completely normal for everyone, lively kids, smiling mothers, organized teachers, uniformed curators telling big stories about small animals. But for Joy, each act became less comprehensible as time twisted around her. She finally lost it in the African Hall, live people surrounded by dozens of stuffed, dead animals. Her skin dissolved and she was bones in the desert with the wildebeest and Thompson's gazelles, the lions returned to their diorama after having devoured them all. Her eyebrows were melting into her cheeks. The boundaries of her body began to grow indistinct and her hands clenched and released.

Time to go.

She somehow was able to check out with the teacher and mumble a goodbye to Jake. She felt his eyes on her back as she fled the hall. She covered her mouth with her forearm and bit down hard on the fleece jacket, then twisted her arm with the sleeve in her teeth so her hand covered her whole face and she screamed "Jenny, Jenny, Jenny" silently into her arm.

She kept moving, and after some time she heard some things and felt the stones of the path pressing up against the bottoms of her feet; she was near the carousel. She thought she might have a chance to catch up to present time and maybe even go back to the museum, but instead she just kept slowing and slowing until taking each step was like lifting an iron boot up and down. Just before things ground to a complete halt she found a bench and sat in the sun and wind. Across from her was a tight grove of tall, green trees and a thick spread of bushes with red berries and little white flowers. Her back was pressed against the bench slats. Her feet were flat on the ground. Her knees were touching each other. Her hands lay unmoving on her thighs.

The feeling on her cheek, she remembered, was called warmth. Something physiological was happening. Photons struck her cheek and some chemistry in her brain reacted, like the touch of oh-so-tiny

Jenny brushing her cheek with sweet little baby fingers. Wind tousled her hair, her split ends tickling her cheek like baby Jenny's perfect little fingers on the distended skin of her lactating breast. She saw herself from afar, a statue of a woman in fleece and a ball cap, leaves eddying in the wind, collecting at her feet. Alone, in the park, nothing to hold, framed by the daytime, pressed against the bench by the weight of air. Time forced her shadow slowly across the ground. It was heavy, this piling, pressing time, diabolical, indifferent.

Before, time was a framework, a reference, a scorecard. Mother of two, wife, lover, daughter, cyclist, artist, designer, businesswoman, school volunteer, purposefully moving from appointment to chore to meeting; fit, smart, attractive, potent, passionate, committed, blooming with glorious maturity. Now she was a twisted scarecrow, skin hanging loosely on her own skeleton, pecked by crows as artifacts of memory piled up in the house along with Jenny's third-grade notebooks, torn jeans, and old Halloween costumes.

I even have to flee the life of children.

When Jenny first met Jake she ran into the room and sat right next to Joy on the birthing bed. She put Jake in Jenny's lap, and she held him with the most careful gentleness. Danny took Joy's hand and put his other hand on Jenny's head and they basked. A mother, a father, a daughter, a son, a wife, a husband, a brother, a sister; in that moment, all Joy had ever wanted.

Today she had wanted to go on the field trip, to be normal, to let the kids pull her back to the Common World—but that world no longer was hers. Only in the Other World was purpose alive, to fall through those clouds and embrace the quest that was her calling, to scheme and seduce and battle to win back the life that no longer was hers.

And the Joy she was now, on the bench, on this day, was ready to fall.

She closed her eyes and let herself go. The wind rushed and the clouds roiled and she was at the altar, in the dress, armor glistening, sword in her hand, balanced on two feet, and oh, so ready to fight . . . but then there was barking, a bounding ball, and the bench pressed her thighs.

Her heart pulsed against her ribs, and the breath she had been holding escaped in a whoosh. Her sword hand was throbbing, the shadow weapon suddenly amputated, a tool irrelevant to the Common World. How tenuous is this world we all are so invested in, that we love so much: Only a fantasy, built on artifice, bound together only by the thinnest threads of agreement woven between the unsuspecting. Why settle, when she had a chance or a right or a mandate to end her complicity, to step into the Other World and live the quest—battle, starvation, slavery, rape—any sacrifice worth it for the chance of seeing Jenny again.

Reluctantly, she began naming the intruding sounds—clanking collars, bouncing balls, occasional barks and snarls followed by raised voices as some canine disagreement got settled. Dogs. Loving, loyal, and living. Dog people—a community, of a sort. She could become a dog person. None of the other dog people would know. She just needed a dog. The right dog. Cute, smart, hypoallergenic, a dog she could waste all her time taking care of and walking and cleaning up its drool in the house and its shit in the yard. *Then it dies when Jake's in high school and the world crashes down around his ears once again. No.*

* * *

Rabbi escorted her to a leather easy chair beside a low, round Formica coffee table, opposite his desk. He was wearing an old brown corduroy suit and a soft yellow shirt with tie loosened, cuffs unbuttoned. The jacket was on a hook behind his desk. The office was lined with inexpensive walnut-stained pine bookcases, and packed to the gills with books. Her eyes drifted over some of the titles, recognizing Maimonides, Spinoza, Wiesel, Kushner. The shelves behind his desk held dozens of large books with Hebrew lettering on the spines. *Talmud?*

Joy had called him from the park and he said that she should come. She could always come. She told him about the Other World and about escaping the museum and about what had happened to her on the bench.

"I feel like the eternal battle between good and evil is going on inside me, like I can change the future of the universe. And I have to do the laundry?"

She met his eyes accusingly. He remained silent.

"She's out there someplace, and I can go find her. But I lose everything."

"Jenny's death ripped your world open," Rabbi said. "It makes a lot of sense to me that you are feeling things you never felt before. Your vision might be true, or it might be false. That's not for me to say. What I do know, though, is that you are alive in this world, here," he rapped his knuckles on the table, "a very substantial place, inhabited by your husband and your son and your parents and a lot of other people who love you. Even if your vision is true, it doesn't seem to me that you have the freedom to go off and pursue it."

She swept her hands in the air as though shaking muck off them. "Crap. If this is enlightenment, they can have it. I never asked for it."

"That's a little dramatic, don't you think? Maybe there's something in between."

Is this my reality? Is this the world I'm going to live in? Always a foot in the world of the dead, spending my days babbling about god and truth and right, twisted by the lost right to my own child's life?

She pulled her hair.

I could rip it out strand by strand and I wouldn't even feel it. Why not throw myself off the cliff? Is God there? Is Jenny?

"I guess that's what I'm doing now," she said, "living in between, but I can barely do the minimum here. The draw to there is strong."

"Joy, I'm a rabbi, so I'm inclined to take your experience at face value. You might be crazy, but you don't have to be alone and crazy. Respect your vision, but stay connected to your family, and keep coming here, saying Kaddish, wrestling with your grief. What happened to you is terrible. Only time passing is going to get you someplace else."

This sounded reasonable to her, but the choice beckoned over and over again. Yield! Follow! Go! and maybe die. Stay, and maybe shrivel, become a crazy old woman cloistered in a dark room above a seedy bar, surrounded by dark, musty books in Latin, Greek, and Aramaic, veiled in black, wrapped in layers of purple organza and lace, forever seeking, needing only the right spell to find communion with the lost spirit of her dead daughter. She knew it was completely crazy. Yet it seemed equally crazy to become willfully deaf, dumb, and blind and live fifty more years with the answer forever concealed by the belief an answer existed.

"I just don't know if I can be patient enough. But now, I have to go pick up Jake."

He nodded.

"Proves your point, I suppose," she said.

"You are his mother."

"Hers too," said Joy.

11.

WHEN JOY APPROACHED the school on foot she stopped behind a tree she knew had a clear view of the front door. Fortunately, most of the other parents were as busy as she used to be, in their minivans and SUVs, dutifully lined up, on the phone, wrapping around the block, motors running, blocking traffic and killing the planet.

Joy watched the choreography. The school doors flexed open and closed and, class by class, the kids came out, the littlest ones first, lined up against the building with both straps of their backpacks on their shoulders, some precious piece of art clutched in each hand. A small army of teachers' aides with clipboards checked the cars, checked the list of approved guardians, took a signature, walked across the sidewalk, retrieved the appropriate child, opened the back door, tucked the child into the car seat, pulled the lap belt tight, signaled the driver, and moved on, repeating the procedure, car by car.

The top of her son's head appeared as Jake took his place in line. She looked in the other direction and saw the city bus two stops away. She became visible, cutting between two cars, offering a halfhearted wave to the barely recognized mother in the driver's seat. Her back to the pick-up line, she took Jake's hand. She signed him out with the teacher, was handed some form or another that, stuffed into her pocket, was promptly forgotten.

The bus rolled up as they arrived at the stop. They got on.

"What did you do in school today, Jakey?"

"We saw a movie with Big Bird. He sang a song."

"What was the song about?"

"Friends."

His best friend is dead, and they made him watch that video.

But whatever damage it caused had already been done. "Friends are important; they can help you a lot."

"I guess," Jake said, staring at his fingers.

She wouldn't believe herself, either. She sat him in her lap and played a little counting game with their fingers, his little body's warmth temporary insulation from the chill of her dread. Soon enough the bus arrived at Chestnut Street. They got off and went to the coffeehouse. She got him a cookie and milk and herself a latte, taking it to an outside table shaded from the late afternoon sun. She sat across from him. He seemed happy with his cookie. She flipped through the free *SF Weekly*.

"Mommy, where's Jenny?"

Ah, she thought. "I wonder that all the time, honey. I don't know. I wish I did."

He looked at her with a very serious expression.

"Is she still my friend?"

"She's still your sister, and she loves you very much."

"I can't play with her now."

How do you even talk about this with your child?

"No, sweetie, you can't play with her, but you can play with us."

Jake took another bite.

"Will you play Sliders with me?"

In Sliders the kids got into a sleeping bag at the top of the stairs and tobogganed down, screaming with joy, falling at the bottom into a giant heap of every pillow in the house.

"Maybe you can play it with Bobby when he comes over. Or with Amanda when they come to visit."

Jake got quiet again. He wanted to play Sliders with Jenny. He wanted Joy be Jenny. She couldn't be Jenny. She couldn't make him be Jenny to her. *How will this ever be okay?*

They walked three blocks and turned the corner. She remembered when she and Danny first came to see the house. Right size. Decent neighborhood. Close to the water and to the bridge. She loved how Alhambra Street's gentle curve broke the monotony of the urban grid. And she had loved the house, in the middle of a short block, its brick parking spot and stairs and front porch, the garden from the building next door providing a bit of separation between their otherwise connected houses. They would be settled and peaceful and happy ever after.

The house was quiet, as it always was, now. She sat down at the kitchen counter with Jake and opened his schoolbook.

"Let's see what you have for homework, Jake." There was an assignment in the homework pocket—the front side of the page had letter recognition exercises, the back side numbers and shapes.

"Which side first?"

"Letters."

"Okay." She watched him work through the page. He didn't need any help. *He really is reading already,* Joy thought.

"Ready for the math? How many triangles?"

"One, two, three . . ." They went through the worksheet together. Finished it. The silence began to extend.

"Can I watch a movie?" Jake asked. There were rules about TV, once: Never in the daytime, an hour at night, movies on the weekends. Joy couldn't think of anything else, right then.

"What do you want to watch?"

"*Sword in the Stone.* Can you watch with me?"

"For a while. Daddy will be home soon. I should get dinner started before that."

Joy turned on the TV, put on *The Sword in the Stone*, got him Teddy and a blanket, sat down with him. He settled. She patted him on the shoulder and kissed the top of his head. She went to her office and closed the door.

Falling to her knees, Joy clapped both hands across her mouth and screamed and screamed. She squeezed every muscle she had into the tiniest possible space; a little ball rolling on the floor. She unsqueezed, writhing. She banged her head with her fist. The tears came now. She kicked the air. After a time she stopped the crying and rolled onto her back, body heavy, limbs flat on the floor. *Shivasana*, corpse pose. Joy was ready to lie there forever.

The front door opened and closed. The metal studs of Danny's briefcase hit the wooden floor of the entry with a chunk. Hinges squeaked as he hung his coat in the closet; his shoes clattered when he dropped them at the bottom of the stairs. His footsteps got louder and then quieter. He must have turned in to the den. She waited, wanting him to come and get her, to see her now. But the seconds creaked by and he didn't and she was glad he couldn't see her now.

She lay on the floor, flirting with the Other World, but dinnertime forced itself upon her. She reached up to the surface of her desk and pulled herself to her feet. Her shoulders wanted to stay hunched. She let them. The reflection in the cold screen of her monitor was scary. Tight lips in a parallel line, red eyes, stringy hair . . . She tried to clean up a bit, gave up, then went to the kitchen and started making noise herself, tossing bags of vegetables onto the countertop.

He came out of the den and closed the door behind him. "How many times has he seen that movie, do you think?"

He was away from her, on the other side of the counter. She turned to him.

"Look at your face," he said, his voice cracking. His arms rose, as if he wanted to embrace her, but the counter blocked his way and seemed to stump him. She watched his face and wondered if his hell felt like hers did.

"I didn't know what else to do," she said. "I picked him up, we went for coffee, he did his homework. He wanted to and I just said okay."

"No problem. Everyone gets a pass this year. How'd the rest of the day go?"

"It sucked."

"I called; you didn't pick up."

"I walked. I didn't take my phone."

"I wanted to talk to you." Danny picked up the newspapers scattered across the counter from breakfast and walked across the room to deposit them in the recycling bin. "Did you ride your bike today?"

"No, I thought about it, though."

"That's progress, I suppose."

"I suppose."

"I'd be happy to see you get that going again."

He used to complain that it took her away from the family on the weekends, but it didn't, really, she was home by ten, or noon on the longer days, and then they would always do something together.

"I guess I would too," she replied.

"You aren't doing as badly as you think. Be nicer to yourself, please."

"Yes, sir." She straightened and saluted.

He stared at her with his you-must-be-an-alien-from-outer-space look. "Wrong thing to say?" he asked.

Of course it was, she wanted to scream at him. *Don't tell me how to do this!*

"Sorry," she said.

He turned away. She heard the pop of a cork, the shallow gurgle of the pour, the splash of wine in the bottom of the glass. He handed her a glass and held his up to her. They clinked; a habit they had. He looked at the mail. Taking shape on the counter was a dinner for which she recently had recovered capacity—rice in the cooker, a pile of neatly cut vegetables, the wok on the stove, butter melting in the pan for cheese sauce.

"How was work today?" she asked.

"Marginally productive," he said. "Sometimes, I can go for five whole minutes without remembering." His hands lifted as if he were going to make some kind of an expressive gesture, but then fell limply to his sides. She saw his suffering again but the counter between them was still too wide. He took a sip of wine. The rice cooker dinged and shut itself off. Joy put two tablespoons of water in it for the rice to finish absorbing. The wok sizzled as she poured just a bit of water and soy sauce over the vegetables. The top went on to steam. She turned the heat off under the cheese sauce and gave it a few more stirs.

"Looks like we're going to buy that company in Chico," he said.

"Will it take you away?" She couldn't keep the quavering from her voice.

Am I scared of everything?

"Probably some nights, but not two in a row, I hope."

He did the work this time, crossing the floor, hugging her with one arm. She was surprised.

This once was something I expected. Something I earned.

She pecked his cheek. "Can you set the table? We're about ready."

He set three places. She watched him; her shoulder still resonated with his touch. She went into the den were Jake was curled up on the couch, Teddy gripped between his arms, the blanket twisted around his legs and up over his head and shoulders. He looked no bigger than a watermelon. She stared at him and he stared at the screen; the future King of England and founder of Camelot was a fish.

"Dinner's ready, Jake."

No answer or movement.

"Let's turn it off. I'll come watch the rest with you after dinner."

"Daddy, too?"

"Okay. Daddy too."

Danny came in.

"I committed you to *The Sword in the Stone*. Not too much is left."

His face didn't move and she was afraid, but he only said, "It's fine, Joy, really."

He squeezed the same shoulder and stepped past.

"Uppy!" Jake said, reaching up to him.

Danny untangled his son from the blanket, lifting him and Teddy high in the air, hugging him close. Jake wrapped both arms around his father's neck. *Off the hook,* she thought, and felt shame battering her heart.

After dinner they watched the rest of the movie. Jake sat between them on the couch, Teddy in his lap. Joy and Danny had their arms entangled over the back of couch, behind Jake's head. Joy watched her man. His face was hard. He did not look like her lover, like anyone's lover, but more like the bust of a minor heroic figure placed in an isolated gallery of an out-of-the-way museum, to be discovered by accident, away from the popular works. A feeling washed through her, not love, really, maybe empathy, or maybe something only transactional, like the satisfaction she got when she received the check for a particularly complicated job, efficiently done. She patted his forearm; he squeezed her back. The movie ended the way it always did.

Jake wanted Joy to put him to bed. She tried to gird herself against what she knew was coming, what had been played out many nights since Jenny died. She went upstairs with him. She laid out his pajamas. He put them on, then went into the bathroom to brush his teeth. She watched him, avoiding the mirror, the mother he had now. He got into bed. She sat next to him and picked up *The Horse and his Boy*, Book Six of the *Chronicles of Narnia* by C.S. Lewis. Jenny loved those stories.

Joy thought of the game Jenny had played with her brother: Jake the haughty younger brother Edmund, and Jenny the elder sister Susan, the archer perched on the brink of womanhood; the one who stayed behind. Joy read a few pages, remembering Jenny's joy at the boy Shasta's constant discoveries under the gentle guidance of the talking horse Bree. She wondered if Jake would be able to take any risks, now that his guide was dead.

"Time to sleep, Jakey," she said.

"Read me another chapter," he said, wheedling, rustling fitfully against her, pressing against her legs and ribs, wrapping his arm inside hers, trying to crawl inside of her clothes.

"No, honey. It's bedtime. You have school tomorrow."

Jake grabbed at her arm, keeping close. Allowing him that part, she gently disentangled the rest of herself from him, turned out the light, leaned over to kiss him goodnight. He was holding on for dear life, reaching for her from the midst of her broken children.

"Stay with me," Jake said.

She sat on the bed. He held tightly onto her arm. She gently caressed his hair. Each time he seemed to settle she moved away, but he held more tightly.

"Shh, Jakey, sleep," she begged.

"Sing to me."

"All right, one song, but you have to go to sleep then."

"Okay, Mommy." He seemed satisfied with his victory.

She followed the script, sliding off the bed onto the floor, her arm moving down his until she held just his hand. Playing his part, he allowed it. She knelt next to the bed, kissed him, then turned around and sat, his hand still in hers, blessedly facing away from him.

"Bows and flows of angel hair, and ice cream castles in the air. . ."

Joy sang all the verses. Jake vanished to her as she soldiered on, singing one-part harmony against the absent voice of her daughter. When his hand finally relaxed she gently let go of it, crawled across the floor, and pulled herself up on Jake's doorknob. She stumbled into their bedroom and threw herself down on the bed, clenched fists shoving her pillow into her face.

Footsteps on the stairs; a hand on her back.

Danny caressed her shoulders. "Joy?"

She didn't move. She didn't talk. She hated his kindness. The hand went away; footsteps receded.

Footsteps returned, a rustling from his closet, the squeak of the door as he closed it, the exhale of the bedding as he lay down. She forgave him, rolled over, her face twisted into the shrew's. He didn't ask. She told him anyway. She hated that song now.

Sorry, he said, and rolled away and turned out his light. She went to the bathroom.

When she returned she lay on top of the covers. He was curled up under them, way over on his side of their king-size bed. His breathing was soft and even, but she knew he was still awake. Maybe she should say something, or try to touch him, but to lift and reach and roll? Such willfulness belonged to the living. Everything was dark. It didn't feel like sleep, but she woke up later, shivering, and crawled under the covers. She tried to move closer to Danny, by infinite halves. Eventually, she slept.

12.

DANNY'S GRIEF WAS becoming indiscernible to her. Maybe hers left no room to see his. Back at work since January, his daily habits had fully reasserted themselves—setting the coffeepot, reading the paper in the morning, stopping off at the gym after work three times a week, reading business magazines and law journals at night. They orbited together at dinnertime, planning Jake's next day. Danny would note the plan in his calendar. If Joy had to do something out of the usual routine, she would often receive a reminder call the next day from his secretary.

At least I still have my husband. There he was, in her bed. She could see the hair on the back of his neck growing out below the sharp line of his last haircut. Before, she would have pointed that out to him; now she wondered why she ever had thought that merited her attention. He never used to worry about her, before, or if he did it was well masked, sounding more like a companionable comment than a diagnostic inquiry. Now he kept asking her and she kept telling him it was okay, whatever it was that needed to be okay. But nothing was really going to be okay, so it was okay to stop listening.

She had always listened. Her presence had been reassuring to him, a touchstone; now she wasn't. She lightly caressed his shoulder. He jerked away from her touch, hand rising to bat hers away as if it were a stray mosquito. She sighed. She had no tears for this, their separation. It was the slightest thing.

Oh, Danny! The beautiful children we once were! Our plan, my plan, to build a life together!

She had challenged him, after he had proposed and they had moved in together, to map it out on big sheets of paper tacked to the walls of their Berkeley studio apartment: career goals, income goals, when to have two kids, saving for college, for retirement, making sure it all fit, no barriers in the way of their gloriously imagined future. Such happiness! So well earned! The living of her daughter was urgently entwined in all those plans, and her death collapsed them all.

On their first weekend away together, Danny took her to a pretty little place in Carmel, a room on the top floor with a private patio open to sky and sea. She already was in love with him, but that first night shocked her. He took her for drinks and dinner, but she wanted only touch. She barely made it back to the room with her clothes on, flooded with a blind passion that obliterated time and caution, body and soul completely exposed. Abandoning herself like that was scary, in retrospect. But exquisite. She had wanted him—them—and nothing else.

But now they were something else.

Their bed was big and they were using it all. Some nights the middle was untouched, mutely denying the hot, mobile sex that used to happen there. She thought about the photo album hidden in her dresser. "Our Kama Sutra," Danny had called it, red-faced and stammering after she teased the fantasy out of him at a beachside restaurant the first night of their tenth anniversary trip to Hawaii. "Don't get your hopes up," she said, but he had a new digital camera. He was taking a lot of pictures and they were making a lot of love, and before the week was out Danny got his wish.

The resort photographer had found them twice, and two of his gloriously tropical shots usually sat on her dresser. In the first she was nestled against Danny's chest on the beach, their feet in the water, her right arm up around his neck, his right arm draped casually over her hip, hand spread very low on her belly, the fingers of their left hands entwined at her side, wearing the smallest bikini she had ever owned. The second was in the evening, Danny in his finest alohawear, she on his arm, her short white sundress cut low in the front and back, contrasting vividly with her tanned skin; she had been naked under the dress.

When she took the photos off the dresser and put them in the drawer with the book she told him it would just be for a while. Danny had groused, but hadn't really objected. She knew it must have upset him. He had told her over and over again that he had never felt as rich as he had that day. He had a small print of the beach photo on his desk, facing him. She was embarrassed that his visitors might see her practically naked, but she liked being his all the same. Now her marriage was reshaped by something untouchable. They shared its presence, this untouchable knowledge, binding them together and pushing them apart.

Joy got out of bed. She nodded at the shadow woman in the bathroom mirror, barely visible in the darkened room. Mostly the world looked like this to her. She put on her fleece and left the bedroom. Checked on Jake. His breathing was an unexpected relief each morning. She didn't know how long she still would have him— she'd only been a mother for ten years, and half of her children already were dead. She watched him for a while. Jenny's door was closed. Her hand moved to the doorknob; the block *J* rattled softly. She promised herself that she could go in later.

The pilgrimages had started when Danny went back to work and Jake went back to school. It was something very private. She tried not to do it every day, but some days she did it twice. Like a junkie. Joy would wait until her boys were away, until the beds were made and dishes washed. She approached Jenny's door. She opened it and stepped inside. First, she checked that the bed was made, pillows fluffed, things still neatly arranged on the shelves. She vacuumed and dusted and washed the window. Then she would lie flat on her back on the floor, arms and legs spread, trying to remember. Some days she would crawl into Jenny's closet or open a drawer and dump the clothes into a pile to rummage around for a smell or a taste, but everything was clean, waiting for that preteen girl who would never come home.

So she played. She sat on Jenny's bed and talked with Jenny's dolls. They had a tea party. She sat at Jenny's desk. She leafed through Jenny's school art. She sat on the floor by the bookcase and read Jenny's books. She added a coin to Jenny's penny collection. Played solitaire with Jenny's favorite cards. Made a bracelet with Jenny's bead set. It helped, for a while, but she could never really hold it, and the boys couldn't know—it was hers.

She went downstairs and sat in the den, staring at the row of unopened photo albums, comforter wrapped around her, her left hand on Jenny's table from Handcrafts Day Camp summer before last. How proud Jenny was to bring it home, cleverly assembled and sanded smooth. Later that summer Joy and Jenny had painted the table on the back deck outside Joy's office. Jenny wanted to paint it like a rainbow. Although Joy had thought she'd end up with a kaleidoscope, Jenny's focus was impeccable, painting thin stripes up the legs, carefully keeping the colors in order. Joy cleaned the brushes between colors, smiling at the paint dripping on Jenny's shoes, collecting under her fingernails and coloring the dangling strands of her curly black hair.

One day Joy found the baseball Danny had muscled up to catch at Jenny's first Giants game. She had let it sit on the counter for a few days. Danny moved it the first day, but Joy put it back and he let it be. A few days later, she brought the table down from Jenny's room. She first put it in a corner of the den often hidden by the door, but the table found its way to a coveted spot by the couch. She put the ball on it and then moved the little pink double picture frame with tiny white flowers on the corners, displaying a sweet picture of the four of them and a sweeter one of Jenny holding Jake as a baby. Danny called it their shrine and he added other things that once were Jenny's: her first pair of tap shoes, perfectly polished; two of her favorite candles, one in the shape of a blue globe, decorated with stars, and the other a tall, braided Havdalah candle from her grandmother; a Chinese dragon backscratcher she had pleaded for on Grant Street one day, because her back itched; a cheap ballpoint pen with four colors that, at three, she thought was just amazing. The *chai* necklace she had been wearing when she died.

Joy was picking these things up and putting them down when she heard Danny padding down the stairs, barefoot. The moment was reassuring. She hoped she wouldn't be forced to leave him and become a crazy old lady. He came into the den with a cup of coffee and she showed him her empty hands. He gave her the cup, then disappeared back into the kitchen, returning with a second cup and the *New York Times*. As he sat their eyes met.

"Thanks," she said.

They took sips.

"How long have you been up?" he asked.

"Not too long. It was just getting light when I came downstairs."

"Been here the whole time?"

"Here and there."

They took a couple more sips.

"Watched Jake breathe for a while. That was good," she said.

He nodded. "We've been lucky with him so far."

They were quiet. Danny opened the paper.

The clouds of the Other World blew up between them and she watched the paper attenuate; his face appeared beyond the type which floated unattached, suspended between them, where she knew the rest of the paper must be. *X-ray vision*, she thought. *Okay. the more of me that's in the Other World the less of me is here so I can see through the spaces.* She looked down at her coffee cup, through the liquid, through the bottom of the cup, through the surface of the table beyond its legs, her attention sucked into the vast roiling chasm that spread out below.

Danny coughed, and the paper firmed up again as she remembered that he was reading it. His presence was a place to plant her foot in this world. *What is in his mind?* He went to the junkyard and cleaned out the car. The car must have been filled with Jenny's blood. *How can he live with that?* Joy realized she never had really asked him about that part. Probably she should, but he could bear it, her Danny. He could.

"Danny."

He looked at her over the paper.

"Something really strange has been going on. I feel like half of me is living somewhere else."

"You don't say."

She soldiered on. "Not like that. Much more. Please listen."

He apologized and put the paper down. She told him everything about the vision she'd had on the path, how another world had opened up, a real one, as if she were in both places at once, and how it felt like Jenny might be there. She told him how often it appeared to her, like on Thanksgiving, and how it felt like the universal war between good and evil was being fought in her chest. She told him what happened after she left the museum the day of the field trip and about talking to the rabbi and about maybe becoming a prophet or a seer or a seeker or a crazy old lady and about how it felt like a calling and a secret and a threat. She told him about having X-ray vision and having seen his face right through the newspaper.

"So do I go look for Jenny?" She didn't like what she was seeing in Danny's face.

He took a deep breath. "Do you really think you could see her again?"

"Feels like it."

"But you can't, Joy."

"I don't know that. It wants me."

"I want you. Who wins?"

"It's not like that. Something different."

"Joy, she's gone."

"Rabbi took me seriously. It seems so real to me," she said.

"That's crazy." He stood up and paced the room. "I don't like this at all."

"It's not about you, Danny."

He stopped and studied her.

He's getting mad. I shouldn't have said anything.

"It is about me, Joy. If it is the world of the dead, to go there you'd have to be dead. I want you alive."

She stayed quiet. *Would I have to be dead? How could he understand?* The feeling was hers still, even after she told him. Her sword hand twitched.

"It feels real," she said, which now sounded kind of lame.

Danny sat. He retrieved the paper that had fallen off his lap and very deliberately folded it. He set it on top of the other sections on the ottoman and straightened the pile. Then he sat up straight in his chair and clasped his hands in his lap.

"It might feel real, Joy, but it's not."

"I don't know that." Truculent.

"Shit," he said.

Danny found the *Times* magazine, flipping to a particular page. He took a pencil out of the coffee table drawer. He laid both in her lap.

"Think about something else, please. Here. Do the crossword."

"The Saturday one is too hard."

"It's Sunday today," he said.

"Whatever. It's too big."

He turned back to the paper.

"Daddy!" Jake called from upstairs.

"That's your son, Joy. Remember him?"

That hurts.

Danny came to her. He put his hand on her shoulders: Gently. Lovingly.

"We both are crazy now. I can't be a part of your vision. I don't like that. Please stay with us. Why don't you go make breakfast?"

She stood and turned to him. "Stop patronizing me. I know what's next."

"Do you? I don't have a clue." He spun away on his heel. "Leave me a note if you go on your vision quest, okay? I'll have to arrange babysitting." He disappeared upstairs.

Maybe I should go so he would have to deal with it. Serve him right. Maybe he's just biding his time until someone else comes along. Maybe I should do him a favor and follow the vision just so he can be free of me.

Instead she made oatmeal with raisins. Danny and Jake were upstairs for a long time before they came down, but when they did the oatmeal still tasted good even though she had to reheat it. When she went to hold Danny's hand, it was rigid and clammy. *I made that,* she thought.

After breakfast, Danny cleaned up and she walked Jake up the block to Bobby's house. When she got back Danny met her at the door. He still was holding a dishtowel.

"This other world of yours? I'm frightened. I don't trust it at all," he said. "I feel like I have to keep the family from exploding when all I really should have to worry about is at the office."

"Please don't be mad, Danny. I can't help what I'm thinking."

"We have a living child too."

"Don't say that. I'm putting my time in with him."

"You can't just punch the clock," he said.

"That's not what I'm doing." But if it looked like that to Danny, maybe it was and that's all she was going to be able to do for her son. "I love him, Danny." A plea.

"Am I going to lose you to this?" he said.

"Not unless you throw me out. But I didn't choose this. I'm sorry if it hurts you."

He shook his head impatiently. "Your questions have no answers, Joy. Rabbi said that too. Where is she? Why did she die? Did we do it? They don't help."

"My daughter died eight weeks ago and this is the thing that's happening now. Please deal with me."

"That's all you'll let me do anyway."

"That was really unfair." She turned and walked down the hall into the kitchen. He followed. He didn't apologize, but the petulance was gone from his voice.

"When my grandpa died I remember seeing my dad through the door of his bedroom, sitting on the bed with his head in his hands. That became what grief looks like to me. But it doesn't work for me, putting my head in my hands. It doesn't work for me to do what you're doing, whatever it is. I don't see how it isn't just going to be there, every day for the rest of my life. It's going to be a lot harder to manage if you go south on me."

Manage. That's it?

She had nothing more to say. She started to turn away but he pulled her to him, wrapping her up with both arms. It was real, and she felt it, but she was stiff and he let her go.

It's going to be really, really hard, she thought, *to get through this together.*

13.

THE FIRST DAY Joy went back to the gym it was 10:30 in the morning. The time was chosen carefully—she'd be very unlikely to see anyone she knew. In the deserted spinning studio, she adjusted a bike and got on it. Memory haltingly returned to her legs, from under the layers, but the yearning of her long-unused muscles overtook any resistance and she surged power into the pedals. Sweat was soon pouring off her. She rode straight tempo until her lungs exploded. She sat up, legs tingling, cooing down as her breath returned to normal, she thought that she really, really wanted to go riding.

Tomorrow. Tell Danny. I'll be safe.

Outside the studio she filled her bottle and leaned on the wall, stretching her legs. But then a hand clasped her shoulder and some woman's husband trapped her between the wall and the drinking fountain.

"Hi, Joy, how are you doing?"

His voice resonated with the low notes of a passing engine. He wrapped his arms around her for just a bit too long, giving her a paternal pat on the back and a little too much of a rub.

John's son Max was in Jake's class at school. "We're okay, we're managing."

"I can't imagine what it's like."

She wanted to slap him. Instead she said, softly, "It's fortunate you don't have to."

He blundered on. "I'm glad to see you," he said. "When my aunt lost her father she was in bed for weeks. It's brave of you just to be here."

John waited briefly for the thank you that was not forthcoming. He tried again.

"Jake seems to be doing well. I was on a field trip last week; he was involved, asking questions, talking to Max."

"He's a brave boy. Pretty resilient."

There was a silence.

He said, "We made you a dinner one night."

"Thanks. I'm sorry we couldn't respond separately to everyone," Joy said.

"Oh, no, I didn't mean . . . We'd love to have you over when the time is right."

She was getting anxious, which must have come out in her voice when she said, "Okay, that could be nice."

A welcome musical voice and bright flash of orange and yellow leotard caught her attention. "Namaste, Joy. Nice to see you back."

Rachel was Joy's friend and the club yogini. Joy had worked with her privately and in classes for the past year, using yoga to balance the effects to cycling. Rachel wasn't Jewish, but she'd come to the house every shiva day.

Joy ducked under John's arm and hugged her.

"Hey, Rachel. Got any time now?"

"I do, actually."

She nodded apologetically at John, who said, "I just wanted to say hello. If there ever is anything we can do, please let us know. Give my best to Danny." He headed off to the weight room.

"You okay?" Rachel asked.

"Yeah. Thanks, though."

"No problem. We try to reduce to a minimum the amount of shit women get in this club."

Joy chuckled. "That wasn't shit. He's a friend, I guess. Doing his best, anyway. I'm sorry I never finished the poster."

"No worries. Something else happened to you."

Joy valued the unadorned acknowledgement.

Rachel said. "We used your design anyway. I got the studio open."

"Congratulations." It was nice for Joy that she meant it.

Rachel took Joy to the yoga alcove behind the water fountain.

They spread a couple of mats and began their asanas. Joy felt something she remembered, a yielding to gravity that led to the center of the earth—not to the other world. *Maybe,* she thought, *I can have more of these moments again, ordinary moments in my life.* She exhaled deeply and felt trust in this woman who spent her life in the palpable world of gravity and touch and feeling. Maybe Joy could touch and feel in that way too; it was a good choice to come to the gym today. *I'll have to tell Danny,* she thought. *He'll be relieved.*

They were sitting in the Twist when Rachel said, "I have a confession. I just told my kids about Jenny yesterday."

Rachel had two daughters, both younger than Jake.

"What?" Joy looked at her uncomprehendingly.

Rachel untwisted herself. "When it first happened, I didn't know what to do. Even though they didn't know Jenny that well, they looked up to her. I didn't know what to think or how to talk about it. I want to protect my kids from pain, and I was just afraid that there would be nothing to say. So I said nothing. Please forgive me."

Joy wanted to be mad at her, but what she felt was compassion.

So she said, "That's all right, there's nothing to really forgive. It's hard."

"I was thinking about myself, actually," Rachel said, "not them. I didn't want to have to tell them why it happened. I don't know why it happened. I guess I thought I'd figure it out with time, but I didn't."

"There was no reason it happened. It was an accident. I left her in the car and boom. It doesn't fit in the world at all. It just happened. It could happen to anyone."

"That's what I was afraid of saying to them. Anyway, I'm sorry. Hearing this now must be a drag."

"No, it's a relief, actually. Hardly anyone is honest with me. At least you didn't ask me how I can do it."

"No one can do it," Rachel said.

"No." Joy moved to the next asana.

"Here," Rachel said, "twist your foot a bit to the left. Lower yourself into that hip. Good. Don't overdo it. Now five long breaths."

They finished the routine.

"Coming here has got to be weird," Rachel said. "Why don't you come to my home studio instead? No charge."

"That's very kind, but I'm fine."

"No, Joy, I mean it. It's a lot nicer than the gym. Let's make a plan. Invite a friend if you want. Thursday mornings?"

"That's very kind. Thursdays work, thanks." Joy remembered gratitude. She tried to seek out John and apologize. But he was gone already.

My job in everyone's life is to threaten their children with annihilation. But maybe they'll survive if they just pretend it's okay. The Angel of Death will overlook them. When the Bay Bridge collapses again in the next earthquake, they won't be on it. When that tree falls down, it will hit someone else's car. Their parents will die peacefully in bed and someone else's will live with Alzheimer's for twenty years. But then they see me and I'm just like them, with a family just like theirs. Rachel's giving me yoga because her kids are alive. *An outcome of Jenny's death: A deeper friendship with Rachel.*

* * *

Early the next morning Joy put on her bike clothes and took a cup of coffee down to the basement. Before she took her road bike off the hook she cleaned and waxed the frame. Then she took it down and wiped off the saddle. She lubed the chain and checked the brakes, spun the wheels and pumped the tires. She found the tire tools and pump and attached them to the bike. She put on her shoes and her helmet and glasses and went with the bike out the basement door and around Danny's car on the parking pad, just like a thousand other mornings, before. She mounted and pushed off the curb and rolled slowly down the street, clicking in to each pedal separately, running up to a big gear and standing to push the pedals slowly but strongly across the first street. She thought she probably shouldn't be too ambitious for her first day back, so she rode ten miles to the other side of the Golden Gate Bridge and back.

What her legs and her breath remembered made it really familiar but she felt displaced; those feelings belonged to someone else. *Have I lost this, too*, she wondered, until she crossed the top of the bridge's arc and found space to ride a good cadence in the right gear for only two minutes. *My heart can be broken and pump hard at the same time*. Not exhilarating, but effective.

Back at the house, Danny toasted her with his insulated travel mug. "To the Common World, perhaps," he said, and kissed her cheek on his way out the door.

14.

THIS TIME HIRAM brought Danny's mother with him.

"Joy," Hiram said, "you need to proceed with the insurance claim. However you feel, you can't turn your back on this money."

"It won't bring her back, Daddy. I'm not going to sit there in court and tell the whole story again while some attorney argues that my negligence killed my daughter."

"For God's sake, Joy, this is not going to end up in court. Or even arbitration."

"If I hadn't left my car there she'd still be alive. If I'd brought her in to the store with me she'd still be alive. If I made her wait five minutes until we got downtown she'd still be alive. If I parked on the other side of the street she'd still be alive. If I asked her about it before we left the school she'd still be alive."

"And if you never had her in the first place she wouldn't be dead either!" Hiram snapped. "Would you have given up the years you did have?"

Of course not. No. Even with this.

"Hiram, control yourself." Elaine's face was tear streaked.

It's hard for her, too. She touched Elaine's arm.

"Honey," she said to Joy, "think about the money being for Jake. You don't have to spend a penny on yourselves. Danny's business is doing great. You can work as much as you want to. The process will mostly be pro-forma: those guys are going to want to settle. You told me Bob has called you? Talk to him." Bob Davidson had been a high school classmate of Danny's and was a well-established personal injury lawyer.

"Call him, Joy," Hiram said. "You're an athlete. A little pain for a lot of good. Suck it up."

The disability insurance that came with their credit card allowed for a payment in case of the death of a child. Danny had told her about it and made a copy of Jenny's death certificate to send to them. The payment was equivalent to the payment for losing a finger on your non-dominant hand; less than the funeral had cost. After just a few weeks there was a check. Joy opened the envelope but she couldn't stand looking at the check with the memo line: Re: the death of Jennifer H. Rosenberg. She had tossed it into a drawer in the kitchen. Danny had found it a couple of days later. He opened the envelope and held the check up in the light and asked with his eyes. She just said, "Oops," but still wouldn't touch the check. He had to deposit it.

After the parents left Danny found her in her office. He squeezed her shoulder and she squeezed his hand and he said, "Was that hard?"

"You knew they were coming," Joy said.

He nodded. Joy thought she should be angry about that.

"The only way I could get Hiram off this would be to shoot him. At least I got him to wait a few weeks and to do it with my mom."

"Thanks, I guess. Dad can be blunt. You want me to do it?"

"Yes. I want you to do it. The money is for Jake. It's only a deposition. Just tell the story."

Joy nodded. *They're right. The world actually is a very dangerous place.* It was much more obvious, likely even, they would suffer some other loss soon, that one of them would be disabled, the Big One would trash their house, or Danny's business would go south, or something, but they would still be responsible for Jake.

Maybe everyone was right and it wouldn't be too bad. Maybe the lawyers would feel sorry for her, dragging her back out on the street again. Maybe she'd remember some detail she had forgotten the last 5,000 times the memory had replayed itself in her head. Maybe that would be okay. Maybe it would be worse. Maybe reliving it over and over, day after day, was her purgatory, round and round in an endless loop for the rest of her damned life.

Probably won't make a goddamn bit of difference anyway. I'll always be the one who left her in the car. Of course, what do I know? I can't even set the table.

15.

JOY WAS CLEANING up noisily from a multi-pot dinner when Danny came downstairs after putting Jake to bed.

"Hey Joy," Danny said, "Keep it down. Jake's going to sleep."

She slowed down.

"Why do they always want to know how I can do it?"

"Who?"

"Everyone who hasn't talked to me yet."

"Prurience, I suppose."

"Well, I'm sick of it."

"You don't have to tell them the truth."

She shook her head. "Sometimes I do."

"Only just enough of it. Not everything."

"I can never remember the clichés when I need them."

"Let's make a list."

He went into Joy's office, coming back with a small drawing pad and a selection of Joy's art pens.

"You give great pen," he said.

"Wives with benefits," she said. "You're in a good mood."

"Nothing like doing a cooperative activity with your spouse to strengthen a marriage."

"Thanks, Dr. Phil."

"Good place to start," Danny said. "Here's one."

Danny wrote the number one on the top of the page and followed that with: I didn't get to die, so I have to live. Then he wrote: 2. You live with the hand you're dealt.

"Pap," Joy said. "And it sounds so bitter."

"We are bitter. But I guess the goal is to deflect further questioning." He wrote: 3. Oh, you develop a certain grace.

"I've got one," Joy said. She took the pen and wrote: 4. I have to be here for Danny and Jake; we still have a life to live.

Danny said, "Yecch."

"The question I hate is how many children do you have?"

"I used to ask that all the time," he said. "Now I never do."

Joy remembered asking that question herself, when pride dominated her narrative. Now it looked like arrogance. Her family's new life was an experience impossible to share. "If I lie I deny Jenny. If I tell the truth they feel bad. Then I have to soothe them, so they can run home to cuddle their live children and I get to feel guilty about disrupting their perfect little life."

"You aren't responsible for how they feel, Joy."

"Of course I am. I have the dead child. I don't feel that nice anymore. I want to tell them to fuck off, it's none of their goddam business."

"Whoa," Danny said. "Getting serious now."

He went to the freezer and brought out the vodka and two shot glasses. He poured.

"Nasdrovya."

They knocked them back and clunked the glasses on the table. He wrote: 5. Fuck off, it's none of your goddam business.

Joy smiled. "Okay, that one stays."

Danny wrote: 6. I have a six-year-old son.

"Shit, Danny, really?"

"It's the truth, isn't it?"

"Not the whole truth."

"We can't deny it." He refilled their glasses.

I can't admit it, either.

"*Nasdrovya.*" The glasses hit the table.

She took the pen: 7. I have two children, a ten-year-old girl and a seven-year-old boy.

"Oh man, this one is dangerous," Danny said. "They're going to ask me about her soccer matches."

"But don't you ever imagine—"

"No. I can't. She'll never get any older. Then Jake will get older than her."

She felt a little dizzy. "That's going to be very weird. So how do we tell the truth?"

The bottle was on the move again.

"*Nasdrovya.*" Clunk.

He wrote: 8. I have one child, a seven-year old boy. We lost our daughter last year.

"No way I'm ever saying that."

She wrote: 8b. I have two children. My son is seven; we lost our daughter last year.

"I hate this so much," he said.

Joy hated it too. "This is the one we have to live with now, I guess."

"I don't know that. *Nasdrovya.*" Clunk.

He wrote: 9. My daughter is dead. She took the pen and added: You'd better be nice to me.

"Playing the dead child card," he said.

In a different time they would have laughed at that. They stared at the list for a while. There was nothing else to add. She tore off the page and copied the list neatly into her sketchbook. Danny kept the original; he said he would put it in his briefcase. When the silence got too thick he took her hand and led her up the stairs.

She came to their bed naked. He saw, and took off his pajamas. His arms came around her, seeking her breasts, but she took his hands and pulled them to her waist, in a hug. She arched her back toward him and he found his place. They fucked quietly, in their bed. He might have come. The earth did not move. The next morning, even though he was asleep, she kissed him right on the lips.

16.

JOY'S REFLECTION STARED back at her from the polished door of the stainless steel elevator: smart black suit, white shirt, black hose, black shoes, but no jewelry, no makeup. Just the look her attorney had ordered. Her hair hung in wet strands. Hollow eyes sunk deep into her face, mouth turned down, like a Disney hag who's been found out at the end of the story.

Davidson had filed claims with the various companies. He told Joy the other side had been expecting a claim and were happy to agree to arbitration, but that he did not think it would come to that; they would be motivated to settle. And he was aware of Joy's desire to get it over with. He filed a brief, with her sworn affidavit, but the attorneys for the other side wanted to depose her anyway.

The law had established protocols for valuing the loss of children. "You'd be surprised how often kids are killed in accidents," Bob said. Joy wasn't, of course. The cases generally were decided on an economic basis. The lifetime loss of the comfort and succor of a living child was impossible to value because the adult capacities of any given child were unpredictable. Each family, too, was different.

Because of Joy and Danny's education, Jenny's life was given a higher value. The assumption was that she'd be educated as well, therefore generating more income over the course of her life and yielding a higher net present value for the settlement. Additional discounts were applied for the delayed start of her earning years due to graduate school and estimated time off for pregnancy. Actuaries used charts that would determine the net present value of her lifetime accrued earnings at a range of estimated inflation-based discounts.

"We might have been able to ask for more," Bob told them, "if Jenny was older with a career earnings path already established. We'll add in your loss of earnings due to bereavement, therapy costs, funeral, all the extra expenses, whatever you can estimate."

"Documented?" Danny asked.

"Nope. At this stage it just has to be reasonable," Bob said. "They want it over with, too."

"We've had a lot pain and suffering," said Joy.

"Can't get paid for that, but I will be bringing it up," Bob said, "very emphatically."

Bob's firm's entry lounge was beautifully appointed with modern art on the walls, dense pile carpeting, carefully placed easy chairs and couches, today's newspapers arranged neatly on the coffee tables. She picked a chair by a large tree, sheltered from the door. A few minutes later what must be her interlocutors came bustling in, overcoats flapping open, briefcases dangling from leather-gloved hands. The receptionist led them away.

A chorus to witness my public stoning.

Joy was the only witness. Bob came to get her.

"Why are there three of them?" she asked.

"One each from the contractor, the property owner, and the scaffolding company. Only one of them will ask the questions, though. Remember, tell the truth, but only answer the questions you are asked. If you can only say yes or no, do that. Don't offer opinions. Just like we practiced. Leave your backpack with the receptionist."

The little lost waif.

* * *

In the conference room, the lawyers' faces were lost in the glare from the wall of glass behind them. Joy took a chair opposite the middle one. A spotlight from the ceiling revealed his face. He looked about fourteen. Davidson sat next to her. A tape recorder sat in the middle of the table. An older woman sat at one end, fingers poised over a stenotype machine. Out the window it was a bluebird day. Joy could see the Campanile on the Berkeley campus, miles away across the water. She remembered young lovers walking up Strawberry Canyon, behind the campus, and for a moment she felt Danny's hand in hers. She forced her attention to the faces. The middle guy's name was Stephen Duckworth. He introduced the others and went over the procedures.

"I apologize in advance," Duckworth said, "if some of my questions seem probing or insensitive. I just have a job to do here. I hope you can forgive me if anything seems hurtful."

Joy gave him her crazy-ass witch stare. "Stephen, the whole thing is hurtful. Don't fool yourself that you're being nice to me. Just get it over with."

Bob laid a cautionary hand on her shoulder. Duckworth looked away. The silence extended.

Score one for the defense.

Duckworth looked at Bob, who raised an eyebrow and tilted his head toward the table.

"Anything else?" asked Duckworth. "No? Then let's begin. If you need to take a break for any reason, just ask."

The recorder was turned on. The stenographer stood, said the date, and turned to Joy.

Stenographer: Do you swear to tell the truth, to the best of your ability and recollection?

Mrs. Rosenberg: I do.

Steno: State your name, please.

Mrs. Rosenberg: Joy Sarah Swartz Rosenberg.

Steno: Are you the mother of the deceased, Jennifer Hannah Rosenberg?

Mrs. Rosenberg: Yes.

Mr. Duckworth: Mrs. Rosenberg, we are here to interview you as to the circumstances surrounding the death of Jennifer Hannah Rosenberg. Please answer each question to the best of your ability and recollection. Please describe the events of the day in question.

Mrs. Rosenberg: I picked my daughter up from school at 3:10. We were going shopping at Union Square. We were driving down Bush Street. She was thirsty. I asked her if she could wait until we got downtown, but she wanted something now. I saw a convenience store and a place to park on the curb across the street, next to the construction site.

Mr. Duckworth: Please describe what you saw.

Mrs. Rosenberg: The building has been under construction for many months. It must be six or eight stories tall. A scaffold was set up on the sidewalk, covering the front of the building. There were things piled on it at various levels, drywall and wood beams and roof tiles. The curb had no cars or trucks. That's where I parked.

Mr. Duckworth: Please continue.

Mrs. Rosenberg: The day was really windy. She wanted to stay in the car. I let her. I crossed the street and went into the store to buy a bottle of water. When I was in the store I heard a terrible crash. When I looked outside the scaffolding had collapsed on my car, with Jenny inside. I ran outside. There was a huge cloud of dust in the air. I remember coughing and choking. I tried to get to her. I tried to pull the steel away with my hands. Some people were trying to help me but nothing could be done. My hands were bleeding. The car was completely buried. I was screaming and crying and telling Jenny I was coming to get her. Officer O'Reilly took me to her car.

Mr. Duckworth: You remember her name?

Mrs. Rosenberg: Yes. She took me home. Subsequently, she visited us with the final police report.

Mr. Duckworth: What happened next?

Mrs. Rosenberg: A fire truck arrived.

Mr. Duckworth: How long did it take them to arrive?

Mrs. Rosenberg: I have no idea. I was distraught. It seemed pretty soon.

Mr. Duckworth: What happened next?

Mrs. Rosenberg: Nothing happened. They were keeping people away from me and the rubble. The officer took my statement. I kept asking where Jenny was. I didn't understand why no one was working on the pile.

Mr. Duckworth: Jenny is the decedent?

Mrs. Rosenberg: Yes, Jennifer. We called her Jenny. The firemen couldn't do anything; they had to get a piece of equipment, like a backhoe or something. I kept wanting to get out of the car, but the officer kept me inside, except when I threw up. I called my husband. He left work to get our son. He was still at school. The pile was huge. Dust was blowing around. My throat hurt. I thought she was dead. I hoped she was alive. I thought it took forever for the backhoe to come, but I learned later it was only fifteen minutes. So it came and eventually the paramedics got to the car. I was just sitting there watching, feeling helpless. I somehow was holding the bottle of water I bought for her. A huge piece of wood stuck straight up. I found out later it had stabbed her right through the car's roof. They wouldn't let me go to her. I demanded to know what had happened. They told me she was dead. They thought she had died almost instantly. They gave me her backpack and her phone. The phone still showed the game she was playing, asking if she wanted to play again. I was relieved that she had finished the game she was playing. I called my husband again and told him she had died. We decided to tell Jake, our son, at home. Officer O'Reilly took me home. My husband and son arrived very soon. We told him together that his big sister was dead.

Mr. Duckworth: Mrs. Rosenberg, please look at this photograph. Does this look like what you saw when you exited the store?

Steno Note: Fifteen-second pause.

Mr. Duckworth: Mrs. Rosenberg?

Mr. Davidson: Joy, do you need anything?

Mrs. Rosenberg: No. Yes.

Mr. Duckworth: You are identifying this picture with yes?

Mrs. Rosenberg: Yes.

Mr. Duckworth: Mrs. Rosenberg, were you aware that you were parking in a construction zone?

Mrs. Rosenberg: Yes, although I didn't really note it when I stopped. I saw no work going on, and I was going to be there for two minutes.

Mr. Duckworth: Work was being conducted inside the premises, behind the locked gate.

Mrs. Rosenberg: Okay.

Mr. Duckworth: Mrs. Rosenberg, let me show you this photograph, taken by the contractor two days before the incident. It clearly shows the "No parking, construction zone" sign. Can you read me the hours on the sign, please?

Mrs. Rosenberg: 7AM to 5PM, Monday through Friday.

Mr. Duckworth: What time did you park there?

Mrs. Rosenberg: About 3:30.

Mr. Duckworth: So you parked in a clearly marked construction zone?

Mrs. Rosenberg: Yes. I already answered this question.

Mr. Duckworth: Mrs. Rosenberg, have you had any experience with construction?

Mrs. Rosenberg: What?

Mr. Duckworth: Have you worked in a construction firm, or had any work done on your home while you were living there?

Mrs. Rosenberg: We had our house painted about eight years ago.

Mr. Duckworth: Did the painters use scaffolding?

Mrs. Rosenberg: Yes.

Mr. Duckworth: Did you receive a document such as this one?

Steno Note: Trifold brochure *Living Safely with Scaffolding* entered as Exhibit 1.

Mrs. Rosenberg: I don't have the slightest idea. My husband managed the job.

Mr. Duckworth: Are you aware that construction zones are inherently dangerous places?

Mrs. Rosenberg: We were outside the building. No work was going on where we were. No trucks or other equipment were parked. I thought they were done working for the day. I drive by there many times a week. Workers park their trucks there all the time. They eat lunch in their trucks. They talk on the phone in their trucks. Without hardhats. I don't believe this was an extra dangerous place to leave my car. Scaffolds are not supposed to fall down in construction zones and kill little girls either. If we'd been walking through the covered sidewalk under the scaffold at the same time she'd be just as dead and I would be too.

Steno Note: Twenty-second pause.

Mr. Davidson: Joy, do you need a minute? No? Let's move on to the next question, please.

Mr. Duckworth: Mrs. Rosenberg, did you often leave your daughter unsupervised?

Mrs. Rosenberg: Very rarely. More recently as she was getting older. She was ten years old.

Mr. Duckworth: Why did you leave her at this time?

Mrs. Rosenberg: I was only running into the store for two minutes. She was playing a game and wanted to continue it. I locked the car door.

Mr. Duckworth: Did you believe this was safe?

Mrs. Rosenberg: Yes. I did not anticipate your client's property falling on her.

Mr. Duckworth: No one anticipated that.

Steno Note: Fifteen-second pause.

Mr. Davidson: Mr. Duckworth?

Mr. Duckworth: Mrs. Rosenberg, you are making a claim for lost business income. Please describe your claim.

Mrs. Rosenberg: I have a design business, and work on contract for a large range of clients. My work includes business development, finding new clients, as well as executing design projects for existing ones. I have lost revenue during the time I've been out and my inflow of new business also will be impacted due to that lack of activity. I expect to go back after six months, but to lose the equivalent of a full year's revenues.

Mr. Duckworth: Why are you unable to work sooner?

Mrs. Rosenberg: Are you really asking me that?

Mr. Davidson: My client is a professional with nearly fifteen years of experience. She is able to evaluate her own capacity to work to expectations. Her claim is quite fair.

Mr. Duckworth: Have you submitted all the expenses related to the claim?

Mrs. Rosenberg: Yes. Except therapy will be ongoing.

Mr. Duckworth: We understand. Mrs. Rosenberg, is there anything you would like to add?

Mrs. Rosenberg: Yes. Jenny's most important role in life was as big sister to her brother Jacob. He has not had a voice at this table, but he is as much a victim as Jenny. He is suffering the largest part of this loss. My husband and I have decided that any settlement is going into a trust for him and hopefully his children.

Mr. Duckworth: Thank you, Mrs. Rosenberg. That concludes our questions. Mr. Davidson has sent us a letter in which he described the decedent as a unique and special child. Did you have any exhibits you wish to include today?

Mrs. Rosenberg: Yes.

Joy opened the portfolio that had been sitting on the table in front of her. Little pieces of Jenny's life began to fill the table. Her report on the California Missions. The program for the tap recital she never got to be in. The letter from the synagogue scheduling her now-cancelled

Bat Mitzvah. Her school evaluations. Medical exam. Duckworth dutifully noted each one, peeling a number off a roll of stickers and pasting it carefully to the top of each paper. They circulated through the lawyers to the stenographer, who placed each one facedown on the copy machine on the shelf behind her. When the machine spit out the paper, she compared the copy with the original, made a note in the stenograph, stamped the copy and initialed it, and returned the original to Joy, one by one.

Dead child street theater, Joy thought.

Steno Note: The deposition concluded at 10:47 AM.

After debriefing in Bob's office, Joy's backpack was delivered and she used Bob's private restroom to change into jeans, socks, and sneakers. It wasn't enough, so she took off her fleece and her shirt and stood at the sink in her bra with her pants down low on her hips, below the counter so they wouldn't get splashed, and rinsed and soaped and then scrubbed really hard at the skin on her face and her chest and her underarms with the high thread count towels Bob's firm provided. Her skin had reddened in places, but she couldn't see it when she put her shirt back on. Downstairs was a brisk March day.

Decedent, she thought. *Fuck.*

It took two hours to walk home.

17.

WHEN JOY GOT pissed at him, she thought that Danny had his shit way too together.

"That's an uncharitable thought," he said. "I hold it in all day. I can't talk to anyone there, no matter how nice they are. I'm still the boss."

"Maybe we should go to a support group," Joy said.

"Do you want to?"

Absolutely not, she said to herself, but she said, "It sounds like something we should try, at least. You could talk there."

"You, too."

"Maybe."

"Okay," he said, and within the hour he had found a group and a schedule and talked to the leaders on the phone.

The closer it got the more uneasy Joy felt, but Danny seemed to be looking forward to the experience. Soon enough Danny was leading her down Waller Street, then down a narrow alley made even more inconsequential by the dark, looming wooden bulk of the church. Maybe it will fall on us, she half-hoped, but it didn't. They descended five steps to a blank brown door. A piece of notebook paper was thumbtacked there, scrawled with the words *Compassionate Friends* in thick black marker.

The room looked like an afterthought—spare space the architect had discovered during construction that could be made usable with a little more excavation, a concrete slab, and a few sheets of drywall. Two small transom windows provided the only ventilation. Against the opposite wall, below a couple of tacky pseudo-spiritual posters, a tired gray plastic folding table held a bubbling teakettle, a jar of instant coffee, a basket of assorted teas, three cocoa packets, and a collection of mismatched coffee mugs. A stained laundry sink sat in one corner. Twelve brown metal folding chairs were arranged in a circle on the worn linoleum floor patterned with triangles. Three other couples and two single women occupied the room. A tall, lean middle-aged man in a stocking cap came over to them, accompanied by a slight but stunning woman with long silver-streaked red hair and an impish smile.

"You must be Joy and Danny. Thank you for coming," the man said. "I'm so sorry for your loss."

"It happens," Joy said. "It happened to you."

"To everyone here," he said.

They all shook hands and he handed them two already-prepared nametags. "My name is Benny, and this is my wife Deborah."

"Deb, please," said Deborah. "We share the hosting of this meeting with two other survivor couples. Our son was seventeen when he was killed by a drunk driver, fourteen years ago."

They didn't seem sad at all. Danny led Joy to a couple of chairs. She slid hers against his and again slipped her hand through his arm, holding on firmly. She kept her jacket on. Introductions proceeded around the circle. Drunk-driving victim, drunk-driving perpetrator, cancer, overdose, suicide, construction accident. Seventeen, sixteen, three, fourteen, twenty-one, ten. Joy's shoulders buckled under the weight of these children—and their killers.

From among them she heard Danny talking. "My phone rang. I saw it was Joy calling and I felt happy, I always was happy when she called, but on the phone she was hysterical, crying, gasping, choking out the words. I had never heard her sound like that before. I was scared; something terrible had happened. When I understood what I screamed, 'Where is Jake?' I was terrified that both the kids were in the car, but he was at school. I wanted to go to Joy, but she just kept repeating that I needed to go get Jake, to be home when she got there. I told my secretary 'Something happened' and just ran out. I left my jacket and briefcase and everything. I got in my car and somehow drove across the bridge, but when I got to the city, Joy called again and it hit me. I pulled in to the parking lot and cried. I was hitting the steering wheel with my fist, but I knew I had to keep it together for a little while longer."

He's keeping it together now, Joy thought. She looked at the other men in the room, wondering if that was what they all did. Only Benny was actually looking at Danny.

"I called my parents in Calistoga," Danny continued, "my brother in LA, Joy's dad, and Joy's two closest friends. I called my secretary and told her what happened and to cancel all my appointments, that I wouldn't be in for a while. I called the school to tell them I was coming and could Jake please be ready and outside. Then I remember I took five deep breaths, I counted them, and started driving.

"When I got to our son he could tell that something was wrong, but I tried to be cheerful. Protect him for another five minutes, I guess. A police car was in front of the house. Jake wanted to know why. When we got inside, Joy was there. She looked wild, her hair was everywhere, she was all dusty. She jumped on me. Jake was scared. When the police officer left, we got into a close huddle and Joy said there was a terrible accident, that Jenny had died. Jake asked if he could ever see her again. Joy collapsed onto the floor, and I had to tell him that he couldn't. No one could."

Someone asked, "Were you alone?"

"Not for long," Danny said. "The people I called started showing up. We just talked and cried and sat around. The rabbi came. We picked something to bury her in—a dress she might have hated. I gave her my childhood prayer shawl. Then we had the funeral, and we were zombies for a month. I went back to work after that."

For a moment, he slumped. His head dropped toward her and Joy stiffened, ready to carry his weight, but he lifted his head up and continued.

"After we talked to the rabbi, my father drove me down to the site. Joy's car had been taken away, and the contractor was cleaning up the mess. I stood in front of the store and watched them working. I didn't want Joy to be on that street alone. A few days after the funeral I went to the police holding yard to clean out the car."

His voice quavered. "I tried to avoid the bloodstains on the passenger seat but I couldn't, so then I really looked, visualizing her sitting there, looking down, earphones in her ears, hearing a noise, then the board spearing through the roof. They think it hit her in the head and knocked her unconscious before she got cut open."

They both cried.

"We didn't view her body."

Joy held his arm tighter. *The day he came back with the car things. Did he talk? Did I listen?*

Deborah passed them a box of tissues.

Directly across from them a young man's arm enveloped his wife. Their three-year-old child Susie had died of cancer two years earlier. The woman wore a worn brown corduroy housedress under a beige cotton cable-knit sweater. Her hair was brown and hid much of her face. She was too thin, but Joy empathized. She could be pretty, if she bothered.

"When Susie died," the young wife said, "the world ended. She had been sick since she was six months old. We're from a small town in Illinois. We grew up there, and walking around I saw her everywhere. Everybody saw me, too, but nobody talked to me about our daughter or how we were doing. It was like she never existed. You were supposed to get over it, but I couldn't stand not talking about her. Mom took down all the pictures she had of Susie. When she came to our apartment she turned my pictures around so she couldn't see them. After a few months we left and came out here. She probably had the cancer even before she was born. How can we have another baby?"

Her husband, a burly young man with a Marine haircut, gave her a protective squeeze. Joy saw him and Danny exchange a glance—an impromptu alliance of husbands babysitting their shattered wives. The honor and duty of men.

Before the silence in the room got too deafening, Deborah said. "Nothing is wrong with you, it was just a terrible thing. It's not your fault, it's not Susie's fault; no one knows why this kind of thing happens. You're young, you still can have children."

"How do I know they won't die too?" The young woman was sobbing.

Deborah sidestepped the question. "I have referrals to good doctors. It would take time but you'll find a way. You have friends in this room."

Is this what I have to look forward to? Two years and still shattered? Will I still be playing in her room? Going to the cemetery and saying Kaddish all the time?

Instead of saying how the girl's testimony had terrified her, Joy said, "It must be so hard to leave everything behind and be all by yourselves. I can't imagine doing this without our parents and friends."

The girl looked as if Joy had just stabbed her.

"That's why we're at a support group," her husband said, patiently. "Some of us just aren't as lucky as you are."

He shook his head at Danny. Honor and duty. Danny shrugged and pulled on Joy's arm.

Lucky, she thought. *Lucky?* Joy stopped listening as the sharing went around the room. Almost everyone spoke. Not Joy. A brief, nondenominational prayer concluded the meeting. Joy practically ran out of the room.

"What just happened in there?" she said when Danny caught up. "I thought I was trying to talk to her."

"You said the obvious. You don't like it when people ask how many children you have."

"I'm glad we don't have to depend on this group."

"A little humility might not be so bad for you, you know."

She flared. "Like I haven't eaten enough shit already?"

"I meant the Other World thing. You think you're wrestling with God, and she just wants to have another baby."

"Drop it, Danny, okay?"

They walked to the car in noisy silence.

"I liked telling my story," Danny said. "I don't really think I've ever told it so completely before."

"I never heard the whole thing, either, not like that. You remember it so concretely."

"Yes."

"You still haven't told me what the car looked like."

"No."

It must really hurt, remembering that. Like I remember the dust.

He gave her the space her prickliness demanded; but with Jake he was alive, vibrant, the man she had married. *He's the counterweight to my nuttiness.* Joy couldn't cry for Danny, yet she held onto him with all the strength she could muster. She had read that more than eighty percent of couples who lose a child break up. The pain was so often unbearable. Yet they bore it.

"I'm sorry I yelled at you."

"Okay," he said. "You kind of got ambushed in there."

"You're too nice to me. I was kind of a jerk. Would you like to go back?"

"I think so. I can go without you."

"No, Danny, I will if you want to."

But they never did.

18.

"I WANT TO clean out her room," Joy announced. She could not get Susie's mom's continuing devastation out of her mind.

"When?" Danny asked.

"On the weekend. You have to help me."

"Of course. What about Jake? He'll want to help too."

"Doesn't sound like a good idea."

"Why not?"

"He could get upset. Or maybe he won't want to get rid of anything."

"We can't protect him, Joy. It's his life, too. I'm going to ask him. Besides, he's her heir."

That stopped her. Danny was right. It was embarrassing that she couldn't think of Jake as having any agency in this change. When Joy was a little girl, her mom always was reorganizing Joy's drawers or her closet and usually took out clothes that she thought Joy shouldn't be wearing anymore, which had upset Joy once she got old enough to push back. This was kind of like the same thing. Probably she should be worried about that in her relationship with him. *What do you think, Jenny?* she wanted to ask, but the Other World was getting farther and farther away.

When she went to tuck him in Jake was reading *Goodnight, Moon*.

He finished that one and asked her which one she wanted him to read to her. She picked *Sophie and Lou,* which was romantic and didn't have any children in it. When he finished, she roused herself.

"Time to sleep now, Jake." It was a lot easier without the singing.

"Mommy, what's going to happen with Jenny's things?"

"We'll look at everything. Some things we'll give away, some we'll keep, some we'll save. I don't know, exactly."

"I haven't been in her room in a long time. It's weird."

Joy had never seen him go into Jenny's room after she died. If he wanted something, he would ask Joy to get it.

"It's good to change it now," Joy said. *For me, too.* She'd played all the games and read all the books and had completely run out of conversation topics relevant to Jenny's dolls.

"I want to help you, Mommy. I want to show Teddy Jenny's things," Jake explained, "because if he wants to keep something I want him to have it."

Joy got worried she'd have to fight with Teddy over everything, but maybe what she really was afraid of was Jake handling it well—or seeing her handle it poorly.

"Maybe a few things, honey."

"I'm still sad, Mommy."

"Me too, Jacob, me too. But it's better to remember than to forget, don't you think so?"

Jake tucked Teddy into bed before letting Joy do it to him.

"Mommy, will Jenny know what we're doing? Will she be mad at us?"

"When she was alive we gave away clothes and stuff she didn't wear or use anymore, so she's used to that. We won't throw away anything that you want to keep."

"I just don't want her to be mad. Can we put more things downstairs?"

"We'll see," she said. She leaned over to kiss him. Jake rolled over and pulled the covers up. Joy kissed the top of his head.

What a brave boy.

* * *

On Saturday, Joy said Kaddish like on every Shabbat. The week's Torah portion was deep in Numbers, *Bamidbar*, with its repetitive descriptions of the *Mishkaan*, the temple to be built to house the tablets of the law, deep in the innermost Holy of Holies. The room could be occupied for only a few minutes once a year, and only by the high priest, who faced sudden death if he screwed up the observance or wore the wrong thing. A place of unforgiving power. Aaron's sons died in there.

Really, though, how much holiness do you need? Do it every day and it isn't holy anymore, it's ordinary. She'd been looking for something that she destroyed by looking for it. *Maybe I'm an apostate for taking apart my holy place,* she thought, *but Jenny never had been there. It's good for it to be a room again. Besides, there's still the cemetery.*

The next morning, Danny didn't make waffles. He had more than one heavy duty, black, self-closing thirty-three-gallon garbage bag on hand for either trash or the things they would run down to Goodwill tomorrow. He had some file boxes. Joy brought a whisk broom and the Dustbuster. When they were ready, Joy opened the door.

"Pretty clean in here," Danny noted.

"I've been keeping it up," said Joy.

Danny photographed everything from every angle, embalming Jenny's history—the blue pastel bedroom set with the little dolphin cutouts, each wall as it stood, each detail as it now was: the top of the dresser, the desk, the candle shelf, the pile of dolls, arranged just as Joy imagined Jenny would have her things if she still could have her things with her, where she was.

Clothes first. They started a trash bag and a giveaway bag. No bras. Joy was both pained and relieved. Joy lifted Jenny's rainbow knee socks with the toes.

"I remember those!" Jake said. "Jenny would slide around on the floor and then pick things up with her toes. I want them!"

Danny got one of the storage bins. "Here, Jake, things we want to keep we'll put in here."

"I want them in my room! My things here!"

He put the socks next to him on the bed.

"Okay, honey," Joy said. Maybe he'd keep less without a box.

T-shirts. Five school walkathons, Giants and Cal teams, Amanda's eighth birthday, vacations . . . Joy examined each one before putting it into giveaway or trash, keeping only the Giant ones that soon would fit Jake. He'd have his own walkathons. Danny saved the Presidio Golf Club polo shirt he bought Jenny the second and last time they went. He looked at Joy wistfully, shrugged his shoulders, shook his head, and dropped it into the save bin.

"Each thing brings something back that I just have to let go again," he said. "Do you remember, in one of those dead child books someone had taken all of the things that made them have a memory like that and put them all into a special dresser? Then they walked by it every day for twenty years and never looked at anything."

"Let's not have a dresser then," she said.

Joy said hello to Jenny's favorite doll, her confidante, Belle/Beauty. "I remember sitting in the hall outside her room, eavesdropping on Jenny's long talks with Beauty. She taught Beauty how to read."

"Jenny would read to me and Beauty at the same time," Jake said.

"Do you want Beauty in your room?"

"No, Mom." He cuddled Teddy tightly.

She looked for Danny, but he was holding the top hat from Jenny's tap show.

"Maybe I'll keep Beauty in my office," she said. "It seems disrespectful to put her in the basement."

Jake sat on the bed and watched. They lifted everything up so he could see it. Some things had a memory in them, but mostly he sat quietly on the bed, Teddy in his lap, watching them work. Joy felt relieved. He was like a little Buddha, serene. Maybe he was upset on the inside, but she didn't believe it. He seemed to be aware of how much they were depending on him.

They finished the dresser and started on the bookcase. Jenny had provided Jake with reviews of every title in her library. Jake told them which books he wanted. Danny picked up the stack of keepers and took them right to Jake's room.

Jenny had kept Things She Loved on the middle shelves where she could see and touch them every day. Things like the odd little juggling frogs Carly got her when she taught Jenny how to juggle. Surprisingly substantial, they were dirtier on the heavy side, the palm side. Joy sniffed them, but they just smelled old.

Jake and Teddy bounced on the bed. "She gave us a show, me and Max and Bobby. She wore her funny socks and a clown nose and she juggled her frogs and made a penny vanish and then found it behind Bobby's ear!"

Joy laughed and said a thank you to Carly. "How did she do that?"

"I don't know," Jake said. "We made her do it two more times and couldn't figure it out!"

"Then it must have been magic," she said. "Your mysterious magical sister. Do you want to keep the frogs in your room?"

Jake grew quiet. Danny squeezed her shoulder.

The frogs went into the save bin.

Shopping for candles was something she and Jenny had done together. Each candle was a repository of everything they had been doing and talking about and seeing on the day it was acquired. Disneyland, Yosemite, Marine World. Each candle was wrapped in paper and saved. When Jake went to the bathroom Danny whispered that they'd probably never even look at them, and that Jake was going to have to clean them out of the basement when they died. Joy wanted to scream, *What the hell else can we do!* at him; but she only shrugged as she wrapped up the next one and put it into the bin.

Danny was holding the *Coins for Kids Handbook.* One day Jenny had started sorting Danny's jar of pennies, pouring them out on the floor, stacking them by date or decade into paper cups she had run down to the kitchen to get. She had been amazed and happy when

Danny showed up the next day with a stack of coin cards and the book. Her enthusiasm had infected him too.

"She was amazed that numismatics existed. Then she had to find out everything," he said. The shelf held a dozen coin cards, one for each decade from 1900. "I think I'll take these to work."

Joy got afraid. Parts of her daughter were getting strewn all over town. But the coins were part of Danny's story with Jenny. He deserved them. He would care for them. The top of the dresser had photographs of the family, of Jenny and Amanda, of Danny and Joy dressed up.

That one Joy remembered. "She was proud of us that night."

"I think she just wanted to use the camera," he replied.

"Oh Danny, no, no." She put her arm around his shoulders. "She was loving us to bits. Jakey, do you remember this?"

"You look happy in that picture, Mom. I like it when you're happy."

Joy's sword hand twitched, but Danny kissed the top of her head just then and the clouds settled. He picked up the fancy little basket their artist friend had made for Jenny's fourth birthday. The basket had a couple of shells and a redwood cone woven into it.

"Maybe this should go on the shrine table," he said.

"We can put some of the loose things in it." Joy wrapped another candle.

On top of the dresser were things she'd made. Each one took the time it needed to be passed back and forth between them until its story was told. Joy searched each piece over carefully, looking at every side for the mark of finger or brush that said, "Jenny was here." Jake would show it to Teddy; sometimes he would put his finger in the place where Jenny's had been. Then one of them would carefully wrap it in paper and place it into the bin with the candles. The little blob of clay Jenny, age three (or was it two?), had insisted was a mouse. Her Hebrew name carefully hand-painted on a tile from the do-it-yourself pottery store. The wooden bookends she made in after-school one week. Joy thought that Jenny likely would have tossed some of this stuff this year, but she and Danny didn't throw one of those things away.

Outside, the sun was setting. The bookcase, credenza, dresser, closet, and nightstand were done. Jake had retreated to his room. Joy could hear him reading to Teddy. Danny pulled the file drawer out of the desk, and they sat on the floor with it. Neatly arranged by grade and subject was Jenny's work product—homework study sheets, reports, drawings, stories, and poems. The file from the deposition was on top. Joy and Danny sat together, looking at each page, one by one, discarding the exercises, figuring out the drawings, reading each other Jenny's second grade poetry and one-paragraph stories full of previously unrecognized meaning now that her story was complete. It amazed Joy how Jenny's stories showed the arc of her life blooming and leading to its ending.

"How could she have known?" she asked him.

"She didn't, but we do, so that's how we see it," Danny said as he passed her the box of sheet protectors. They fossilized the wisdom of their child inside a three-inch, D-ring dime store binder.

Finally, they were done. The giveaways: four bags of clothes, one bag of dolls, some boxes of books and games. Three bags of garbage. Danny wanted to sell the furniture on eBay but Joy refused to have people in the house to see it. The credenza was going to Joy's bike room, and Goodwill was coming for the rest. In the middle of the room were stacked four plastic storage bins with a single three-inch binder, half full, sitting mutely on top—the complete life output of a ten-year-old.

That's it. How did Jenny ever fill up this room?

They gathered Jake and went for dinner to the neighborhood Italian place. After they ordered, Jake played a game on Jenny's phone. *His phone,* Joy thought. Danny and Joy drank a bottle of wine before their food came. He ordered another one.

"How do you feel?" he asked her.

"Exhausted. Relieved. Intoxicated." She waved her glass at the boys. "To fellow travelers."

"Maybe drinking is the right move," he said, waving back. "At least we're not driving."

They talked about what to do with the room. Joy thought it should be a guestroom/library. No TV. Danny agreed about the TV but said it would be nice if he could have a more permanent home office. Probably both of those things could be accommodated, they agreed. A guest room/library/office. He asked if she wanted to move her office there, but the idea filled her with dread. She told him it was because clients occasionally came to see her, but really she was afraid she'd never go downstairs again.

Their pasta came. Jake took his earbuds out and Danny helped him get started on his food. Joy watched them. It felt like a normal moment. Then she saw the empty chair. Some restaurants must have tables for three.

"Earth to Mom! Earth to Mom! Your food's getting cold!"

Indeed. Her plate was still full. She blushed though the haze of the wine.

"Oops! Sorry, guys!" She took a bite. "Tastes good." She took another bite. "What a thing to do today, huh?"

"Yeah, Mom," Jake said. "We're really special. I bet everyone wants to be just like us. Not."

19.

JOY HAD A hangover the next morning. She put on her bike clothes but kept finding other things to do. She ferried the bags and boxes down the stairs, then went back upstairs to view the deserted room. *Danny can help me move the credenza,* she thought, but she took out the shelves and rubber-banded its door handles together. She wiped down the rest of the furniture. After she closed the door she took the block *J* downstairs to the shrine table. Then she put the four boxes in the basement and the notebook in the den with their photo albums. She stacked the giveaway bags and boxes by the front door. She drank more coffee and read the paper, then went into her office.

Sometime during *Shloshim*, Danny had told her he had dreamed of Jenny as a young adult, happy and smiling. Joy had tried to draw that Jenny, a portrait in charcoal and pencil, long black hair falling below her shoulders and off the bottom of the page. Joy found the drawing on the shelf of her drafting table and tried to imagine the privilege of knowing this young woman. Then she looked again and frowned. The eyes never were right.

Danny called to her from the kitchen. "Were you moving boxes?" He came into the room. "Nice legs. You didn't get on the bike."

"Never got around to it."

"What have you been doing?"

"Wandering around. Did some swearing."

"Well, it's not like having her room together made it any easier."

"No."

She felt his hands on her shoulders. She lifted up the drawing to show him.

"That's good, Joy," he said. "We could go back upstairs, if you want."

She felt his hands slide slightly down toward her breasts. His fingers ran between her ribs, lightly massaging. She like his touch, but the drawing had the bulk of her attention. She stopped his hands. Danny kissed the top of her head and sat in her office chair while she perched on the stool looking out the window.

"When you told me your dream I thought she had come back. Then I had my vision about the Other World. I thought that if I could draw her it might be a talisman or something that she could find more easily when she wanted to come visit us. I hated it because I couldn't get the eyes right. But now she doesn't have any eyes. Should I draw her without eyes?"

"No," he said. "Eyes, please."

She closed the drawing pad and slid it back under the desk.

"I thought if you dreamed her alive maybe it could be true. I did that in her room. I kept waiting for her to talk back to me."

He was very still and said softly, "Yeah. Sometimes I get lost too."

They went back to the kitchen. Joy got a dust rag and returned to her office, grateful, today, for her husband. She wiped Jake's dinosaur off the wall. The world tightened, forcing her attention ahead toward a foggy, featureless future. The Other World crumbled forever, its warriors dead and buried, it mysteries unsolved. In brief equilibrium she floated, untethered, a moment of perfected wisdom, of submission rather than glory. She was surrounded. Jake's kind sweetness and bewildered sadness; Danny's duty, his loyalty; her dad, her bike, her business, the persistence of the world. Committed to the Common World, functional but floating until maybe, when she was many years out, the capacity to believe in what she was feeling might be restored.

She opened a new page in her sketchbook. She wrote at the top: Losing Jenny is irredeemable. But I remain alive.

Then she made a list.

1. Be Jake's mom.
2. Work.
3. Ride the bike a lot. Do yoga.
4. Keep house (with help).
5. See Dad once a week.
6. Help Danny. Somehow.

She put the pen down and studied the page. After a while it still seemed good enough, so she took a piece of art paper and her calligraphic pen, cleanly copied the list (except for the somehow), cut the page neatly from the sketchbook, and taped it to the wall above her monitor. She heard Jake padding down the stairs, and, temporarily satisfied, went into the kitchen to execute on her first deliverable.

20.

ON JAKE'S SEVENTH birthday, ten months almost to the day after she lost his sister, Joy invited Danny, Carly, and the three local grandparents to mark the day. No one, Jake included, wanted a party, even though Carly did do some tricks. He got just a few presents. Rose sent a beautifully illustrated young adult history book called *The Jews Come to America!* Hiram got him a baseball bat. With subdued fanfare Danny lifted the top of the cake plate to reveal the year-old poppy-seed cake from the bottom of the freezer, the last one Jenny had made. Elaine compensated for the freezer burn with a decent lemon-vanilla icing that she layered on thick. It was a Bundt cake, so Danny couldn't write a message on it, but they had seven candles, plus one to grow on, and chocolate chip ice cream.

Joy thought it macabre to use that cake, but Danny pointed out it was the last thing that Jenny could give her brother. *Until he uses the funds from the settlement,* she thought, *which really is macabre.* When it was time to sing, Joy called Lizzie on the speakerphone as she had promised, and Lizzie and Amanda and all their family joined in a rousing "Happy Birthday."

Jake's birthday was on a school day. He didn't want a party in his classroom like usual because Jenny had come down to his classroom when it was his birthday in kindergarten and first grade and now she couldn't. Usually, the mom brought cupcakes and the kids sang happy birthday after lunch. Joy said no to the teacher twice. That refusal percolated upward, and the head of school called Joy to tell her bringing birthday cupcakes would be good normalizing behavior for her son.

"Except he doesn't want it," she said. "We didn't do one at home and he doesn't want a party at the school either."

"But Joy, he'll be the only kid without one. If it's too much, I'm sure one of the other mothers will bake the cupcakes for you."

Are you really that stupid? Joy wanted to say, but instead she said, "That's very thoughtful, but it's not the point. Nothing is normal. Our first party is not going to be at school. Okay?"

And the head asked if Joy was really sure and Joy said yes and then she said goodbye nicely before she slammed the receiver down on the flash button.

Maybe I should keep Jake out that day, in case they can't control themselves.

Joy avoided school events as much as possible. When she had to go to one she actively followed a spontaneously developed practice that minimized the inauthentic contact so characteristic of such gatherings. Park a few blocks away. Wear neat but nondescript clothing. Style-less. Baggy. Show up at the last possible minute. Keep her hair loose, partially covering her face. Take a seat in the back, go to the bathroom right when it was over, dawdle, then drift through the crowded hallways, sliding off the conversations already begun, until she could get to Jake. And vamoose.

But today was *Forward!*, the day kids and parents got the educational and fundraising plans for the year. Joy walked Jake inside to his classroom. She bent down to kiss him but he was already gone, backpack hung on the hook neatly labeled with his alphabetically ordered name. He didn't look back. The teacher, who had taught Jenny, looked up at Joy and flashed one of those deeply empathetic teacher smiles, full of care, hope, and regret all at once. Joy gave a halfhearted wave and turned away from her son.

She made her way to the auditorium, slipping in the back door and leaning against the wall, alone. School leaders were pitching the annual fundraiser. From where she stood at the rear of the auditorium she could feel the rustling in the room, the men making sure their wallets were still in their pockets as their women whispered to them about doing their part.

Would have been me up there, before. Busy Little Beaver.

The pitching over, parents and kids traded locations. She watched the sixth grade parents, Jenny's class, going up the stairs to the science classroom and wished that she was walking up the stairs with them. No one looked for Joy, the exile, stranded in the desert like Hagar. In Jake's classroom she tried to lose herself against the wall, but the teacher would have none of that, pushing a nametag on her. "Joy, Jake's Mom," it said. The tag had little heart stickers on it.

The teacher briskly organized them into pairs to do one of the introduction to algebra exercises the kids would be doing this year. Joy was paired with the father of a new student. He seemed nice.

"So, how many children do you have?"

He didn't know who she was. She had six more years in the school with him. "Jake is here. We lost our daughter last November."

"Oh, you are the Rosenberg family. They told us about you when we got admitted to this class. What a terrible thing. I'm so sorry for your loss."

"Thank you," Joy said. She wondered what the school told incoming parents. *Walk softly around those Rosenbergs? Give little Jake a pass when he does something weird? I should ask them. What right do they have to tell people what to think about my family?*

"I hope somebody pays," he said.

"I'm paying," Joy snapped. She fixed her gaze on this hapless and unwitting man, letting the witch take over. Fear spread across his face. Beads of sweat formed at his hairline. She held his gaze just long enough to drive her despair into him, then, just before his head exploded, she hooded her eyes, looked away, and became a socialized woman once again. From the top of her mountain, she smiled, and making the generous gesture of king to subject, asked him, "Do you have other children here?"

She immediately forgot his answer.

He avoided her at the next classroom event.

21.

CONVENTIONAL WISDOM WIDELY promulgated in grief
books promised some relief after a year, as the mourner lives for the
second time those specific days that already included her bereavement.

Joy wondered who the hell they were talking about.

Most days she was able to cook dinner. Danny would pick up
something she'd ordered if she couldn't. They found Jake a therapist,
not because he seemed abnormally sad or withdrawn, but more
prophylactically, as if a problem was expected and they had better make
some room for it to arrive. Elaine thought an outlet outside the family
system might provide greater access to wellness, and Joy saw no reason
why that might not be true. But Jake seemed okay. He was reading a
lot at night. Joy thought maybe she was not as afraid of losing him, but
on too many nights too much of her got in his way and Danny would
tuck him in.

After Jake's bedtime, Danny would work in the office/guest room/
library. Some nights Joy would go downstairs and work too, far from
him, but other nights she'd sit with him in the room that used to be
Jenny's, drawing in her sketchbook or reading novels that all too often
surprised her with a dead child in the plot. Then she would find herself

in some kind of suspended animation, seeing the pages through the dust of the minimart doorway. Sometimes ten pages would go by and she'd have to backtrack to find out what had happened. Danny thought she maybe should read non-fiction, but Joy didn't see how it mattered. Jenny still was dead.

Joy generally went to bed first. If she still was awake when Danny came in, most nights a whispered kindness ended their evening. Rarely, he would come to bed with an insistence she would always allow. She thought if she could keep her body close enough to him, her spirit might eventually come around too. But if his need wasn't urgent, hers never was, and then they would go to wherever it was they went now that they couldn't go to where they once went anymore.

Yoga at Rachel's studio was lasting. Joy appreciated having a new friend who accepted that remaining alive wasn't actually her doing. Days she didn't feel safe on the road—she owed that much to Jake— or wanted to avoid the eyes of men, Joy rode the trainer on her back porch, headphones blasting Velvet Underground or Talking Heads.

The first morning she had returned to work the habit of years reasserted itself. She sent her boys off. She washed the breakfast dishes. She went upstairs, showered, and got dressed for the office. At nine, she sat at her desk. She opened her accounting program and generated an email list of all her past clients. She cut and pasted email addresses from the few inquiries that had come in during the past six months. She loaded her letter template. Her logo was multicolored and flowerish. Joyful.

When she started the business, she had agonized for weeks if she should call it Joy Design, JoyDesign or Joydesign! The decision had seemed dreadfully important, and she had thought that the wrong choice would consign her to the bush leagues forever.

The ridiculous things I worried about, she thought, not unkindly. *It didn't matter at all.*

The email read, "Dear Friends and Clients: Thank you so much for all your thoughtful kindness and concern over these past six months. I'm writing to let you know that I have now reopened my office and am available to work with you again for all your design and production needs. As always, you can reach me by phone or email at the contacts below."

She stared at the text for a while. *I should be nicer.* She added, "I hope everyone is doing well and looking forward to a happy summer. Warmly," and pasted her signature at the bottom. She touched the return key and the message whooshed away into the ether. Then she modified the letter and sent it to all the ad agency account managers she knew, and finally she modified that one and did a little more individual customization to send to friends and colleagues who had the kind of connections to be able to refer her for work. Then she placed some phone calls to her most faithful clients and agency people. She had two conversations and left twelve voice mails. That all took about two hours. She reviewed her website portfolio, but she had nothing to update it with. With no other work do, she went upstairs, changed out of her work clothes, and got on the bike.

She was surprised and gratified that only a week later she had four jobs. Her old clients seemed genuinely happy to have her back.

Joy had told Carly she didn't know why. "They probably pity me."

"People are glad to do something for you, Joy," Carly agreed, "but actually you're damn good: fast, smart, competent, creative, attentive, and easy to work with. Just like before."

"I suppose," Joy said, because it seemed to be a good way to think about it, now that she had no pride anymore.

When she felt in control of things she kept it simple. Stay in her office, ride her bike, feed her boys, try to be present for the people who loved her. That's what she wanted.

Her girlfriends double-teamed her. Carly never asked how she was feeling, just about Jake and how work was going and how things were with Danny, and her own work and man troubles, and when all else failed would just kiss her and walk with her companionably, arm-in-arm. Lizzie, on the other hand, made it her mission to inhabit as much of Joy's interior as she could, asking a million questions. Joy felt both loved and exhausted when she got off those calls.

Hiram came for Shabbat dinner nearly every week, and surprised Joy by joining in the blessings. He told her that despite having lost Rose to religion (not that there weren't other reasons, of course), he could respect the tradition. "My mom actively didn't want me to learn Hebrew," Hiram said. "My generation needed to be Americans. Not Christians, but like Christians, kind of. Assimilated. Not that I missed having a Jewish life or anything. How can you miss what you don't know?"

Joy liked her ordered Shabbats. The quiet, the shul, the peaceful walks with Danny in the afternoons while Hiram still had Jake off to wherever they had gone in the morning. Sometimes she would sit on a park bench with her husband, he with a novel or magazine, she with her sketchbook and pencils, and she would draw landscapes with empty places in them.

Danny didn't like those drawings. "They're weird, those empty spaces."

"They fit," Joy said. "They're a part of the drawing."

"I hope the world won't always look like that to you," Danny told her. "I thought work would fill those empty places."

"Not for me."

"Yeah. I'm too busy to stop for them, even if they are there."

"I know," she said. "That's your thing. I feel like I hardly see you."

"It isn't so different than before, is it?"

"I guess not," she said. "I just feel more alone."

"I'm still in your bed every night."

"I go to sleep alone a lot," she said. "You stay up too late."

"You get up too early." He snapped that one off, but then lowered his tone. "Joy, honey, we talked about this when we bought the business. Dead child or not, I can't back off now. A few more years until it's big enough to sell. Then I can do lawyering and consulting and we can go do the things you made me write on the wall of our apartment."

The plan was perfect, and she followed it—grad school, magazine jobs, athletics, friends, and Danny was there, at home, when she wanted him.

"Jenny dying wasn't part of the plan."

"No." His voice shook.

"Maybe I need you more now."

"Look, you're working. You're riding. I'm working. Jake's in school. We're managing."

There's that word again. Like routine can make this life graceful.

"Coping, you mean."

"So call it that. Does it matter?"

She wanted to touch something, but her hands bounded off of each other, opposite poles of a magnet. "So everything just goes back to the way it was? Like she never existed? Maybe her life didn't mean anything at all."

Danny looked exasperated. "Of course it did. We don't lose that because she's dead."

"How do you know that? Her being alive has just made Jake's life harder."

Danny's face stiffened. "Did you really just say that?"

The dust billowed. Joy paced. "Her death is having more consequences than her life. Was she born just to die? Just for us? Just to have a perfect childhood?" Joy could not stop. "Never becoming an adult, never dealing with ambiguity, never seeing my failings, never seeing her period, boys, college, never knowing her children."

"It was an accident, Joy. Stop this!" Danny was almost yelling. "Her being dead is what's hard. She wasn't born just so she could screw over her brother."

Standing in the minimart doorway she reached out for him, but he went into the bathroom and closed the door.

Joy fell to the bed. She pulled her knees to her chest and moaned, "I'm so scared, Danny, I can't lose you, too, I can't lose Jake, what's happening?"

The toilet flushed. She sat up.

He opened the door. "Did you just say something?"

"No."

"I'm going downstairs."

She heard the TV click on. She wanted him to come to her; she was lonely. She wanted him to stay away; she was afraid. She touched a hand to her sex; indifference. After nothing else happened for a while, Joy got herself ready for bed. He didn't come back before she fell asleep.

22.

SCHOOL WAS CANCELLED for a staff in-service on this beautiful spring day. Joy always used to look forward to these days and planned her work so she could maximize her time with the kids. *Kid.* Jake pulled his mother up the stairs and into his room and opened his overstuffed game cabinet.

"Let's play one of Jenny's games." He pulled *Connect Four* out of the cabinet.

Joy sighed.

Jake looked at her sternly. "You said!"

"I'm sorry, Jake. I was just remembering."

Joy took the box and set up the stand.

Jake started to cry.

She reached out and held him. "It's all right, Jakey, it's okay. What's the matter, honey?"

He stomped his foot. "Mommy, why can't you just be happy?"

Fuck me, Joy thought. She had no answer for him.

"You're right, Jacob. I'm sorry. Let's play. Do you want to be red or blue?"

Joy's afternoon hung in the balance.

"Blue."

Earlier, Joy had walked with Jake down to the Marina Green. While he played with some kids in the playground, she did some quick sketching to get the juices flowing, then drew a few ideas for a new job she had. After an hour or so they went and played some catch out on the field. Joy had a glove Danny had gotten her as kind of a joke when he bought into a Giants season ticket group a few years before. But now that Jake was getting more serious about baseball she was learning to throw and catch along with him. When Joy got tired of that they lay down on their backs on the thick grass, holding hands with their heads almost touching, and watched the big kites coasting on the trade winds high above their heads, shocks of bright color against the rapidly moving clouds. When Jake got hungry, they went home.

After Jake beat Joy two out of three in *Connect Four*, but lost to her in double solitaire, she let him watch a movie. She went into her office to render the sketches she'd done in the park onto the computer, but she kept finding herself looking at movie trailers and reading lifestyle articles at Cosmopolitan.com. She felt bad that Jake was alone in front of the TV. On a normal off-day, Jenny would have been with her brother. After reading her fourth column, she called Lizzie.

"This is normal now," Joy said. "Today he asked me why I couldn't be happy. What do I tell him? I see other families with both their kids and I feel so jealous. Why do they get to be happy?"

The photos of a bygone era taunted Joy from the wall.

"Why do you get to be happy? Why do you get to have all your kids and I don't?"

"No one can answer that, Joy."

"I know. Please forgive me."

"Joy, sweetheart, I thought about this a lot at the beginning and decided that whatever happened, I could take it. I won't lose you. I won't hide my kids from you. Amanda is your goddaughter and she loves you and is already talking about going to Berkeley so she can be closer to you."

"I keep thinking," Joy said, "about that young couple who got chased out of their hometown because no one wanted to deal with their dead child, and here I have you getting on a plane every time I turn around and sticking your nose in my business. I obviously have to handle shit like this if I'm going to get back into living again at all."

"Shit like this?" Lizzie snorted. "You mean, sympathetic and sustained support from people who love you? You Danny and Jake have a really bad deal. But none of us got to pick that."

"It wasn't supposed to be like this! I get one of my kids killed, now I'm sucking the life out of the other."

"Stop! Jenny would be outraged if she heard that!" Lizzie voice was barely controlled. "Don't be stupid. Go do forty pushups or something. Get yourself the hell out of this line of thinking."

"That was unfair." Joy resented the invocation of Jenny's name. "My relationship with Jake feels incomplete without her."

"That sure sucks for him, huh?"

It must. I should let his therapist know about this. What does Jake tell her about me?

"Jealousy is new. I don't like it," Joy said, "but I feel it. Maybe I'll still end up a zombie."

"I don't think so. The last time I was there you definitely had lips and there wasn't a single drop of blood anywhere on your outfit. You're working, you're riding, you're homemaking. Let that be enough for now. I've always admired your focus, Joy, but try to chill out, please. Please?"

"I love you, too, Liz," said Joy, and hung up.

Joy stared at Jake's baby picture on her office wall and wondered if she really was exacerbating or even creating his sadness. But when she went back to the TV, Jake cuddled in next to her, just a mom and her boy. She watched the rest of the movie with him in a comfortable silence.

"Daddy will be home pretty soon," she said.

"Mommy, we don't have to play Jenny's games anymore if you don't want to."

"I like to, but sometimes I remember her when we do, and it makes me sad."

"I like when you play them with me, but I don't like you to be sad."

"I'll play them with you anytime, Jakey. I told you that I would, and I will."

"I wonder if Jenny remembers me."

"Do you remember her?"

"Sometimes in my room I pretend she's in her room, doing her homework, or maybe she's at her friend's house. I wish she could teach me how to play some of her games."

"She wanted to be a teacher. She really liked teaching you things."

"Who's going to teach me those things now?"

Joy held him tighter. "We'll all do it, me, Daddy, Grandpa, your teachers. Amanda and Sarah, when they come."

"I don't like being by myself all the time."

"Let's be sure you see your friends more. Maybe this summer you can be in a baseball league."

"Okay. Can Grandpa come?"

"Sure." *I couldn't keep him away.*

Jake got off the couch.

"Wanna hear me read my book?"

"Can you read it to me while I'm cooking? It's going to be time for dinner soon."

He pushed away from her. "I'm going upstairs."

"Bring your book down. I'd like to hear it."

As the heat of his presence dissipated, Joy wondered what her mistake was, exactly. She didn't deserve his resentment. She was taking care of all of them. Then she wondered if she should cook at all. Maybe she should call a babysitter and go and meet Danny for dinner somewhere, if Jake was going to be like this.

Instead, she went upstairs. Jake's door was open. He was lying on the floor, his book clutched to his stomach. He didn't look at her as she walked in. She sat on the floor next to him and touched his arm.

He turned on her.

"Am I ever going to get to be a kid again?"

"Jake, lovey, I know you miss her. I wish it hadn't happened."

She pulled at him. He crawled into her lap. His whole body relaxed and she remembered that she really was his mother and that had to be enough. They sat there for a long time, hugging. She sang him the sweet little songs of his infancy.

Danny found them there when he got home. Jake twisted around and held out an arm to him. He found his way into the pile and they all hugged, gradually losing their balance and tipping over into a laughing heap on the floor.

"Looks like we should go get a pizza."

"Get it delivered," Joy said.

She knew the length of her husband's hip under her hand and the wide press of his hand, somehow well under her shirt, warming her back. No one was letting go; they were so packed in that she had to get his phone out of his pocket.

When the pizza came, they unfolded and he went down to get it and some paper towels and they ate on the floor of Jake's room. Afterwards, Jake read to them for quite a while; then he wanted Danny to put him to bed. Joy wanted to go in to Jenny like they used to do, two kids for two parents, but the only place to go was their bedroom. She sat at her vanity. Jenny's jewelry box was there. She had it open when Danny came in.

"I haven't been to the cemetery in three weeks," she said. "Do you want to come with me tomorrow?"

"It's Monday," he said. "I'm going to work. Aren't you?"

"Yes. But I can go out there early."

"I'll get Jake ready and take him to school," Danny said.

"It's your day anyway."

"No credit for excess beneficence, eh?"

"Nope. But if it makes you feel better I'll check the manual."

Joy and Danny fell asleep holding hands.

* * *

In the morning the fog was still settled closely over the streets. Dew dripped off every tree. Puddles formed in the potholes. Drops layered the windshields of parked cars and formed a film on Joy's glasses she had to wipe off constantly. Spinning south in a small gear at a high cadence, Joy wondered if Jenny would appear today. *Soon I probably won't be coming at all,* she thought. *Maybe just on the yartzeit, and probably not alone. I wonder if I'll ever stop looking for her.*

As she crested the ridgetop the fog was losing its struggle against the slow heating of the morning, the high wall of gray slowly retreating to the west. Down below, in the valley, the row of cemeteries leaned against the base of the mountain, thousands of headstones glistening in the morning sunlight. She screamed down the descent of Hickey Boulevard, then made the left turn and rode two blocks to the cemetery. Up the driveway the auto gate was locked. Joy passed her bike under the bar and remounted. She put herself in a big gear, to make it hard, and standing, ground up the road to the shul's small section. Olive trees were interspersed among the silent headstones, many bearing the names of families she knew, people she saw at the shul sometimes, for one of their yartzeits, commemorating the day of the death. *That's every day, for me,* she thought. The commemorants were always surprised to see her in the pews. They'd ask, isn't Jenny's yartzeit in the fall? Yes, she'd say, with a generous smile. We're coming most weeks these days, and leave it at that.

Jenny's spot up the hillside had been isolated when they buried her, but newer graves were drawing her more fully into the community of the dead. Joy took off her shoes and socks to walk on impossibly thick, receiving grass, spongy under her feet. The stone needed tending. Joy took her sweat rag and cleaned each engraved letter: *Loving Sister, Daughter, Friend—In Our Hearts Forever.*

Jenny's name and dates were inscribed in Hebrew and English. Other visitors, following Jewish custom, had left small stones on top of the headstone. Joy carefully lifted each stone and cleaned underneath it before putting it back in its place. Then she was done. Not much you can do for your daughter after she's dead.

"Hi, sweetheart. I'm here," Joy said, out loud.

She lay face down on the grave, arms and legs spread, the top of her head touching the stone. She launched her spirit into the grave, questing, searching, demanding, reaching out for any sensation, any remainder of Jenny's spirit still residing in what was there, her body, the coffin, the things they had put in the grave, the first dirt, the vault, the rest of the dirt, the grass. Was the coffin rotting yet? The clothes, the body, were they merging together? Were the maggots returning the body to the earth? She heard the wind in the trees, felt the sun on her back; all else was silence. Joy grieved for the end of her line of women. She wanted to squeeze herself into the grave, get lost in the chorus of missing lovers, mothers, daughters lying here, to stand with her daughter in the endlessness of their dead dreaming.

After that didn't happen Joy sat up, rolled her jacket into a ball and sat on it. She pressed the entire side of her body against the headstone, wrapped her arm around it. Down the shallow hillside below her, the carefully tended grass punctured by the silent rows of witnessing stones. A plane roared overhead.

"Should we get on that one, Jenny?" Joy said. "I bet it's going to Tokyo. We can walk the Ginza, eat sushi."

Will they have a rainbow roll?

"I'm sure they have all your favorites . . . then we can get on the bullet train and climb Mount Fuji."

A mountain? I'm not a super jock like you, Mom.

"Oh, c'mon, you love to hike."

For an hour maybe.

"Oh, all right. Let's get on that one and go to Hawaii instead."

That's a much better idea. I love the water!

"We can go snorkeling, but you'd better remember to put on your sunscreen more often this time. How about surf lessons?"

You're on, Mom!

But I'm not, actually. She's still dead.

Encased in a quart-sized Ziploc bag and tucked into Joy's jersey pocket was their tattered copy of *A Horse and His Boy*. Opening to a random page, she began to read out loud, to Jenny's tombstone. Down the hill a bit, the sprinklers began to sputter. Soon they would reach her. The present returned. She stood. Turf rolled under her bare feet as she walked the line of headstones. She always finished her visits by pausing briefly at the gravesites of other children, marking her visit by placing on each memorial a stone she had brought. Ellen, age twelve. Oren, age ten. Aryeh, age sixteen. There rarely were stones on those graves. *Where were their parents? Dead? Moved on?* The air was still; the suddenly hot sun beat down on her. She turned back to Jenny's place as the nearby sprinkler began to turn. Everywhere Joy went, Jenny was dead. Only in the cemetery was this normal. She retrieved her bike, donning her shoes and her helmet. She looked at the now-shining headstone.

Joy waited, loath to leave, but no magic butterfly landed on her shoulder, bringing the secret of touch—it was time to go home.

"Oh, my love," Joy said, "my dearest sweet baby, I wanted to give the world to you. Who gets that now?"

23.

CARLY AND JOY sat in Joy's kitchen after a late afternoon walk by the Bay. Carly's face was ruddy from the wind and damp. *She is still a beautiful woman,* Joy thought. Out the back window, fog rolled over the neighboring rooftops and a brisk west wind rustled the trees. Joy had made some lemon spritzers. Non-alcoholic.

"Isn't Jake's birthday coming up?" Carly asked.

"Yes," Joy said. "Eight years old."

"Want to have a clown?"

"I was thinking yes," Joy said.

Carly the clown had provided the entertainment at most of Jenny's birthday parties. She wanted to do Jake's parties too, but when Joy had two living children she worried that Jake would feel eclipsed by his sister if the birthday parties were always the same. So even though Carly did his third birthday, they had a zoo party when he was four and a pottery party when he was five and took all the kids to the movies when he was six. *Another wrong thing I worried about.* "Hooray!" Carly clapped. "I thought I might have to wear the clown costume to the office."

"Or maybe to court." Joy always had loved Carly's absurdities.

"It wouldn't be so off base, given what we actually do there."

"Jake's getting a little old for clownies," Joy said. "This is probably his last one. Maybe you can be a clown for Danny's birthday."

"I'll need a grownup costume."

"Just don't forget the red nose!"

"For Danny, maybe that's all I'll wear."

"He'd like that."

"Wow, girl. Is that an invitation?" Carly asked.

Joy was overcome with the thought that Danny deserved more than she was giving him. *Wouldn't it be easier if it was Carly instead of some stranger?* But she said, "No, better not, I think."

"Oh, honey." Joy's voice had given her away; Carly heard the whole story in a sentence. She came around the counter and enveloped Joy's whole body in a hug. She pulled her head to her shoulder and stroked her hair, holding her close, like a lover, like a mother with her baby, planting light kisses on her head. Cradled there, Joy saw an alternate future: Leave Danny, room with Carly, go on dates, have some kind of reasonable sex with the occasional hook-up, take Jake on alternate weekends as the family-that-was slipped away. She imagined waving to Jake as he grew away from her, leaning on his father and grandfather, romantic love denied him because his mother couldn't love him freely after his sister died. She saw herself alone at seventy, at eighty, Danny with a new family, Jake living across the country, visiting his elderly mom in assisted living every couple of months when business brought him out to San Francisco.

"The regular costume is good for Danny, too," Joy said lamely, but Carly only took out her calendar. Together they picked the date for Jake's party.

* * *

On the Sunday of the party, Joy put on makeup and dressed in a full-skirted sleeveless dress in a summery print. At Jake's request there were helium balloons everywhere, tied to things or pressed against the ceiling with their colored ribbons dangling, parading down the hallway and into the backyard. Danny said Jake was trying to lift their spirits. Joy said she'd try to lighten up. All the boys had arrived, the food ready, and Carly was leading games out in the backyard.

Danny came looking for her. "Hey, pretty girl. Come play some games."

"Do I have to?"

"Yes, you have to."

Joy was silent. She didn't get off her stool.

Danny leaned against the counter. "Okay, Joy, two minutes. What's up?"

"Do you remember his sixth birthday, when Jenny hosted his friends' big sisters?"

"I do. They got into your closet and put on a fashion show."

"I remember how happy I was, that she had these friends, like me and Lizzie, that she could have her whole life. When I see them at the school now I can't even recognize them as the same girls."

"Girls change fast at this age," he said.

"I don't want to lose these boys, too."

"Joy. Do not go there. It is statistically almost impossible that these boys will do anything other than outlive us."

"Are you sure?"

"Of course not, but for the purposes of this conversation? Yes. You can commit to them." He stood and extended his hand to her. "Come outside. Pin the tail on the donkey."

She had to, then. Jake, dressed in his buckskin tunic and jeans, with a feather in his cap, came running over and threw his arms around her. That had been a wonderful surprise, and she wondered why it was surprising at all. Jake is such a sweet boy. *I guess I have been pretty good with him recently. I just keep forgetting. Danny's so steady,* she thought, *he's good for me.*

Jake dragged her into the center of the circle. "It's my mom's turn now!"

Carly tied on the eyeshade and got Joy spinning. Blindfolded and dizzy, she stumbled, but Danny caught her, both of them laughing.

"Nope, go that way!" He whispered, "It's fun, isn't it?"

She had to admit it was. The boys were screaming, "More left! More right!" She ran into the donkey and took off her mask; she had pinned the tail a little too low and angled to the front.

Danny laughed and Carly leaned over and whispered, "See? Your subconscious is talking! You can't postpone it forever!"

Joy laughed too, whispering back, "Maybe Danny will get lucky tonight!"

He did, and he was full of endearments. Joy liked that, and she liked wrapping herself around him, and after, she was able to stay in his arms for a pretty long while before rolling away.

When she thought about it the next day she thought that love really was mysterious, because that night she dreamed that she went to the cemetery and lay down on the grave to reach out for Jenny's spirit like she always did. She floated up and in the sky she saw Jenny with the impossible-to-imagine undrawable eyes. In that funny way people can analyze a dream while they're having it, she thought she should be afraid, but she felt at home there, floating in the air with Dead Jenny beside her.

24.

EARLY THE NEXT MORNING before she got on the bike, Joy took her coffee into the office and found the drawing, which looked just like she'd imagined in the dream, but nothing like Jenny had ever looked or probably even would look if she'd ever gotten to grow up. She wondered why she thought only of the-absence-of-Jenny, or what-Jake-had-lost, or her never-to-be-born grandchildren.

Jenny doesn't even live in my imagination. At least my heart still beats on the bike.

These days, along with the dust and the screaming, what she remembered from the accident was the moment before the crashing; how proud she had been to stand at the cash register and buy water for her daughter. Proud that she got to take care of her. When she told that to Rabbi he had said that she was nobly pursuing Jenny's welfare that day, and what happened can't be understood. What happened was both brutally simple and beyond our comprehension, he had said, and that she needed to find some way of holding it that she could accept.

I only left Jenny in the car. Doesn't seem so bad. Was that my sin?

The wind blowing in from the Golden Gate had its hand on her chest as she pedaled straight into it. Portraying her intentions as noble seemed like a really overblown way to talk about shopping for shoes. She didn't know how noble she actually was, because as much as consequences followed the moment, consequences of other moments led up to it too.

Maybe arrogance was my sin, she thought, *But I'm not arrogant anymore.*

No, agreed Dead Jenny, *you're not arrogant anymore.*

It seemed perfectly normal to hear that voice in her head. She wanted it to be Jenny, but it spoke in Joy's own voice. The road spun her into a right turn. Parking barriers swept by on her right, white dashes and blank spaces against the green backdrop of the field.

Maybe the shopping trip wasn't about what Jenny needed, but about what Joy needed, like Rose needing to control Joy's wardrobe when Joy was a little girl. Joy could still summon the rage she felt when her mother had been through her dresser again. *Maybe my mistake was that I made Jenny too independent of that inheritance, and she had to die because I wasn't faithful to my mother and my sin was making her different.*

Except you really were different, weren't you, Jenny?

I'm not Jenny, said Dead Jenny. *You made me up.*

Joy knew that to be true. The bay crashed against the rocks at Fort Point as Joy squeezed the last bit of distance out of the available road. Sweeping through the 180-degree turn at its end, she rose out of the saddle and sprinted back the way she came, back up to speed.

Jenny had devoted many hours to decorating and loving her sneakers, but they had holes. They really needed to be replaced. Otherwise her arches would fall and then she'd have flat feet and a sore lower back and probably bunions and a lifetime of podiatry visits.

You were the mommy, Dead Jenny said, *so you could have done it anytime.*

I could have. But I wanted her to feel agency.

But maybe the worst thing was telling Jenny they needed to buy some boots, which was true, because Jenny had outgrown the ones she had and winter was coming, and there would be Thanksgiving, and year-end events at school and holiday parties, and maybe even some rainy days. Joy had hoped that while they were shopping for boots they could find the exact same sneakers that Jenny loved and get her to replace them.

Sneaky. Was that the lie?

Everyone lies about something, said Dead Jenny.

Joy deftly avoided a drain grate. But really, she didn't know what Jenny wanted that day, even though Jenny liked going shopping with her. Maybe the whole plan was the sin and she should have left her at school with the crappy sneakers.

I'm sorry. I wish it had been me.

You don't get to be dead, said Dead Jenny. *I'm dead.*

What did you have to go and die for?

I've always been dead.

Joy lifted the bike onto its storage hook in the basement. She heard the front door close as the boys left. Body heat flooded her face as she reached down and opened the clicklocks on her shoes; she wished Jake still wanted to do it. *He's going to grow up, hopefully.* Sweat dripped from her headband onto the chair, Jenny's tiny red folding chair that came with the little Ikea art table Danny bought for his sweet girl. She placed her shoes and helmet on the cabinet, Jenny's former credenza. *Maybe Jenny died so Mommy could have some bike room furniture.*

Joy wondered if she should be worried about having this person in her head, but it seemed just fine to her. *She had always been dead. What does that even mean? I guess a mystery voice in the Common World is closer to reality than slaying dragons in the Other World,* she thought, even though she was psychologically sophisticated enough to know that whatever it was came from her. She heard the car start and drive away. She looked at her watch. Jake would get to school on time.

It's Monday, she reminded herself. The chart of Danny's schedule tacked prominently to the wall said he had to visit the Danville office. The schedule had appeared during the first winter, when she forgot she had promised to pick Jake up and they'd had to pay an extra hundred bucks because the school charged five dollars a minute for every minute after six. Danny said he didn't care about the money, but Jake had gotten worried, which was the last thing he needed. He had unveiled the schedule the next day. It was kind of embarrassing and Joy had tried to have a fight with him about it, but her heart wasn't really in it.

I should make him stop. I'm not a zombie now.

You just used it, said Dead Jenny. *You should be grateful.*

Am I a disorder in his world?

Joy peeled off her sweaty clothes right there in the basement and left them on the washer. Barefoot and wrapped in an old beach towel she detoured through the kitchen, poured some juice and Recoverite into her water bottle, and went upstairs.

Danny had put the Hawaii anniversary photos back on her dresser. Did he mean to seduce or mock her? Impulsively she opened the top drawer of the dresser and took out Danny's Kama Sutra. When they came back from Hawaii, she had made him give her the memory card with the photos. "Ask me if you want to see them," she said. "I'll let you. I just don't want it to be a secret."

He did ask her twice, even though it shamed him, and the third time she looked at the pictures with him. She saw how happy he was to own that memory so she learned some bookbinding skills and surprised him with a top-rate, richly bound book for his fortieth birthday. It was exactly what he had imagined, and he quickened rapidly as the pages went by. Joy, wearing his favorite little nothing under her terrycloth bathrobe, had been ready and welcoming.

The testimony was there on the pages, flirting with his camera on the beach, partial nudes taken in found moments of privacy, purposefully erotic poses from their forest walks, and the explicit record of their last couple of nights, beach to jungle to hotel, dressed to undressed, him in her mouth, his head between her legs, her legs draped over his shoulders as he folded her in two. His favorite took a full page—she in his lap, both of them facing the camera, clutching each other's hands, penetration obscenely visible, their faces transformed. She saw his face, hard with passion and soft with love, and her face, alive, so alive. A soft puff of air caressed her hand as the cover closed.

Naked then, naked now. Out of the shower Joy stood, dripping, staring back at herself from the mirror. Danny lusted after her from his photo on her vanity, jaunty in a fedora. She imagined how he actually felt about her: Anger, empathy, desire, sorrow: lover, partner, troubled friend. She called him.

"Hi, Danny. I was just thinking about you."

"Thanks," he said. "Heard you come in when we were leaving."

"Yeah, I didn't quite get back in time."

"Jake looked for you this morning."

"Danny, I've been out in the mornings since he was a little boy."

"He's angry about it now, I think."

Did he really want the conversation to go there? "It's got to be okay, Danny. Help me out here. Maybe I'll take him to the movies later."

More kindly he said, "He'd like that. I can meet you for dinner after."

"Maybe just pick something up. It'll be too late for him otherwise." Joy paused, wondering if she should try to talk to him now.

"When I was on the bike this morning," she said, "I was thinking about that day again and how I might have lied to Jenny about the shoes."

"You've talked about that."

She couldn't tell him about Dead Jenny yet. She promised herself she would, soon.

"I felt different this time. I didn't beat myself up so much."

"I'm glad to hear that."

"Then I came in the house and looked at your book."

"Our book," he said. "Maybe you want to be the woman in the book."

"Oh, no." she said. "I'm not that woman now."

Her voice sounded peculiar to her own ears, reed-like, plaintive, mournful, like the high register of an oboe.

"I can't really have this conversation now, I'm on the freeway." He sounded broken too; his words grated, like a hangnail catching repeatedly on a sock. "Jenny's dead, but everyone else is alive."

"You're angry."

"I guess, some, but that's not all of it. Are you okay for today?"

The dismissal in his voice hurt her. "Sure, fine. Got some work. One day at a time."

"Okay. Love you." He hung up.

"Fuck. Fuck. Fuck!" Joy threw the phone at her pillow. *I lose my girl and my son wants what he can't have and my husband wants what he once had and now I'm having conversations with a ghost.*

I'm not a ghost, said Dead Jenny. *You made me up.*

That's a relief, I guess.

Dead Jenny rolled her empty eyes.

Everyone tries so hard to be good. I try hard to be good. This is not good. Maybe I should try something really, really different, like moving to Patagonia or studying for the rabbinate.

Instead she got dressed and went to the office and for a few hours just put it all on hold. It engaged her enough that she left Jake in afterschool and asked Danny to pick him up like usual.

At home Danny was gentle and attentive, cooking and cleaning up and letting her play games with Jake. They put him to bed together. He was kind, and it was enough, but then when she came out of the bathroom he said he had been thinking about something else ever since they talked on the phone. Would she . . . and he took out the book. She said, "Okay, sure, I can look at that with you," and they got onto the bed. When he moved his hand down between her legs she said, for no particular reason that she could name, "No, not for me tonight, but I'll do you." So he lay back, and she kept her hand slippery, and it was nice to get him off while they looked at the book together.

25.

THE GRANDSTAND CREAKED and moaned when Joy stepped onto it. She had seen the thin tubes of steel making a framework under the splintery wooden benches: scaffolding. Joy remembered how hot her chest had felt when good and evil were raging there. She missed it. *Maybe I'll feel that again when I die,* she thought. Joy found a seat next to her dad.

It had surprised Joy when Jake got mad at her for skipping his first Saturday morning Little League game. Danny went to the game with Hiram, but Joy went to the shul like she always did. But it was just a habit. *He's absolutely right that I should pick him over shul.* She felt strange being out in the world on a Saturday again, displaced. *This must be the feeling that Mom just couldn't stand feeling anymore.* Joy wondered if that would happen to her. *Pretty ironic way of getting to know my mother better.*

Maybe thirty people were in the stands. Joy was wearing jeans, sneakers, and a vintage Giants cap of Hiram's. Her *I'm a Little League Mom* T-shirt showed a graphic of a little boy swinging a bat with a full-skirted, bobbed-haired generic Mom in the background, clapping. *Irritating graphic; sexist message.* Joy decided that she would design the shirt next year, but she had worn it today to help the other parents know she was qualified.

Boys' voices ricocheted around the field. They were running and throwing and she enjoyed watching their bodies work. At Jake's birthday last year she could barely even look at them.

Only Jenny had to die so Jake could end up playing baseball here today.

Whoa there, said Dead Jenny.

It was true, Joy thought grudgingly, *that he was getting into baseball anyway.*

After their warmups, the boys gathered in the dugout. The coach announced the lineups for the scorekeepers like Hiram, and the game got underway. After a few pitches came the dull pinging sound of aluminum on rawhide; a ball bounded through the infield for a single. Hiram noted it on the scorecard. Joy wondered if her attendance at every game was noted on a scorecard too.

When she first had asked Danny about skipping the Saturday game, he said, "Jake seems to be so disappointed in you. If it was me, I'd be showing up at everything."

"I show up at a lot more things that you do."

"That's not the point. We're talking about how Jake feels, not about how you feel. You are judged according to the special Mom scale."

"It's a moving target, Danny," Joy had told him.

Jake's at-bat—a ground out to shortstop—brought Joy back to the game. Hiram noted the put-out on the scorecard.

"You remember," Joy said to him, "that Jake wanted to ride the bus to school by himself?"

"Of course. He's been doing that on Fridays, right?"

Joy had thought it was dangerous, but Danny was supportive and Hiram found statistics that said it was no more dangerous today than when Joy had done it at age eight. You're more likely to have a car accident driving him, Hiram had said. Besides, anything that supported Jake's experience of himself as an independent actor was great and no time was too early if that was the benefit.

"No one even lets kids be capable these days. I had a job when I was nine."

"Dad," Joy had said, "you cleaned up your father's shop."

"Still," he said, "I did it. He paid me."

So Joy had yielded, walking Jake to the stop and watching him get on the bus, and he made it to school every time. Joy's anxiety was not salved at all.

"I've been walking with him, but yesterday he wanted to walk alone too."

"Okay," said Hiram. "That's good. Did you let him?"

"Yes. But I followed him." *Spied on him.*

She had shadowed him the four blocks to the bus stop, sneaking out of the house right behind him, running to the corner and peering around it, walking in the street next to the parked cars, ready to duck if Jake looked back her way, running across Chestnut Street against the light, in front of oncoming traffic.

"He stopped at every stop sign and made eye contact with the drivers and crossed with the light. He waited at the stop until the bus came, and he got on it."

"That was it?"

"I called the school and he was there. Everything was fine."

Following him is not the same as protecting him.

Hiram was nodding. "He's got a hard road," he said to Joy, "being so alone."

Dust billowed in front of her, but it was only a kid sliding into third base. Sunlight stabbed through the cloud. "Daddy, stop. We have this conversation every week. I'm doing the best I can."

He's parenting his daughter, Dead Jenny said. *Cut him some slack.*

As parents do, Hiram stayed on point. "It's obvious how much Jake loves you and you him, but he misses the old you. He tells me that. And he's pissed, Joy. He tells me that, too."

"Do you think I don't know it? I was pretty pissed at both of you, if I recall."

"Not at his age. You were a teenager, and we were ready to be divorced. You had a reason."

Joy was admiring the way her father had slipped that admission into the conversation when Jake stroked a liner past the third baseman and down the left field line. They jumped up and cheered, applauding him as he waved at them from second base. Two runs scored.

When they sat down again for the next batter Hiram said, "I remember you having a harder time with your mother."

"You would, Daddy."

"I wasn't quite ready for you to grow up."

"You fixed that on vodka night."

"So I did. It has to be worse for Jake, though, with you and Danny suffering so much."

"We'll be okay."

Hiram shrugged and said, "I hope you aspire to more than okay. It's a terrible thing that she died, but you have a future."

Joy tried to forgive him for that. She leaned her head on his shoulder. The familiar smell of him opened a door and behind it were the girls she once was: Cute Joy who wore those dresses while she climbed trees and fought dragons. Proud Joy, so self-reliant, so capable, redecorating her room at the age of eight. Sweet Joy, resilient when her pride was wounded, angry when things were unfair, kind to her friends, loving to her daddy. And then Grown-up Joy brought him Jenny, a different girl, tougher, smarter, more direct, the sweetness of molasses instead of sugar, Pirate Jenny with a harder center, leaving Grandpa empty-lapped because she wanted to sit next to him and figure something out together.

Jake's team came in from the field. Jake looked at his grandfather and made a little signal. Hiram signaled back.

"What was that?" Joy asked.

"Keep the bat level through the zone," Hiram said, demonstrating. "You try."

She felt jealous; the world of men was beginning to take her little boy away. *I have enough to worry about. Soon Jake will be old. How much will he need his mother then?* But Hiram was her daddy, and truthfully, she was grateful. He made it so much easier for her, and Jake loved him. She practiced the signal.

When they were lying in bed that night she told Danny that he had been right, and she wondered why she ever would have chosen shul over parenting.

"That's not really what you were doing, is it?" Danny had asked her. He gave her a hug and a kiss. "You were just trying to do anything to make sense of it. And neither of us can say we're not grateful for the shul and the rabbi."

"That's true, but the effect of it was to take me away from Jake."

"True, but I was off-base. You spend a lot of time with him. The effect was to let him spend more time with his grandfather."

"It has a different valence now. Why do you go to shul?"

He rolled onto his side and looked at her. "Being with you at the shul reminds me how hard grief actually is."

"And you appreciate that? Sounds like the booby prize."

"You know me. If you weren't struggling I'd probably just be working all the time and end up losing both of you."

"That is a very strange way to be charming," she said, and wrapped herself around him. Joy fell off to sleep feeling more satisfied that she wasn't that much like her mother after all.

26.

ON A DAY just before the end of the school year Jake came home from school and went right upstairs to his room. Thinking it odd that he hadn't gone to the kitchen first, Joy went upstairs and knocked on his door.

"Are you all right, Jake?"

She heard no answer. She opened the door a crack.

"Don't forget you have to go to Annie's today."

"Do I have to?"

"We need to leave in an hour."

She closed the door. *I hope he works it out.* Joy went to her office to work on a newsletter design for a law firm that recently had come to her practice. Her current draft looked boring. She saved the file and opened a new copy of that template. She looked again at the name of the firm and at its logo. Challenging herself to do something different, she altered the frames, tweaked the font, tried a little pixilation, and fiddled with alternate color palettes. After an hour she had to remind herself that it wasn't her newsletter, it was a fixed-fee contract, and it was time to take Jake to his therapy appointment. She saved the PDF, wrote *Newsletter scheme C, final draft* in the subject line, and sent it off.

Danny has certain things right about working. I'm good at it. I do get involved. I want what's best for my client in spite of what they might think. Referrals keep coming. I might need an assistant. I was foolish to wait so long. Then she had to laugh at herself, still worrying about that although she'd been back for over a year.

Good. Cut yourself a little slack, said Dead Jenny.

I like it when you're nice to me, Joy told her.

When she knocked on Jake's door, there was no answer. So she said, "I'm coming in," and opened the door.

"Time to go, Jake."

He was flat on his back, juggling a single baseball. She knelt next to him and put a hand on his arm. He yanked his arm away.

Joy was pretty sure touching his arm was something that had been fine last week.

"Jake, I can't help you if you won't tell me what's wrong."

"I just don't want to go, Mom. Please?"

"You need to go."

"If you love me, don't make me go today."

"It's because I love you that you need to go."

She winced. That was a real Mom thing to say.

Jake obviously thought so too. He screwed his face into a sneer and said, "Well, I don't want to go, Moouummm."

He bounced his baseball off the floor past her and it banged off the wall.

"Jake, that's a hardball! You'll put a hole in the wall!"

She barehanded the ball on the bounce and put it on top of the bookcase, out of his reach. He opened his toy cabinet and started dumping things out onto the floor.

"What are you doing?"

"It's my room and I can do what I want to!"

"No, you can't. You're almost nine years old and you share this house with me and your dad and you can't just throw things all over the place like this. What do you want?"

He crawled away from her, burrowing into the huge pile of his and Jenny's stuffed animals in the corner of his room. Joy waited until the burrowing stopped, then tried again.

"You've been liking going. Why not today?"

Last week Jake had come out of Annie's office singing.

"I just don't want to."

"What do you want to do instead?"

"Nothing."

"You can talk to her about this."

Jake, in his most nasal and sarcastic tone, said, "Oh Annie, my mom always says she wants to talk but then she stops in the middle so she can do something else and she makes me come talk to you instead."

Instead of throwing the ball at his head Joy said, "You have to go, honey. We all have to do things we don't like to do sometimes. I'm sorry if I hurt your feelings. I make mistakes, too."

"I don't care. I just want to stay home today." The conviction had drained from his voice.

"It'll be okay. Here, put on your shoes."

"I'm not going to say anything at all today. I'll just play one of her stupid games."

"That's just fine, honey."

Jake crawled out of the soft pile. She handed him his sneakers. He stuck his feet into the toes and stood up, crushing the backs. He turned his back on her and shuffled out of the room. She heard him going down the stairs. The front door slammed. Her heart rose in her throat. She ran to the window and saw him sitting on the front steps. Joy felt relieved he was angry. Normal kids got mad at their moms. But growing up with a dead sister was not normal. Every year he had to experience his loss all over again in a more mature way.

Every time I think of Jenny while I'm with Jake he can tell. No wonder he's mad. Joy had never been angry with Jenny for dying before. *What a selfish thing to do, leaving me to clean up the mess.*

When she got in the car with him Joy thanked Jake for going. He said you made me do it, and she said you're right, but I appreciate it anyway. Fortunately, the Giants were on the East Coast and they could listen to the ballgame for the ten minutes it took to drive to Annie's office.

Joy had the fifty-minute hour free while Jake was inside with Annie. She regretted not planning the hour. Other moms cherished their rare private time, but improvisation was still too much for Joy. She wondered if she should go to the little coffeehouse to have a cup of coffee and fiddle around with her phone, or if she should sit in the car and listen to the ballgame so she could give Jake a full report when he came out, but she decided to go into that cute little clothing store on the corner that was expensive but had really nice clothes and buy something for Carly, whose birthday was in a couple of weeks.

As she put the shopping bag into the back seat she heard a door slam. She turned and saw Jake step out onto Annie's porch. His body was elongating, she realized, stretching toward the end of boyhood. Soon enough he would be a man, lost to her in the particular way that only her child could be. When she started the car the radio came on. The Giants were ahead. Jake was annoyed that she wasn't able to report on what happened in the game, so before they drove away she looked it up on her phone.

27.

JAKE'S LITTLE LEAGUE team held its autumn practices on an old field pockmarked with a hybrid assortment of grasses, weeds, and brown spots, surrounded by a high chain-link fence. Joy, in purgatory, waited patiently at the gate, watching the last drills.

"I don't want you to come in when you get here, Mom," Jake had said.

"Jake, I'd like to get to know these people. You spend a lot of time with their kids."

"I don't like it when you come in right at the end," he said.

You are still too busy with me, said Dead Jenny.

It's not about you, Joy told her. *Jake can have his way here. I'll just keep showing up.*

She watched the last fielding drills and foul-line to foul-line wind sprints. A final whistle and the boys headed for the benches, collecting their fielding gloves and batting gloves and bats and various pieces of discarded clothing and haphazardly stuffing their gear bags. The bleachers creaked and rustled as parents stood. Everyone headed to the gates. Jake put on his backpack and slung the gear bag over his shoulder.

She watched him, beaming. *My son can walk!*

Dead Jenny liked that.

Joy hadn't told anyone about Dead Jenny and didn't think she was going to. Carly would want to be included in the conversation. Lizzie would want to analyze its roots. Rabbi would be encouraging. Danny probably would bring down the men in white coats, even though keeping it a secret made Joy feel as if she were cheating on him. Yet Joy understood that she and Dead Jenny were going someplace, together. She knew she wasn't crazy, only that she was alone.

Her conversations with Danny often ended up in the same place.

"Get out of your head," he said. "Focus externally. When I start feeling hopeless I just take a breath and look at your picture on my desk and then make the next phone call."

"I'm glad my naked body is so soothing," she said sourly. "Maybe I should become a calendar model."

"Hey, I only look at your face. Besides, you told me you liked it."

She remembered liking it. *Honor my body. Find my sin. Pray for forgiveness.*

Danny had been encouraging about that, too. "Prayer can't hurt," he said. "Judaism is full of stories about miraculous intercessions in the face of overwhelming odds."

"True," she said, "but these stories have lasted thousands of years. Moses and those guys were real heavyweights. You don't hear about that anonymous Israelite mother from Bumfuck, Canaan, who smote her own child with self-absorbed indifference."

"Joy, you are the only person in the entire world who thinks it was even remotely possible that you mothered either of our kids with self-absorbed indifference. Can you pray for deliverance from that?"

She thought that was kind of a good idea, but when push came to shove it still was easier to get ragged on by Dead Jenny. Well, Yom Kippur was coming up. Maybe then.

"Should I get a job instead of working for myself? That way I'd always have something external to answer to."

"You'd go crazy. I still think hiring someone is the way to go. You can get enough work."

"I could," Joy said, and saw the crone, executive version, smartly dressed in a power suit, heels, and telephone headset, hair and nails perfect, standing with arms crossed at the picture window of the stylish private office upstairs in the JoyDesign high-ceilinged loft, surveying the staff carrels below, making deals and having meetings and solving problems and being as far away from the design process as she was from Jenny. Maybe she'd display a Solomon-like self-possession in the settling of trivial disputes among her employees. Or maybe she'd just yell at everyone every time she missed Jenny, ruling the roost with an iron fist, everyone terrified of her power.

"I don't want to be a manager," Joy said. "I'm a craftswoman."

"All the more reason to hire someone," Danny said. "You can concentrate on design and rainmaking and someone else can do the production."

"I'll think about it, Danny," she said, so she wrote a job description for an assistant and put it in her to-do folder. She looked up some design competitions and found one that looked good, but wondered if she could sustain engaging with the politics of it, and she was still wondering when the application deadline passed. She reviewed the newsletters she had sent to her clients back when she was avid, but couldn't quite figure out why what she put in was so damn important. *Just a best practice for a small businessperson, a byproduct of pride and ambition.*

Both of which you have, said Dead Jenny.

No, Joy said, *not so much anymore. And don't do the eye thing, please.*

* * *

When Jake reached the gate Joy asked how practice went and reached out to take the gear bag. Jake brushed by her without a word. He opened the rear door, threw his bags inside, got in, and closed the door behind him. She came around and got in on the driver's side. He stayed on the passenger side.

"You're not being very nice, Jake."

"You aren't either. Give me my phone back."

"Why did I take it?" Joy had asked him to take out the earbuds when she picked him up to drive to the practice. When he didn't, she confiscated the phone.

"Because you want me to talk to you even if I don't have anything to say."

"Two months ago you were mad at me for not talking to you, and now you're mad at me for talking to you." She gave him the phone. "Here, Jake."

"Thanks for nothing."

I don't think I was ever such a jerk to my mother, Joy said to Dead Jenny. She didn't like remembering how mean she had been to Rose in those last couple of years before the divorce.

You're kidding, right?

Headline: Woman Strangles Imaginary Doppelgänger.

Joy adjusted the mirror so she could sneak glances of Jake in the back seat. Driving home she could see that he was typing something, but he kept the earbuds in his pocket. An invitation?

"Do you have homework tonight?"

"I always have homework," Jake said.

"What do you have to do? Do you need any help?"

"Dad can help me."

See, Joy said to Dead Jenny. *What am I supposed to do about that?*

Woe is you, indeed, said Dead Jenny.

So I'm a stumblebum. There're worse things.

At home, Joy told Jake she was going to work in her office, but that she would be happy to help him if he needed it. He had to do some online research.

"Remember," she reminded him, "no movies or games."

"Mom, I'm not stupid. I need to have good grades to play on the traveling team, which is like a ton better than having to stay around here with you all summer."

I earned that, Joy said to herself. "I'm sorry I said that. I love you and I trust you. When you're done maybe we can cook dinner together or something."

"Maybe," he said, and went upstairs.

Apologizing made Jake angry, but so did being nice. Danny expected her to be infinitely forgiving, even if Jake was a pill or if she was stressed. She thought she deserved some recognition for the transportation-providing and schedule-maintaining and room-straightening and meal-preparing and chore-doing, all of which they both took for granted, but Jake expected it and Danny was so used to it that no extra credit was available.

Later, Jake came down, said that he was invited for dinner at Bobby's, and left to walk up the street. Then Danny called and said he was going to stay at the office late and that Becky was going out to grab them all something. Joy called Carly, but there was no answer. She thought of calling Lizzie or Rachel, but she looked at the clock and knew they would be busy with their families. She changed her clothes, took a bike and her headphones out to the back deck, and rode the trainer for an hour. Then she showered and, thinking of Carly, put on her nicest jeans and a pretty sweater and went out to Chestnut Street with her novel and sketchbook, thinking she might get a bite to eat. All the restaurants had couples and families in them, and then she thought she might go to a bar where she would get hit on but could at least talk to someone, but that was too dumb. So she bought some takeout and went home and set the table for one and by the time she was done Danny was home and she was happy to see him. When Jake came home he tried to stay about five feet away from her, but Danny kept all three of them in the same room until Jake went upstairs. Joy was grateful and felt open to her husband, but Danny said he needed to chill for a bit, which turned out to be quite a while, and Joy went to sleep alone.

Her weekly date with Carly was the next night. Joy wore a youngish dress. They were in the Balboa Café, sitting at a small table in the bar, when she told her about it.

"What do you expect?" Carly said to Joy. "Jake may be nine years old but he's still a guy."

"And you're the expert?"

"More than you."

That was a good point, Joy conceded. "Who's gonna get their nails done with me?"

"I will," Carly said.

"I didn't mean you."

"I know what you meant, but your world can't end with them. Danny isn't even home that much. Come out with me some night. We can get our nails done first."

"Do I have to wear one of those little dresses we used to wear?"

"You still could, and you'd be very, very popular. Half the guys in this place have been checking you out. I try to be more glamorous now. You'll be proud to be seen with me."

"You always look great. Hope I can keep up."

"Joy, you're a goddess. You can wear anything. Besides, you got out of the game when you hit the jackpot with Danny."

"It feels like the booby prize. Maybe promiscuity wouldn't be so bad for either of us now."

"That's the last thing you need. Things are the same?"

"Mostly it's just kind of dull and achy. Up and down. Having a dead child really sucks."

Joy took a sip and stared out the window at a young mother wheeling her twins down the sidewalk. "I'll go out with you, Carly. Just don't abandon me again." Joy remembered finding herself in one of those little dresses, alone with three boys behind the closed door of someone's bedroom. She kept them at bay but felt hunted, and was furious with Carly when she waltzed back in an hour later with the boy she'd been eyeing . . . and Joy's car keys.

"You never are going to let me forget that, are you?" Carly said. "It only happened once."

"Twice."

"No, it was the same night. That only counts as once. And you did get the car."

Joy had left then, and Carly's boy had brought her home in the morning.

"Why did we think we had to do that?"

"I liked it, Joy. But I never go home with them on the first night anymore."

Joy snorted. They got a second glass of wine. Carly kept pointing out the guys who were checking Joy out.

"Good clean fun, Joy. Not every guy wants to get into your pants."

"Not when they can get into yours, right?"

Carly spit out her wine, she was laughing so hard, and they kept it up while one-upping each other with many details of a few wild college nights they later almost regretted. At home that night, Joy thought that doing more probably was the right thing to do, but why did everyone have to tell her all the time?

I wish, she said to Dead Jenny, *that for five minutes all of you could just shut the fuck up.*

28.

ON ROSH HASHANAH Joy lingered with the story of Hannah, a woman who was loved but couldn't get pregnant. This went on for years. She even got hubby a second, more fecund wife. Eventually, though, her constant, anguished prayer was answered and she bore Samuel, but at a significant cost—she had to give him up to the priesthood at age five. That didn't seem like such a bargain to Joy, five years and out, but Hannah at least knew the deal at the outset, and she at least got to see him a couple of times a year. *I'd make that deal now*, Joy thought, *instantly*.

Jenny had quickened in her like a magic bean; Joy went off the pill and there she was. Now every month another baby was never born, ticking the time away until the plumbing clogged for good. *Maybe I'm actually as desperate as Hannah and don't know it. I still could have another one. Even if Danny doesn't want to I can get him to bed and not even tell him I decided. Just let it be a "whoops" in a couple of months.*

Great plan, said Dead Jenny. *Whoops.*

When Joy was at the shul she tried to think about forgiveness, but it seemed petty to want relief from a small personal problem like hers when God seemed more inclined to grant miracles like Knocking Down the Walls of Jericho, or reward sustainable activities like Getting

Eternally Rich and Fecund Harvests for Hewing to the Covenant.

God is infinitely forgiving, but I don't feel forgiven. Jenny can't forgive me.

No, Dead Jenny said, *dead is dead.*

Can't you ask her for me?

Dead Jenny ignored that question. *Danny forgives you. Jake forgives you.*

I don't know how to forgive myself.

She expected the experience to be singular and cathartic. She'd have some kind of a holy moment and God would immediately and permanently release the nagging guilt that she alone had wrecked their life.

Maybe for you God is more like a cheerleader than a wizard, said Dead Jenny. *No magic for the common mourner.*

Maybe I can get forgiven only after I die. Or after I spend my entire life mindlessly executing on my deliverables.

That piece of paper is already pretty tattered, Dead Jenny said.

I want it a lot.

Stop trying so damned hard, Dead Jenny said.

I'm afraid to stop trying.

Maybe forgiveness never really happens at all, but eventually enough time goes by that the slow accrual of other layers of experience buries the grief and the guilt. Living half a life becomes acceptable because a full life is impossible.

Or maybe forgiveness is already happening in little bits and pieces of chance occurrences, doing something just a little differently each time. Tolerating Danny's absorption in his work. Tolerating Jake's anger. Tolerating her own failures. Forgiveness by attrition.

She had to be more afraid in order to feel her sin. She had to feel her sin to feel forgiven.

She asked Rabbi about it, when he made some time for her in the incredibly busy week between Rosh Hashanah and Yom Kippur.

"Afraid of what?" Rabbi asked.

"Fate? Death? God? I thought I got inoculated against fear because

I now know anything really can happen. I guess I was just dense. I should still be afraid. Maybe that's why I can't find forgiveness."

"God already forgave you, Joy, but He can't save you from yourself."

"God is a terrifying idea," she said.

"You haven't said much about God in our talks," Rabbi said.

"It's hard to believe in a God who left Jenny out of the Book of Life."

"He might have something for you anyway."

"I'm still here. That's enough."

"Doesn't seem to be. What's missing?"

"A purpose beyond breathing, maybe?"

"You already found that when you decided your family needs you."

"That was your wording," Joy said. "I couldn't refute it."

Do you always have to be such a hardnose? Dead Jenny asked.

I feel like a marshmallow.

"You abandoned the Other World for it," Rabbi said.

"That's true." *I had thought it abandoned me.* Joy suddenly thought that maybe just being alive and having Jake and Danny was its own miracle, in a way, when not too long ago her destiny was to become a lonely crone-witch doctor-medium-permanently grieving crazy lady.

"This seems to be your work for Yom Kippur, Joy," Rabbi said, "figuring out what fear and forgiveness have to do with each other."

She said, "I was in charge and she got killed and I can't get around that."

"Maybe that's not the relevant thing anymore. Start somewhere else."

The only work she used to do on Yom Kippur was try not to die of boredom as the day crept glacially by. Now she understood that the holiday itself was a practice, a place to be immersed in rituals of transparency, forgiveness, and submission. The practice of *Tshuvah*, she thought, the active work of self-examination, an annual ritual of my people, thousands of years of penitence and error and renewed penitence and more error. Mistakes are inevitable, unforgiven or not.

* * *

Joy called her mother the morning before Yom Kippur.

"*G'mar chatimah tovah*, Joyeleh," Rose said. May the Book of Life be sealed with your inscription already in it.

"I hope that happens for all of us," Joy said.

"We do what we can, honey. Are you doing okay?" She hadn't called Joy "honey" in a while.

Joy liked it. "Well enough. We're both working and Jake's doing well in school." Joy felt Rose waiting, her calm attention warming the telephone's handset. Hiram had always liked Rose's attention. Joy suspected he had actually let Rose go because having a wife who followed her own mind as far as Rose had confounded him. Now she was Mrs. Pinchas Gelberman, *rebbetzin*—wife of the rabbi. Joy only heard her call him "Reb Pinchas" or "the Rebbe," even in private conversations. He was always studying or teaching, and Rose told Joy she had her own life, so much richer than it ever was in San Francisco, not that she meant anything personal by that. Joy wanted her to feel at least a little bit lonely, so they could commiserate, but Rose said what with being the rebbetzin and all, she had a lot of unofficial duties in their community, plus the Rebbe's family. He had five children and seventeen grandchildren.

"I'm sorry I was so mad at you, Mom, when you left."

"I hurt you, Joy. I knew that, but it was a long time ago. You have nothing to apologize for. Your *tshuvah* is done with me."

Joy wasn't sure about that, but she had to accept it. "I'm not doing so well with Jenny."

"I don't know what to say to that, Joy. Almost four years have gone by. I can't imagine your father lets you get away with that, even if Danny does."

Nailed you there, said Dead Jenny.

"I don't know, Mom. A lot is good. Rabbi thinks I'm not asking the right question."

"He's a wise man."

"I keep trying to do the right thing."

"I know that, Joy," Rose said to her. "May God bless you for it."

They said *shanah tovah*, Happy New Year, and wished each other an easy fast. Joy stared at the phone. Rose hadn't abandoned her, exactly, she remembered holidays and birthdays, but she had made herself a new life. Emphatically.

I forgive you, Mom, for leaving me. It felt true. *Just like Jake wants of me.*

Joy had thought that she had to forgive Mom for leaving her; but Mom didn't think so. Rose forgave Joy for doing the leaving, but Joy never thought it had been her doing. *Mom is holding me. She loves me. Judaism will hold my grief for longer than I will live. When I'm the one who's in the Other World.*

* * *

Yom Kippur started with a short service in the evening. Rabbi's sermon was pointed, droll, and warm. Joy felt grateful he was her rabbi. The next morning she checked off all the boxes. She didn't shower, and when she brushed her teeth she was careful not to swallow any water. She made no coffee in the kitchen. The morning orange remained uncut. She poured Jake's cereal into a bowl and put the milk carton next to it.

Danny appeared, unshaven. "Morning. What kind of a holiday starts at the crack of dawn? I thought it was the alarm for work."

He got himself a glass of water.

"Started last night," she said. "You're drinking water?"

"Yes," he said, "it's hard enough to go without coffee. Hope I don't get smited. Smoted?"

He took a sip. They waited. No smiting occurred.

"Didn't you drink water last year?"

"Yes," Joy said. "Just trying the next thing."

"Whatever," he said. "You can always be more perfect, I suppose."

"Or less fucked up."

He shook his head at that one, but hugged her anyway, and she kissed him.

Jake walked in. "Should I be fasting?" He poured milk into his bowl, then picked up his spoon and took a bite.

Joy put the milk back in the refrigerator. "Kids aren't expected to."

"We fast to remember our regrets," Danny said. "You're too young for them."

"No, Dad," Jake said. "I'm not."

"We all have that regret," Danny said.

"We can't change what happened," Joy said. "Only what we do next. Just like baseball."

There was peace in that moment.

You're going to run out of things to talk about, Joy said to Dead Jenny.

That's the plan, said Dead Jenny.

Yom Kippur services started early and ran past sundown, five services linked, one after the other, with a short afternoon break. Joy and Danny got there at the beginning of the second service. The tired old building looked a lot grander when its rows were filled with congregants, many in long white *kittels*, topped with a wide variety of yarmulkes and draped with prayer shawls.

Repetition is the root of change. Doing the same thing, differently. Maybe something different will happen to me today.

She stood up and sat down and sang and beat her breast and tried to be an open vessel. The *Yizkor* service, memorializing all the dead, came and went around noon, and she cried for her loss. Rabbi prostrated himself three times during the service of the *Kohen Gadol*, and her heart melted toward the ground too. She read the selections and studied the commentaries during the Torah service. She listened to the rabbi and the cantor and the poets. She was tired and hungry and thirsty. After the break they came back for *Ne'ilah*, the final service: as it's said, the last chance before the Gates of Heaven closed for another year. She read the sins, again, *Al chayt shechatanu lefanecha,* beat her chest, again, for thousandth time that day.

> "...we have sinned against you through hardening our hearts, We have sinned against you thoughtlessly, We have sinned against you in our innermost thoughts. We have sinned against you through empty confession, through foolishness, by clever cynicism, through stubbornness, by betraying trust, by succumbing to confusion ..."

Her skin flushed. A rippling rose against gravity, through her feet, hands, arms, legs, head, heart, that pushed open the door of the selfish time and space she wanted to believe protected her loves from her suffering but was her suffering, the sweet glory of her martyrdom to the Moment When Everything Changed. Millions of children were dead, dead in the Holocaust and dead in pogroms and dead by plague and by accident and in simple ordinary dying.

I have to let my one dead child fully live in the world of the dead. She is gone. Danny has his life to live. Jake needs to push against me. And I must stand.

Joy held on to Danny's shoulder to keep from falling. He looked at her; she saw his question turn to softness as she saw in him the softness she felt in her own face. The final *shofar* blast turned her inside out, her loss, for once, on the outside, perhaps to be transformed forever. She sang *Havdalah* with a full heart.

But the next morning she woke to billowing dust and stabbing sunlight and echoing screams. She'd been waiting for so long for a moment of forgiveness, of light, and it had come and gone outside her control, as chance as Jenny's death had been.

How much light did you expect, Joy? asked Dead Jenny. *Can I go now? Not quite yet. Soon, I hope.*

29.

ON THE OUTSKIRTS of St. Helena, vineyards surrounded the winery. When Joy drove down the long driveway to the offices she saw the bare architecture of dormant vines and the road stretching into the distance, and for just a moment she remembered cold wind cutting her face and the rhythm of breath and steady effort resonating in her legs. She felt an archaic, elemental yearning to be on the road, alone, away, just her and Dead Jenny, forever.

Not to be.

Joy had been excited to win this high profile contract, an identity package for a new winery opening up in Yountville, part of a large beverage group with a big budget. She worked crisply with the client and the branding agency to produce something specific yet enticing that would immediately differentiate this particular winery from all the other ones. The blinds rolled up as she finished her presentation.

"So," she said, "you can see that the basic image is strong by itself, but as I illustrated in the slide show is very adaptable to each of the requirements laid out in the brand statement. If there are any questions I'll be happy to take them now."

The five faces around the table were smiling, nodding. She wondered about each of them, if the young woman from marketing was a mother, if the guy from finance ignored his wife, if that older guy, the winemaker, had lost his parents yet, if the young secretary in the short skirt she kept pulling down even thought about why she dressed that way. They left, but the boss was hanging around, checking his phone. Joy waited for it, and as she was ready to go he caught her arm.

"I guess there's no good way to do this," he said, "but I just want to say how sorry I am for your loss. I have two sons and I can't imagine how it feels."

"You're imagining it now," Joy said. "It's nothing to wish on anyone, but it could happen to anyone." She let a beat go by. "I appreciate your kindness, and I do look forward to working together. Maybe I can bring my bike next time."

"Sure," he said all in a rush, "I ride, too!"

Joy, who knew that about him, said, "Oh, you do? We should make a plan."

She said *nasdrovya* to Danny, for the list they had made so long ago. When she got to the car, she called him.

"I did good, Danny. They really liked it, and I've got the account for the foreseeable future, I think. Then the boss gave me his condolences."

"It's about time. You've only had about six meetings with the guy."

"Four," she said. "I did just fine, although I wasn't very gracious. Anyway, he rides, so I started talking about that."

Danny chuckled. "Nice feint. We have two things to celebrate tonight!"

He had called her from his office a couple of weeks before to ask her to go out with him for his birthday. "Another tradition restored," he told her.

She knew what he really wanted. More often than not Joy had given herself as Danny's present, vampy and bare under a range of skimpy dresses and high heels. He would wine and dine her and later in their bed her generous intention often reduced him to grateful tears.

"It still feels like the beginning, Danny. I don't know if I can be like that again."

"We've done pretty damn well, if you ask me," Danny said. "And I love you no matter what you do."

He had put up with a lot. So Joy accepted. Then the presentation had come up for the same day, and she thought of course, this is the way things happen, work all day and then go out with your husband without any kind of a grief break. On the drive home she scouted a road she'd heard was good for riding up there, and got back to the city just in time for her hair appointment. She thought she looked real good when she picked up Jake at practice. Jake didn't notice but most of the dads did.

*   *   *

Joy found the dress she wanted in the back of her closet, a royal blue silk wrap with long sleeves, hemmed a little above the knee, closed with a belt and a couple of tiny snaps. Revealing, but womanly. The slinky fabric hugged her, smooth and soft against her skin. She chose a skimpy bra and panty set that she knew Danny would like when the dress came off later. *What could she be tonight?*

Start somewhere else, Rabbi had said. She had been holding on with such force it had been impossible to imagine how things might look if released. What would Danny look like, then? He was different too, this Danny, the one she had created with her preoccupations. Would he recognize the woman she was now? Would she?

Joy was sitting at her vanity when Danny came back from taking Jake to Max's house for the night. He kissed the top of her head. She took his hand off her shoulder and kissed it.

"We would have been leaving them home together by now."

"Fourteen years old, almost," he said, "We'd be paying her."

"Not for taking care of Jake. She loved him."

"Altruism wouldn't get her to the movies the way ten bucks an hour would. Should I wear a tie?"

Joy thought if he did she could use it to strangle him for his pedantry, but then she remembered that she was trying to abandon the glory of her bereavement so she said, "Only if you want to. It's your party, after all."

He vanished into the shower. Joy finished her makeup, put on the dress, decided not to wear pantyhose, and chose the highest heels she still could tolerate. He came up behind her, a towel wrapped around his waist.

"Those shoes do fantastic things to your legs."

"You'd better like them. I can barely walk."

"You can wear something else."

"What, and spoil the full effect?" She spun a full circle, the skirt flying.

"We'll use the valet parking."

He dropped the towel and hugged her from behind, lightly thrusting, his hands sliding the thin silk over her skin, slowly pulling the dress apart. She could feel him stiffening against her back.

"Okay, you like them."

"I like you," he said.

"Don't we have a reservation?"

"So we do."

She felt grateful. *He really is an extraordinary man*, she thought, *caring, safe, kind. Mature. He loves me. We're still here, together.* He put on an Italian silk suit and a tie that matched her dress.

She whistled. "Looking sharp, counselor."

He offered her his arm. "Thank you, Mrs. Rosenberg. Shall we go?"

* * *

They entered through the revolving door and were escorted to a small table under a window where they sat side by side, with a view of all the hustle and bustle of the busy restaurant. The waiter brought them two glasses of champagne. She toasted her husband; his hand slid under the wrap. He moved it gently between her thighs, but she took his wrist and held his hand where it was.

"Easy," she said.

He put his hand back on the table. Compromising, she relaxed and crossed her knee, letting the wrap fall open, exposing her leg to the hip.

"Nice legs," he said.

"Aren't you getting to be kind of old for this sort of thing?"

"No! Besides, you're still twenty-two to me. Every time I look at you I see the girl who was showing all that skin at the race."

"You could barely look at me."

He blushed. "It's true. I almost blew it."

"You got over it fast enough. It was like two AM or something and I went inside and woke Lizzie up and told her I might have just met my husband."

"That's sweet." He kissed her. "Congrats on getting that job today."

"Yeah, they have a big budget and they're going to use me for a lot of their media. I'll get a lot of exposure. And I got another referral today through the same agency. I think I can work as much as I want to. Maybe as much as you, if I want to."

"I knew it," Danny said. "I guess we'll be eating in a lot of restaurants."

"I hope not, Danny. We need a normal home life. What's Jake going to think?"

"That normal is working hard and eating out," Danny said. He was on a roll now. "He's got money. Besides, I cook."

"Not very much," Joy said. "Graduate school will probably use up his money."

"Weekends, I cook. And we're paying for graduate school. The blood money is his." He paused. "Are we having a fight?"

"No, we're not," she said.

"Good. So can you hire someone now?"

She nodded. "I was thinking I should sub out the excess work instead of hiring. I worry about the next disaster."

"No more disasters," he said fervently. "No more."

They drank to that too. Their salads came, and Joy pulled her napkin over her bare leg. They fed each other tastes.

"It sucks that her being dead is normal," he said.

"The new normal. I can even try to look beautiful and it doesn't feel like a lie."

He slid the napkin off her lap. "It's no lie with legs like that."

"A little chunky in the thighs and butt, don't you think? All that bicycling."

"I've never gone for those willowy white girls," he said. "Hearty peasant stock for me. Drop the babies and pick the potatoes."

"That's not the way to get to where you want to go tonight, Danny." She smiled anyway, then pulled her dress closed as the waiter cleared the salads and refilled the wine glasses.

He lifted a glass to her. "I get a little slack on my birthday, I hope. I remember a few other birthdays where you made me very, very happy."

I could be something like that at home tonight, something close to that, maybe. Maybe he's even right to expect it.

Their main courses arrived. They talked about the news, and the office, and what was up with their parents, and about Jake some more. Joy lifted her napkin this time. He dropped a slow hand, then flicked the wrap open. She let it stay that way.

"I was remembering your vision," Danny said. "I was angry at you for giving in to it, but it scared me. All I could do was hang on to what I knew. I get it now, I think—loosen that grip just a little and the world starts to fade away."

"Hah," she said. "Welcome to the loony bin."

"No," Danny said, "I opted out of that one."

"I'm sorry that was hard for you," she said, "but you're batting a thousand tonight."

She leaned over and kissed his cheek. "I have something for you."

Joy had wanted to get him something unique, like an engraved bracelet, but she knew he wouldn't wear it, so then maybe something practical, but he said one night that he hoped his parents wouldn't give him another sweater. So she called Elaine to tell her to not buy him a sweater. Maybe a nice portrait of her and Jake? But she couldn't schedule that soon enough with their busy schedules, and if she was hiring a photographer it should be all of them and maybe the grandparents too. Then she thought she could get golf clubs or a new bike, but those were too much for a non-zero birthday. She reached into her purse and handed him a small velvet box.

"You didn't have to do this," he protested. "The night is enough."

She hoped it would be.

He tore off the paper with a certain eagerness nonetheless, opened the box, and took out the watch. It was simple and dressy, with a small diamond embedded in the face.

"Look at the back."

The engraving read, *To Danny, my rock. Love forever, your Joy.*

"It's beautiful, honey." He took off his other watch and put it on. She knew his wrist size. "Let's get out of here."

She took his arm. They left the restaurant and walked around the corner to the Embarcadero. Buffeted by the westerlies, they watched the twinkling light patterns play up and down the Bay Bridge cables, then circled back and picked up their car. Joy took her coat off, laying it on the back seat. When Danny sat down she caressed his thigh, leaving her hand there. Crossing right leg over left, she let the wrap open, revealing her thigh; he reached over and gently pulled the other half of the skirt toward him, baring both her legs to the hip. She let her legs fall open.

"That's a great view. I want more."

He pulled the away from the curb.

"Gosh, you're so demanding. I bought you a watch."

"You can return it if there's a quid pro quo."

"There isn't. Danny. Look all you want."

"I'm past looking now."

He drove home with only one hand on the wheel. She liked what he did with his other hand, but she felt both urgent and broken. *Always broken*, she thought. Ignoring the danger, she unclipped her seatbelt as Danny parked in their driveway. He brought her to him and kissed her fiercely. His left hand roamed the front of her body. She felt a tug and her belt came loose. The snaps ticked and the dress fell open, baring her body to him. His hands were all over her. She gave him a squeeze in the place he wanted to be touched.

He came around the car and opened her door. She left her dress dangling open for the short walk to the front door. As it closed behind him Danny reached out and pulled the dress off her shoulders. She turned, and looking straight at him, let it slide down her arms onto the floor. In her transparent lingerie and high heels, she led him up the stairs.

The naked woman in the bathroom mirror was her. Seeking Gauguin, she saw Munch. She wanted to cuddle up with her pillow in her brushed cotton pajamas printed with little bicycles, soft, quiescent, Danny at a comfortable distance. But he was in their bed full of sweet kisses and soft smiles and cheeks made warm by champagne and wine. She joined him, for the sake of the woman she was sure wanted him, coiling around him, kissing, touching, hiding her breasts against his chest. His skin was hot, his muscles were tight, grabby. He was so much bigger than her.

"Go slow, Danny," her fear whispered.

He didn't. His hands scraped her skin. She suffocated in an avalanche of touch. Her body moved itself away from his hands, down, her mouth surrounding his hard pleasure, veins and ridges throbbing between her lips, heat on her tongue.

His hips moved forward and her head moved back. He followed relentlessly. She tried to hold him still, but he was too strong and he was too big in her mouth and she was afraid and she flipped away from his heat and his smell and his eyes, onto her belly, face deep in her pillow, biting down hard, wishing he was a tree, a telephone pole, there to rip her to shreds. He became it, slamming into her again and again, his weight driving the breath out of her. He shoved his arm under her hips and dragged her to her knees. She had to use all her strength to survive his power: used, taken, owned, flooded. After, his strength gone, he dropped his sweaty weight fully onto her body and crushed her flat. Just Danny, once again.

As soon as seemed practical she rolled him off her and headed to the bathroom. It still was Munch in the mirror. When she came out Danny was gone. She lay on their bed, the sheets sweaty and sticky. She felt sullied; she had lied to him. Familiar, ordinary, foreign sounds percolated from the kitchen, the top popping off the teapot, water filling it, the click of the switch; gentle bubbling as water boiled in the machine. Footsteps on the stairs. She levered herself upright and leaned against the headboard. He came in with the tea, still naked, his white-caked cock small and mild. He handed the tea to her wordlessly.

"Happy birthday," she said. *What to say?* "That was intense."

He looked at her. "Yes. Why do I feel like shit?"

Dead Jenny was watching. Joy held on.

"What are you talking about? Wasn't I what you wanted?" She threw her legs open and put her hand there. "Oh Danny, oh, that was so good, oh, oh, more, more."

"Joy, yes, that's real funny. Now stop it. We're in trouble here."

He sat on the bed, put his arm around her, tried to pull her close. She pushed away. He followed her across the bed. She jumped off the bed and nearly ran across the room.

For a brief moment, Joy burst into tears. "Goddammit, Danny; don't touch me!" She took a step, but he didn't move. She sat on the floor. "How could you do that?"

"Do what? What you wanted?"

"I asked you to go slow."

"And I didn't. Usually you ask again. I thought you wanted that."

I wanted to feel something. It was confusing. She wrapped her arms around her knees and held on tightly. "You hurt me."

"You wanted me to."

"Yes." The admission hurt as much as the act.

"Crap," Danny said. "Can we just stop this?"

He picked up his boxers and put them on. He extended his hand. She took it and he pulled her up. She went to her dresser and put on the pajamas. Silently, they straightened up the bed. The tea was

WITHOUT JENNY

cold. He took the cups into the bathroom and dumped them out. He brushed his teeth, then she brushed hers. She washed her face and braided her hair and took her vitamins. They lay in their bed.

"I'm so sorry," he said, after a while.

"Me too," she said. He reached tentatively toward her, and she caught his hand—simply Danny's hand again. She held it softly, warming next to her hip.

* * *

Joy woke up early and got on the bike. She was sore. She banged a fist on the handlebar, missing Jenny, missing Danny, ready to vanish into the soothing intensity of three climbing intervals up the Marin Headlands.

If Jenny was still alive, everything would be all right.

Do we have to go over this again? said Dead Jenny.

Y'know, said Joy, *No. We're done here.*

For a tiny suspended moment the landscape exhaled and Joy felt untethered; then the hill started to bite and she became only legs and breath. Power on, up the hill, watch the monitor, heart rate high and steady, twelve minutes up. Relax. Descend. Repeat. Relax. Descend. Repeat. Relax. Descend. Recover. Return.

When she got home, she was relieved Danny was there. He was dressed in jeans and a T-shirt and his briefcase was open on the counter.

"Good ride?" He poured her some coffee but kept the counter between them.

"I did my work." She paused. "Danny, I don't know what to say."

He put some files away and closed the briefcase. She liked it when he clicked the latches and put it on the floor.

"It got pretty ugly," he said. "I'm sorry for my part. I haven't wanted you like that since before she died, though. I guess that was good. Wanting you, I mean."

"At least you got a good fuck out if it." He winced, and she held her hand up. "It went too far. You should have stopped. I should have stopped you. We both got hurt. Something still is broken. I don't know how to fix it right now."

"Can last night just be over?"

I hope so. She reached across the counter and squeezed his forearm. However many things he had been to her, he had never been selfish. The quiet felt good. She watched him over the rim of her coffee cup. The newspaper was spread out on the counter and he drank his coffee left-handed, his baby finger extended. Just like Danny always did.

"Quite the adventure, eh?"

He looked up and shook his head. "No shit. Who knew we were signing up for this!"

"When do we have to get Jake?"

"At three. I was hoping to spend the day in bed, but we might kill each other."

"Yeah, better safe than sorry. Maybe we should clean out the basement."

"I don't know, there're a lot of pointy implements down there."

They decided to go to a museum.

"Okay," he said, "but what I said last night? I really mean it. No more of this."

"Jesus H. Fuck, Danny. Just can the holier-than-thou shit, okay?"

He put his cup down emphatically. "Joy, I am not going to be the bad guy here. It was an equal opportunity fuck-up. Okay?"

She wanted to punch him. "Okay."

"Okay," he said, and when he smiled the smile she remembered from the coffeehouse that very first night, what she wanted was to spend the day with that boy. For most of the day, she did.

30.

THAT FOURTH SUMMER, Joy often was alone.

She had known it was coming but it surprised her nonetheless. She kept buying food for a full house that ended up in the compost bucket. Jake was away on a six-week baseball tour. A lot of the time that she wasn't working she spent on the bike. She told Lizzie the discipline was a lifesaver, to which Lizzie retorted that at least it was a time sink. Not that she offered Joy any real alternatives. Joy's winery designs were all over the Bay Area, and she was providing close to full-time work to a couple of her graduate school classmates.

Danny had a room in the Executive Stay Hotel and Suites in Stockton and slept there three or four nights a week. The new acquisition was not going so smoothly, he said, but she saw him reveling in an orgy of competence so much more predictable than his life with her. They wore their intimate distance comfortably—householding days, movie nights, and separate bedtimes created just enough present for it all to feel autonomous. Some weeks they didn't talk at all. When he was home they still went to the shul most Saturdays, did things with Jake, saw the parents and some friends. In her grimmer moods Joy saw their life as stepping in the pre-painted footsteps of what families do, guiding them down an inevitable path of ever greater insensibility.

Partners, joined at the hip by the shared space that should have been Jenny.

One Thursday morning her empty house was too damn quiet. She couldn't settle down. Her office looked like a prison, and she didn't have any phone calls or immediate deadlines. Joy's tried-and-true solution to this kind of unrest was to get really, really tired. *Fortunately I have a way to do that.* She got on her bike with a vague plan to head north over the bridge and ride a long damn way.

Ninety minutes later she rolled up next to a rider at Claus Drive in Fairfax, waiting to turn onto Sir Francis Drake.

"Hey," she said.

"Hey. Beautiful morning."

"Supposed to get even warmer tomorrow," she replied. "But you look prepared for anything."

His bike carried fenders, a pair of small but fully packed panniers, three water bottles, a tool kit, pump, spare tire, and lights. A jacket and wind vest were bungeed to his rear rack. He looked tantalizingly familiar to her, but older guys in helmets and sunglasses with two days of graying growth were not uncommon out on the road.

"You never know what could happen. I'm out touring for a few days. Guerneville, Fort Bragg, Lakeport, Calistoga. You?"

"Those are hundred-mile days. Good for you. I'm out for the day, the big loop to Tomales or Valley Ford. Family's away."

"Either one of those is a longer day than mine. You have kids at home?"

"Yeah, a ten-year-old boy. And a husband," she said pointedly, thinking, *at least in name.*

"I'm one of those myself." He held up his left hand to show his ring. "My wife's in New York, visiting her sister. Our youngest is thirty-two. We lost our oldest long ago."

Joy stopped pedaling and reached out to touch his arm.

"I'm so sorry. My daughter was killed almost five years ago."

"Ah." They stopped in the middle of the bike path, by the 7-Eleven about a mile out Sir Francis Drake. They rolled their bikes to the curb. She took off her helmet. He did too.

"I know you. You're Benny. We came to a Compassionate Friends meeting."

"I remember," he said. "Joy. You never came back."

"No," she said, pausing, then, "are you still doing it?"

"Passed it on," he said. "To that Illinois couple, actually. They had a baby."

"That's nice." She plowed on. "Your son was sixteen?"

"Yes. Jason," he said.

"Jason," she said. "Jenny."

"Jenny. I remember," he said. "Scaffolding. You were there."

She nodded. "Still am."

His face went through a set of expressive transformations. "Didn't make any difference, being there?"

"Nope. Couldn't do a thing, anyway."

He looked frustrated. "Jason was going to take the bus, but I made all these arrangements so he could take the car instead. I thought I was doing him a favor."

"I was just getting her a bottle of water." She showed him her helplessness, too. Benny shrugged and angled his head toward the road, raising an eyebrow; she had always liked guys who could raise one eyebrow. She buckled her helmet. They headed up the road.

"I didn't know you rode," she said. "Maybe I would have come back."

"I did it a lot when I was younger. I started again when Jason got interested, in my forties. Since he died, quite a bit."

"Your wife?"

"Not riding. She walks and does yoga."

"Danny says he'll tour with me next summer."

"Is he fit enough?"

"He has a decent enough base, but fifty-mile days probably will be enough for him."

"I'm sure you can find some bonus miles, if you want. Maybe you should ride a tandem." In unconscious rhythm, they stood to power over the little rise after Lefty Gomez Park. "I'm getting a crush on you," he said. "Beautiful, bereaved, and on the bike."

"Charming. Maybe you need to add bummed-out and bitter."

"*Borrring*! Not today. Not out here."

They followed the tilt of the road up White's Hill. The elastic stretched as she pulled ahead of him on the steeper parts in the middle of the climb. Over the top first, she was going thirty when he caught her wheel on the descent. She slowed a bit and they rode side by side.

"It's been fifteen years for you," she said. "What do you tell people now?"

"Eighteen, actually. I tell them when they ask how many kids I have, but not any details."

"I've never met a bereaved parent out here before," she said. "But I've had a lot of talks about religion. Or their other bike."

"Yeah," he snorted, "it's so exclusive, we can have our jerseys handmade. The Dead Child Cycling Club."

"Ride with the club that no one wants to join."

"Very funny," he said. "You still want to see her?"

"Every damn day. Maybe when I die, but I can't say that I believe it. Who knows?"

"*What Dreams May Come*. It only happens in the movies," he said. "I still have such a longing for things to be different."

"And you're eighteen years out. Okay."

"It's just unacceptable. Always unacceptable."

"Yeah." That never was going to go away then. They rode fast for a while, then made the right turn uphill onto Nicasio Valley Road.

"You've got some nonstandard chainrings there," she said.

"Forty-six/thirty. I've got an eleven in the back. Jason wanted to push a big gear all the time, but I haven't raced since we lost him. These chainrings are plenty big for touring. And I had enough to catch you on the descent."

She was really glad he had, but she pushed back. "That's only because you're so heavy."

"If I get too slow you can push me."

She pulled ahead again, but then slowed up and got behind him. He made some kind of a breathy gibe, and she said she thought she should be behind the old guy, you know, just in case. The little climb of Cecy's Hill was enough to shut them up. Benny spun his bulky bike up the grade, his upper body quiet and relaxed, head steady, legs strong and fast. On the wide shoulder out by the reservoir they were side-by-side again. His line was super steady, and she felt confident enough in him to drift her bike closer. They were inches apart. She glanced at him and he was smiling, but his eyes were fixed down the road.

"You ever wonder why you never rode your bike off the mountain?" he asked.

"Wasn't my turn, I guess. And my son needed a mom. Needs a mom. He was six."

"He's ten now? Doing okay?"

"I hope so. He's been really mad at me, but it might be getting better."

"Damn kids really have minds of their own, don't they?"

Joy laughed. "I sure did."

"Touché," he said. "Our daughter Sam was fourteen when her brother was killed. She had a few hard years, but now she's got a career and a serious boyfriend and they come over for dinner every week."

"Sounds like you won the jackpot."

"Yeah, so far. Deborah is ready for a grandchild."

They made the right on Shoreline, up toward Tomales. She slipped behind him again, pacing easily on his wheel; everything felt peaceful and right, there in his draft. *This is how I used to feel,* she thought, *when we were perfect.* Then he flicked his elbow. Sighing, Joy went past and took a turn in the front—can't ride in the draft forever. He said something that she needed repeated.

"My wife was amazing. She didn't blame me for one second."

"Danny went down there the next day. Stood where I stood. I was so grateful to him, but I was pretty self-involved. He just went back to work. I thought he was avoiding his grief, but that's how he could manage it. All I could do was walk. And cry."

"At first I couldn't do much for either of them. Sam made me do stuff with her. Deborah just waited. Pretty nice of her."

"I remember her being a beautiful woman."

"She is that. In many ways."

Clicking up and down the cogset, Joy was in and out of the saddle as the road bobbed and weaved along Tomales Bay. The tide was rolling into the narrow bay in a wave.

"Don't see that too often," he said.

Joy had never seen it. Something inside her shifted and clicked into place.

"You find out you don't have as many friends as you thought," he said. "And then the people you meet after—"

"If you don't talk about it, it becomes this big secret," Joy said. "Your child is dead. It's like the only thing that ever happened to you. Then people want to help, and they're almost always wrong. We don't have as many friends as we used to."

"Thank God for the bike."

"Amen to that, brother."

Joy and Benny rode the last of the whoop-de-do's, up past Miller Park, and descended to Tomales Creek. Settled in again, he asked, "How old are you? How long have you been married?"

"I'm forty-five, almost. We've been married eighteen years."

"I'm sixty-three. Thirty-five years with Deb."

"Wow, sixty-three. You're a really strong rider."

"In a way. My muscles are all slow twitch, all the time!"

Joy laughed. "Well, that's good for bereaved parenting. It is a slow twitch sport."

She didn't at all feel angry with Danny about anything, out here. She loved him.

"You were young enough when she died. Did you think about having another one?"

"We did think about it, but decided it wouldn't be fair to Jake."

"Deb got a dog after a couple years. Sweet dog, but I wouldn't have."

"I thought about that for Jake. I never really thought about it for me."

"It would have been your dog anyway."

"True enough."

They stopped in Tomales for a sandwich and to refill their water bottles. They sat at a tacky plastic table in the window of the deli, catching glimpses of the grocery store across the highway through the steady stream of northbound RVs.

"You keep trying to figure it out," he said. "We must have twenty or thirty dead child books, but there's nothing to know. It was chance. An accident."

"The dead child industry suffers from a lot of twenty-twenty hindsight, but it's hard to accept that it was so capricious," Joy said. "Our rabbi kept saying there's only one reality. All of life led to that one moment and all the rest of life is its consequence. I guess that was advice, but what do you do with it?"

"The death is meaningless," Benny said, "but their lives had meaning. And what we do after."

"Hard to separate that out," Joy said. "Don't think I've done it yet."

They were back on their bikes. Joy had lunch legs and dragged up the hill out of town. She still was ahead of him though. She freewheeled down the other side to let him catch up. Some more minutes went by.

He asked, "How do you handle the triad thing? I couldn't do it for a long time. When Deb and Sam were together I would check out, even if I was in the same room as them."

"Me too. I was a zombie. I could read to Jake, but Danny and my Dad had to think of stuff to do. Dad still sees Jake a lot."

"That sounds nice."

"It is, but I thought I should be able to do it all. Felt like shit that I couldn't."

"You probably did, before. Supermom."

"True enough," she said. "If I only knew."

"Who would? Can't be super when your kid is dead."

"Convince me! I needed my daddy. Jake saved himself, though—he got into baseball, of all things. He's been gone all month. I won't even see him for a couple more weeks. I miss him."

Danny isn't sleeping at home tonight, either, she thought. They rode below Whitaker Bluff. The pawls inside her freewheel stuttered when she coasted. Cows looked up, listening to them pass.

"It had to be chance!" The words burst out of her. "What reason would any God have to take her? I like to think He welcomed her, but was surprised. And sorrowful."

He said. "Faith is such a crapshoot. The first night a rabbi came, and when she read the *vidui,* the confessional prayer, Jason's spirit or God or something holy reached inside my body and slapped my heart with a force I could feel. I just exploded with light from the inside out. God existed. I'm not such a cynic anymore."

"It probably was your son—who else would even care?"

"I thought that, too, but—"

She squeezed his shoulder, then patted it.

"Whatever works, man. Grief is a but-free zone." Her hand was back on the handlebar. "I was so desperate at first. Then I kept refusing to let her be dead and that took up all my time. But she is, and my business is doing great, I'm riding long days again."

"Glad you've gotten it together, Joy."

She had to let that stand as they stood to push over the top of Middle Road. Bombing the descent they rolled to a stop at the Valley Ford Market.

"I guess you have to turn around here," he said. "I don't want to say goodbye."

"Me neither. This is the best time I've had in months. I don't have any deadlines tomorrow. My house is empty. Tell you what, if it's all right, maybe I'll come to Guerneville, find a room, and ride back tomorrow."

"That would be great," he said. "My room has two beds, if you're okay with that."

"Sure, that works." Honor existed among cyclists. She had shared rooms with unknown men on other overnight rides.

They rode the rollers down to Bodega Bay and up the coast to the river against the permanent headwind. She told him about the Other World and Dead Jenny and going to shul and what she used to do at the cemetery and in Jenny's room. He told her about Deb and teaching sociology and about things he wrote in his journals and how he and Deb had gotten involved with Compassionate Friends and then left it behind. But there wasn't much to say about Jenny or Jason. Turning inland onto the flats of River Road was its usual relief, and they traded pulls, hammering the final ten miles to Guerneville.

When they got there they had a beer. The bank thermometer read ninety-seven degrees. At a store he waited while she bought a top and a skirt and a toothbrush and a pair of rubber sandals. In the room she took the bathroom first to wash out her bike clothes and shower. She dressed while he was showering. Danny didn't call her, but if he had, she would have kept a secret. Her travel-team-permitted weekly call with Jake wasn't till Sunday. He would be in Salt Lake City then.

They found dinner at a cowboy-inspired Mexican diner that served arugula tostadas and line-caught fish tacos. A two-piece band played "Corazon, Corazon" at their table. She was tired and a little sore but after eight hours in the saddle every part of her body felt soft and easy. She drank two margaritas. They talked about everything again, and then about everything else. He paid the check, which she accepted after only the weakest quibble. She would get breakfast, she said. He took her hand as they left and she intertwined her fingers with his. Neither of them spoke. He held the door for her when she entered their room. He closed the door, then leaned down and kissed her.

She saw the question in his eyes.

"Okay," she said. "Okay."

She put the whole of her body up against his, then pulled back just a bit, reached up, and touched his face. He blushed. She felt his body soften and mold to hers. They kissed slowly, sharing lips and tongues. He held her with firm and careful strength, as if he were handling a large crystal vase. She felt safe. Regarded. She leaned back into his embrace, smiling, and raised her arms over her head. He took the suggestion and peeled her top off. His shirt followed.

"You are a beautiful woman, Joy. Danny should be spending more time with you."

She had forgotten so much.

"I haven't been very encouraging to him, I guess."

"I'm feeling encouraged," he said, thumb lightly tweaking a nipple.

"This is good," she said. *Help me remember.*

She left any guilt on the floor with her shirt as he led her to the couch. She felt her blood reddening, leavened by his rising desire, illuminating memories in its dull glow, split-second images of intimacies past, of Danny, dressing or shaving or sleeping. She felt her skin open, a generous physicality that softened the ossified edges of her grief. She remembered standing on the back patio, her arm wrapped around Danny, watching their children play, remembered yielding to the sweetness of her babies' need for her, the unconstrained joyfulness of infinitely loving them.

"I want to bring this home again," she said.

"You seem like people who work things out. Did something happen?"

"He took me to dinner on his birthday. I got all dressed up and we had just the loveliest evening, but when we went home I got anxious and he got selfish and it got really fucked up really fast. We'd never had sex where he didn't care how I felt."

"That sounds hard." He caressed her head.

"I was mad as hell. We kind of made up the next day, but not really. I'm avoiding him. I hate it. I want my marriage back."

His hand explored her face. She lightly kissed his fingers as they trailed past her lips.

"After Jason died, touching just seemed irrelevant. Then something changed and for about five years in there we were like kids again. I was in heaven. That's passed now and I don't really get why. I still want her."

He fondled Joy's breasts.

"Not right now, it seems."

"Now as much as ever. More, actually. Just like you, I suspect."

He was right. She tugged at his shorts. "I want these off."

He was semi-soft. She lifted him up, cradled him, held the weight in her hand, let him harden under her touch.

"That feels nice," he said. "Can I do anything for you?"

"Later," she said.

They sat together, his arm firmly around her, her head on his shoulder, her hand encouraging his changing shape. He planted soft kisses on the parts of her body he could reach. She stood, slipped out of her skirt, and reached a hand to him. "We'll have to be a bit careful. It's near my fertile time."

"I remember that," he said. "I hope I won't frustrate you. The plumbing has gotten a bit cranky as I've aged. Although I did have a Viagra in my bag."

"You really are prepared!" She laughed and gave him a squeeze. "Looks like you'll be just fine."

"I want to be, very, very badly!" She pulled him to the bed and they fell on it together, arms and legs reaching, wrapping, grappling, hot and mellow and soft and strong and she was tied to his eyes and saw all her yearning and all Danny's heartbreak, there in him. His touch was soft as her babies' skin. She yielded, luxuriant, truthful, mounting him, hips moving in time with his, looking down at this kind man who so recently had been a stranger. He rolled them over to look down at her, gentle love etched in his face.

"Do you see Deb now?" she asked him.

"I do," he said. "Sorry."

"That's good. You aren't mine."

"No."

They surrounded each other and release vibrated through her core. Breathing quickened and he withdrew. The hot liquid pooled on her belly.

"All okay?" he asked her.

"I'm happy," she said, and she was.

They lay close, skin sticking them together, wayfarers tied in a moment. They found a romantic comedy on the TV and laughed their heads off. Later, Joy rejoiced at his tongue on her. She awoke in the morning, spooned, him already inside, growing easily, persistently. She rolled onto her front, moving him over her, the harsh memory melting away under his tender urgency. When the ugliness was all gone she exhaled; the clock moved them inexorably onward.

Most of what had to be said already had been, and blessedly now there was the bike. They rode without speaking, east along the river in the rising heat of the morning, past the quiet wineries on Westside Road, an hour to Healdsburg. A big breakfast under the misters at the Oakville Grocery and a kind, chaste hug framed their goodbye. He had ninety-five miles to Fort Bragg. She turned south, seventy-five miles from home herself. She rode with focus and strength and enough determination for the painful parts—steadily turning a big gear through the miles of flat valley, attacking Red Hill with a cadence just a little quicker than she would have settled for on another day, charging down the descents like a falcon, a nimble dryad in magical space, immune to the heat, blessed with legs that could do no wrong and lungs of infinite capacity and the rhythmic and muscular heart she had built to power it all.

Grief had usurped her desire, not stolen it. All she had been doing was wanting—not to have parked there and to have been able to buy the shoes, and to have Jenny back and her life restored, and to feel Jenny's body at the cemetery, and to jump off a cliff into another world; and to preserve her grief and to show it off, and to glory in her suffering, and to bury her grief under duty, and for grief to be a way of life and for it to vanquish her, and she had wanted the pain to just stop, and she had had an imaginary relationship with some schizophrenic part of her self, and she had been ashamed to be seen, and she had lived without a soul, and she had pushed her husband away from everything but their shared grief, and she had been afraid to love her son. Even today she still wanted something impossible, the inversion of her loss to a gain; but yearning was yearning, a newly permanent part of her: a yearning that would never be fulfilled. In the physics of emotion her loss was a constant.

But I'm not fated to lose everything.

She was Jake's mom. *I get to love him, even though I'll lose him to another girl. Sunday I can tell him I love him.*

She was Danny's wife. She wanted to sit with him in their house and watch him read the paper. She wanted to call him on the phone and ask him to pick up a pizza on the way home. She wanted him to do something with her that was new to both of them, and she wanted to go to the grocery store and to the museum and to the movies. She wanted to lie on the beach and climb up a mountain and reorganize the basement with him. She wanted to take his hardness inside her, feel his muscles rippling under his skin and wrap him up in her legs and arms and never let go. She wanted to go with him to Jake's wedding. She thought about Benny and how nice it had been and how she didn't feel the least bit cross-threaded about it. The night was a great thing, a nice thing, an important thing, a real thing that she deserved and would treasure. Mostly, though, she thought about Danny and how she had lost him already.

If I want my marriage back I have to get right to work.

* * *

She called her husband as soon as she got home, when she was still hot and smelly.

"I had an interesting couple of days," she said. "I shined on work yesterday and went riding, and the funniest thing happened. I met Benny. Do you remember him?"

"Of course, Compassionate Friends," Danny said. "I liked him."

I hope you always will.

"Well, it turns out he rides! I ran into him in Fairfax. He was out touring for a few days, hundred-mile days."

"Wow," Danny said. "Your kind of guy."

"I guess. He has a really specific bicycle for that," Joy said. "Once we recognized each other we had just the most fantastic talk. We talked about everything. Jenny. His son. Judaism. Grief. Memory. Him and Deb. Us."

"What about us?" Danny sounded guarded.

"The point is," she said, "I want to apologize. I lost you, Danny. After the thing happened on your birthday, I let you go. When we got married I promised you that I never would, but I did. I'm sorry for that, Danny. I want you back. I love you, Danny, but I'm gone if we can't fix this." She ran out of words. There was silence on the other end of the phone, then just when she was going to say something she heard a faint sniffle.

"I love you too, Joy. I want you really bad. Every day. So many nights in this apartment I knew I really could be at home but I was afraid of the nights I lay in our bed ignoring you. I felt bad about hurting you and told myself I needed to let you set the pace, but it was an excuse. I couldn't handle my own feelings. I need you. I'm not a monolith. Now I sleep in fucking Stockton. Stupid."

"We've both done foolish things," she said. "Come home now."

Is that how I'll classify last night? Can't. It was too real to be foolish.

"As soon as I can get away. I've got a dinner meeting."

She heard it first as one more no. But then she chose yes.

"Okay. If I'm not awake, you can wake me up. Gently."

"Deal," he said. "I'll call you when I leave."

"Okay, bye."

"Wait. Did you ride all the way home?" he asked

He wants to know the story. Is he worried?

"No," she said. "A hundred seventy-five miles? I'm not that crazy. He was stopping in Guerneville. I got a room. We drank some margaritas. Then we met up in the morning and rode to Healdsburg for breakfast. He went on and I came back."

It was extraordinarily easy to say that, she thought, and even though she knew that she would tell him eventually, today the memory still was hers alone.

"I'm glad you made a new friend," he said.

"First one since," she agreed.

31.

JOY KICKED AT the aggressive seagull eyeing Jake's bag of popcorn. They were sitting on a bench that fronted the penguin pool at the San Francisco Zoo. For his eleventh birthday, Jake wanted to have a "special date" with her, he said, like they used to. She was touched. When Jenny died Joy had gotten out of the special date habit, and he never brought it up. *You can lose things,* she thought, *without even suspecting it.* Joy was pleased when he asked her and even more pleased to believe Danny's denial of prompting the invitation.

"Mom, I hardly ever remember her."

"What do you mean, honey? What she looked like, or what you did, or her voice?"

He took a handful of popcorn. "All of those, I guess. She used to tell me jokes and stories and all kinds of stuff, and I can't remember any of it. I look at her things on the little table, and I know they're hers, but not really anymore. I wish I could remember doing stuff with her. I wish she could watch me play ball like I watched her tap dance."

"I remember being here in the zoo with you and Jenny and Dad. Do you?"

He brightened a bit. "Yeah. She liked those really big monkeys. She used to make faces at me that the monkeys were making."

Joy laughed. "Right, the gibbons. We'd come here and Dad would tell her to quit monkeying around. She thought it was so funny."

We always were together in those days.

"Can we go see them?"

"Sure. Can I have some popcorn?"

He handed her the bag. "Tell me something else you remember."

The urge to run came and went. *Jake wants to know his sister.*

They started walking, holding hands, blocked momentarily by a gaggle of peacocks crossing the path in front of them. She felt the scratchiness of popcorn salt melting under the heat of their twined fingers. Her little man. They strolled past the elephants and tigers to the big square gibbon cage close to the old entrance to the zoo. Across the way a lone orangutan sat on top of his tall pylon, watching them.

"When you were still a baby, five months old, we had Jenny's fourth birthday at the children's zoo. We had all the little girls from her preschool, and Amanda and Lizzie. We went to the petting zoo, but Jenny wanted snakes. So Daddy got them to bring a python over, and the zookeeper put it on her shoulders and it slithered around her arm. First she didn't quite know what to do, but then she started laughing because it was tickling her."

"Was it big? Was she scared?"

"It wasn't super big, but she was only four. I was scared. I think she was at first, but before the guy put the snake on her he let her touch it and watch it slither on his arm. Plus it had a non-scary name. Queenie. We have pictures at home. Maybe we can find them later."

Joy had not touched a photo album or put any pictures in a new one since Jenny's death. The little envelopes from the photo store were piled up in a shopping bag in the back of the front hall closet. The digital camera made records even more ephemeral.

"Did I eat any cake?"

"No, I was still nursing you. But we also were feeding you baby food. You got pretty interested in food when you were about three months old, and every time we ate you'd fuss, so we started feeding you and there was no turning back."

Jake stood silently. They watched the gibbons swirl around their cage.

"Do you think she knows we're still here?"

"In the world, you mean? Gosh, honey, I don't know. Sometimes I really want her to. Sometimes I just want her to be off being happy wherever she is now."

"Do you think she's somewhere?"

A gibbon flew hand over hand across the top of the cage, swung down to a tree branch, and flung himself completely around it before landing on the platform near the back.

"I used to. I'm not sure now. I've thought about it a lot. I hope so."

"Well, I don't think she's anywhere."

She heard exhaustion and resignation in his tone. She ached for him and for the thing she could never repair. "If she is somewhere, it's really different than here. She can't exactly call us on the phone."

"I don't know," he said. "Maybe I'd hear her voice in my head or something. When I think about her it's just this buzzing noise. Do you ever hear her?"

"In the beginning I wanted to at the cemetery, and in her room. I had a couple of dreams right at the beginning where I thought I heard her, but not for a long time now."

"Mom, you remember a lot more than me. The harder I try, the less I remember. We hardly ever see Grandma Rose."

Joy understood something big. She took her son by the shoulders and looked him in the eye.

"Jacob. Please listen to me very carefully. When you go to school every day I remember you. I have a picture of you on my desk so I think of you over and over again, and when you go on your baseball tour again next summer and Daddy and I go on our bike trip we'll have a picture of you that we'll put on the dresser in each hotel and we will talk and talk about you, and when we come back and you're still away I'll go sit in your room and remember you then too, and when you go away to college and when you get married and when I come over and babysit your kids. You might get sick of me!"

Jake turned his face away from her and rubbed his left eye with his right hand. It was such a Danny gesture. "Let's ride the zoo train," he said.

The rubber-wheeled train pulled up. He grabbed an outside seat. She sat next to him, as close as she dared, and felt the solid contact of their legs and shoulders.

"Jenny used to tell me that when she grew up she wanted to get married and live in a house right next door to us, so she could see you and me and Daddy all the time."

"But I'm not going to live with you all the time."

"She was little. I think it was her way of saying how important you were to her."

It also was Jenny's way of saying she never wanted her childhood to end. Joy would never know if Jenny was having a premonition. Maybe she had been seeding Joy's memory so that this thought could return at precisely the moment Jake needed it. Joy thanked her, just in case she was listening. The zebra-painted cars made a circuit of the wide asphalt walkways that led through the zoo. Jake pointed out various animals as they went by.

"Another animal that Jenny really liked was the capybara. She thought it was a funny word and it was funny that it was the same kind of animal as a mouse except huger. She wondered if people in Brazil had to put capybara traps in their houses like we put mousetraps in the basement."

Joy felt very pleased with that memory.

Jake looked for the capybara as the train went by.

"I can't see it!"

"We'll see it when we come back here to watch the giraffes get fed."

"So did they have to use traps?"

"No, Daddy looked it up and capybaras live near water. They like to go swimming, not make a mess in people's basements."

The train came back to the start, and they went for lunch. The dining patio had netting over it to keep the seagulls out.

"When I think that Jenny is somewhere," Joy said, "what I really mean is that I want her to be here. But that will never happen. She has to be in whatever her own future is and not worry about us."

Jake considered this. He took a French fry, dipped it in ketchup. "I guess it's like the zoo. If we keep needing Jenny all the time, she'll be in a cage too."

He ate another fry. Joy gazed at him with great admiration.

Her phone rang. She dug it out of her purse.

"Hi, Danny. How'd you play?"

Jake looked up. "Tell Dad I want to go with him next time!"

"Here, honey. You tell him."

She handed Jake the phone and watched him tell his dad about their morning. He didn't mention Jenny, but he did say the gibbons were monkeying around.

"Dad wants to know if you want to go out later." He handed the phone back.

"No, let's just meet at home," she told her husband. "We're still going to be here for a while, I think. Things are good, Danny. We're remembering a lot. Really a lot. We have an amazing son."

She put the phone away and asked, "Is Daddy going to take you golfing?"

Jake swirled the ketchup with his last French fry. "We're going to the putting green tomorrow when you're on your bike. Is it time to feed the giraffes yet?"

Joy looked at her watch. "We have a few minutes."

"Can I get an Its-It?"

Cookies and ice cream, plus the French fries? *A little fatty.*

"Not now, Jake," she temporized. "Maybe later."

Thank you, God, for everyone who loved him when I couldn't. Thank you, God, that I can love Jake now.

On the way to the giraffes they detoured past the capybara. The giraffe enclosure had a trough about ten feet high that the zookeepers filled with straw, and the zoo's five giraffes gathered around, under a few tall, scraggly looking palm trees.

"They look so funny from this side," Jake said. "Big heads with no bodies."

He pulled her around to the other side of the trough, where the bodies became visible.

"I don't think I'd like to be a giraffe."

"Why not?" Joy asked him.

"You can't really go and hide anywhere, and people always end up looking at you."

"Do you feel that way sometimes?"

"Not so much now. But I know I'm different. When I hear people complaining about their big sisters, I want to hit them. I don't, usually, but sometimes I have to go sit by myself. Nobody really gets it, Mom."

"No, honey, no one gets it unless it happened to them. But no one really wants to hurt your feelings, either. They're just thinking about themselves, but that's okay. And you can trust the people who love you."

I can, too.

32.

THE BAG OF photos had beckoned from the floor of the closet. Now there was a pile of fifty envelopes on the dining room table. Joy got a pencil and a pad and a bag to use for the discards.

"Okay, Joy," she said, taking a deep breath, "you don't need to agonize over every picture. If we can just label the envelopes that will be good enough."

She picked up the first one. Jake's fourth birthday. She tossed a couple of blurry ones and a couple more ugly ones into the trash, stopping just a bit at a photo of Jenny cutting pieces of cake for Jake's friends, but slipped them back into the envelope, labeled it *Jake's Fourth b-day,* put it aside, and picked up the next one. Jenner Weekend, 1996. She only saved one of the endless shots of beautiful beaches with tiny family members bundled up in jackets and hats and scarves against the freezing winds. Lot of hours playing cards that weekend! One picture had Jenny with two arms raised high in victory after a particularly rough game of Hell, Danny bowing at her feet. She wiped a tear from her eye and turned to the next envelope. Danny's parents' fortieth anniversary. She worked her way through the stack.

Jake came thundering down the stairs.

"Hi, Mom, whatcha doin'?"

"Sorting out photos. Want to see?"

He saw the trash bag.

"Are you throwing them away?" Jake's voice rose, his anxiety apparent.

She pulled up a chair and he sat down. She wrapped an arm around him.

"I only get rid of the bad ones so the albums aren't boring. Let's look at this batch together so you can see what I'm doing."

He was antsy, squirming, holding on to the arm she had around him. Joy put down the packet she was working on and picked up the first one.

"It's your fourth birthday party. Here's you and your two grandpas. Here's me and Daddy. Here's me bringing in the cake. Here's Jenny cutting the cake."

She paused. Jake held the picture of Jenny for just a moment, then turned it over.

"Cool photo, Mom."

Joy breathed a sigh of relief and said, "Work on these with me for a while?"

She opened the next set. Jenny's fourth birthday, with the snake. She showed Jake the picture, and he thought Jenny looked real funny. Jake's sixth was in the next envelope, the last one Jenny was at. She held it for a second, but Jake took the batch right out of her hands.

"Look at this. Jenny and her friends are all dressed up in your clothes! That was so funny. I remember when they came down the stairs like a fashion show!"

"That's a nice memory, Jake, but you got mad at her."

"I did? Why?"

"Maybe you felt she shouldn't be the star of your birthday."

Jake studied the picture for quite a while. He leafed through a few of the other ones. Joy couldn't contain herself. She touched him on the arm.

"Jake, it's okay to feel that way."

He stopped shuffling the photos but kept them in his hands. "Don't worry, Mom. It's just something that I don't remember. I don't want to think about being mad at her, but I guess I'm still mad at her for not being here anymore."

"That's a hard thing to say. Do you talk about that with Annie? I'm mad at myself for her not being here anymore."

"I'm not mad at you. You didn't make the thing fall down. I'm not really mad at her either, but sometimes I just get mad anyway."

"Jacob, it's so not fair that you have to deal with this. I'm so sorry."

"Mom, it's bad for everyone."

They looked at the rest of the pictures of the party. Jake agreed that a bunch could be thrown away.

The front door opened and closed. "Hello!"

"In here, Danny!"

He came into the room. Neither Joy nor Jake looked up.

"Wow, you guys. Wow. What brought this on?"

He tousled Jake's hair, but Jake stayed firmly planted.

"It just seemed like the right time to do it and it's actually kind of fun," Joy said. "Wanna help?"

"Yeah, Dad, sometimes there are some sad parts. Remember this?"

He showed Danny the picture of Jenny and her friends.

Danny took it. "I do remember that, Jacob. That was a real fun party."

Joy smiled and patted his hand. "Today was the best day in a long time, right, Jake?"

"Right, Mom. You didn't make me mad once."

Danny pulled a chair close to them. They went through everything. Jenny's tenth birthday. Jenny's ninth birthday. Jake's fifth birthday. Their family vacation to Maui, with Hiram and his then-girlfriend. Joy and Lizzie's shared fortieth birthday, just a few months before Jenny died. The *purimspiel* when Jenny was seven and played Esther. The PG-rated shots from their anniversary trip. Jerry and Elaine moving to Calistoga. They got everything sorted back into the envelopes and in chronological order.

While Joy scrounged some dinner out of the refrigerator, Danny and Jake went out to Chestnut Street and bought some more photo albums. They ate in the kitchen. After dinner they divided the photos up by years, then helped each other fill the books. Joy went to her workstation and made labels for the binders. Jake stuck them on, and Danny put the completed albums on the shelf in the den with all the other ones, right next to the binder with Jenny's work in it. Then they sat on the couch and looked at the shelf. Things felt, to Joy, impossibly normal.

33.

WHEN JAKE CAME home from school on Tuesday, his eleventh birthday, Joy was busy in the kitchen. It was Indian Summer. She was wearing her Hawaii sundress and singing. The house smelled like freshly baked cake; it sat cooling on a shelf above the stove.

"Hi, honey!" She reached out for a hug. He high-fived her.

"Hi, Mom. Hey, you look pretty today."

"Thank you, sweetheart! Did they do a party for you at school?"

"Did you have to make cupcakes? That stops in the fifth grade. I'm in middle school now."

He made it up those stairs that Jenny didn't.

Jake opened the refrigerator and grabbed a cheese stick and a juice box. He sat down at the kitchen table and watched her.

"You seem really happy, Mom."

"It's your birthday, and it's a beautiful day today, and I got paid for a couple of projects, and Grandpa's coming for dinner."

She realized he was becoming aware of her as a woman. She forgave him when he just said, "That's cool. I'm gonna go do some homework now."

She watched him go without an ounce of regret. She heard a key in the door and looked at the clock. A little early for Danny. Hiram.

"In here, Daddy!" she called.

"That sounded cheerful!" He came into the kitchen. "Wow, look at you. Hot stuff."

"Yes, well, I've turned over a new leaf. Pollyanna."

"Sounds real good to me. If you stop worrying so much then I can die happy."

She gave him a hug. "Not tomorrow, I hope. I'm still getting over the last one."

Joy made a wonderful dinner to go with the cake. After Hiram left, Danny went upstairs and Jake helped her clean up the kitchen before vanishing into his room.

A little later Joy came into Danny's office and sat down. "I have another thing to tell you. Last year, when things were really bad? I slept with someone, just once, one night."

"With Benny? In Guerneville, maybe?"

"Shit. That's embarrassing. Yes. How did you know?"

"I didn't really until just now, but it made sense. I've been able to practice forgiving you, though. I slept with Janine."

First she felt shocked, but then a gigantic wave of relief made her laugh.

"Janine?" Long ago, he and Janine had taken each other's virginity. She was afraid to ask him. "For a while?"

"Just one time," he said. He looked like he wanted to smile.

Phew, she thought. "How'd it happen? I thought she was in Boston."

"Conference in Sacramento. She called me for dinner, and we talked, and she came to the apartment for a nightcap, and it happened. I'm sorry."

"Oh, Danny." She leaned forward and took hold of his knees. "I don't even have the right to forgive you."

He reached over and they got tangled up in each other.

When they got untangled she leaned back in her chair and gave him her best deadpan look. "I never got to see that apartment."

"Probably for the best," he said.

"That can be your special place."

He winced.

"So is this, uh, like an annual conference?"

Suddenly, he looked very unsure of himself. "Rotating. Every few years."

Joy waited two beats. She trembled out, "Uh oh."

Danny's relief was written all over his face. "But I don't have an apartment."

"Well, okay then."

"And she's married again."

They had a good laugh over that one.

"Thank you, Danny. Benny's become a good friend."

"Better than I thought, evidently."

She whacked him a good one on the arm.

"Ow! I get it. We were deranged."

"Look what can happen when people are nice to you," Joy said. "He kept seeing Deb and I kept seeing you. By the time I got home I just wanted you. Us. When I called you I was still in my bike clothes."

"That call changed my life."

"Thank God. Just imagine—"

"Nope. Don't want to. I like how it's turning out."

"Me too."

They each looked at the wall for a while.

"So it was good?" he asked her.

She felt her face flushing. She sort of squeaked out a yes.

"Just once?"

He wanted to know.

She wanted to swallow her own tongue. "Well, the night and the next morning."

He sighed. "Okay. Me too. Like that. But after breakfast, too."

"Three times?" she asked.

"It just seems like once." He was completely red-faced.

"It's okay," she said. She was having a little trouble with her breathing.

"You do everything?" he asked.

"Not everything everything," she said. "A lot, though."

She thought she didn't need to ask him.

"Okay." He sighed again and held her hand.

They were quiet for a while, staring at the bookcase.

"Do you think Deborah knows?" he said.

"Now that you know, he'll want to tell her, if he hasn't already. You get a pass if she needs you."

"I decline," he said. "But you, I accept."

She took a breath and thought this exact moment was the most precious thing in the whole world. They walked together to the bedroom. Before he had even closed the door she was on him with lips and limbs and tongue. Clothes melted away. She became wide as the sky and he was the moonrise and they got lost together for a long time. After, she crawled into his embrace.

"We have got to do more of this," he said.

"Okay," Joy said. "Okay."

The dried sweat on his skin stuck to her body. She smelled him, sexual, overpowering, intense. A few tears slid gently down her cheeks and splashed on his chest. He lay motionless, the hand on her bare hip holding her just so, in the way she knew was him. Peace. An eon passed. A night.

In the morning Joy dreamed of Jenny, the ageless child, eyes bright and shining, running across a field, skirt flying, embracing her mother, and flying off into the clouds, gone again. Grief had no end, yet love was there, next to her, in her bed. She kissed Danny's shoulder and his neck and she followed her own sensation down his chest, his belly, her lips wrapping him up, growing his stiffness, for his pleasure. She felt him wake; she held his eyes, sucking and rubbing until he filled her mouth. His hand found her chin; she swallowed and let him bring her up to him, kissing, tasting, breathing. They fell, side by side, flat onto their backs.

Danny said, "Wow. You can wake me like this every morning."

"Unlikely," she said.

"Darn." He turned to his side and propped his head on his hand. He saw her face. "You're crying."

"I saw her, Danny, in a dream. I love her. Right now."

His face twisted and melted.

"Thanks," he said. He kissed her tears.

After a while, he said, "It's going to be a hot day. How about I stay home? You busy?"

"Nothing that won't keep. Don't have to train. Jake has school."

He levered himself out of the bed and put on his bathrobe. She heard him open Jake's door, and the slight creak of the springs as he sat down on the bed. In the shower, the warm water slid off her back as she reached to the ceiling, opening her chest, pulling the shoulder blades together, arching her back to stretch the front of her hips. She turned off the water.

The dust billowed; the scream echoed; the pain was quilted through her heart. *Dear sweet Jenny,* she thought, banging her clenched fist repeatedly against the wall of the shower.

She heard her boys walk down the stairs. Joy dug around in her closet and found the short denim skirt Danny had liked so much, pairing it with a camisole top. A light blouse and sandals completed the ensemble. She caught herself in the mirror, stopped for a minute. An old friend stared back at her. *Where is the crone now?*

She shook her head. Her hair settled easily around her face.

This is a gift. Ride it as long as it lasts.

Joy went downstairs to find her family.

34.

EIGHTEEN YEARS PASSED, and there was another girl. Jake's girl. Her name was Evelyn, but everyone called her Ev. Her Hebrew name was Chava. She was twenty-seven, grew up in New Jersey, and worked in project management for one of the biotech companies down in Mission Bay. Jake had met her on a research rotation at med school. When he brought her home the first time, toward the end of the evening she had embraced Joy when they were alone in the kitchen and said thank you, thank you for your son. I hope he marries me. From that moment, Joy could only love this vivacious, self-confident, sweet-hearted girl with the open shoulders and runner's legs and wonderfully thick, black, curly hair, just like Jenny's.

After a few months the four of them went to Calistoga for the weekend to spend time with the recently widowed, ninety-two-year-old Elaine, who still was a crackerjack despite being alone in that gigantic house. On Shabbat morning, after Joy rode her bike, Ev came to her and they took a long walk up past the geyser, talking about stuff at work and movies and the news, to a rock Joy knew, overlooking the Valley.

"It's beautiful here," Ev said.

"I spent a lot of time sitting on this rock after Jenny died."

"I guess. I'd walk here every day, if I could." Ev paused. She put a soft hand on Joy's knee. "Jake has talked so much about you and Jenny. He told me he was mad at you for a long time. It had to be so hard."

Joy heard no echoes, no voices, no dialogues; time did not stop; the air was not heavy; the accident played only quietly; loss and regret were layered with what had come since.

"It was," Joy said. "I did the best I could, but I was pretty messed up. People were wonderful to me. But I believed I was going to lose everything—it took years to find a new normal."

Ev's voice cracked. "It's scary, what you had to do."

"In some ways," Joy said, "it's harder now. The ripples of her death just keep expanding. My friends are becoming grandparents. Their kids are great people, and Jenny just isn't. I'm so grateful Jake met you."

"Jake's love can be so fierce. We went away one time and . . . well." She stopped herself, blushing. "I guess he learned that from you."

"That is so sweet." Joy put her arm around the younger woman. She remembered how it was for her, before, that arrogant confidence she had, that cracked into a million pieces. Evelyn was not like that. *I wish I had known that when I was her age.* Joy wondered if she should, but asked, "He's told me you've had your struggles too?"

"What did he say?"

"Only that. No secrets."

"He's so honorable!" Ev giggled, then took two breaths. "I was bulimic in high school and into my sophomore year. I hid it pretty well. It got pretty bad. At one point I only weighed a hundred pounds. I cut myself once." She held up her wrist. Joy could see the faint scar. "My parents saved me, but I took a long time to really stop." She paused. "Giving that dependency up hurt a lot. Becoming real instead . . . but I know I could go back there, if things go south . . ."

Tears dappled her eyelids. Her lips pursed and drew into a line. Joy watched her struggle with it and let it go. Ev relaxed and smiled. "Jake helps me so much. We even make jokes about it."

Joy's heart burst with pride and she wanted this girl to be her daughter in the worst way.

"I was afraid to tell you," Ev said. "But I had to."

"Thank you, honey," Joy said, "for telling me. I believe you. It can't be easy."

"It's got to be easier than what you lived with."

"No one wins that contest. You just work at it every day." Joy took her hands. "I know this—I love my boys," she said, "and they love me. I love Jenny. I have good, good friends. I enjoy my work. I have a strong body." She paused again. "And I love you, *Chavaleh*."

Joy squeezed her tight. She felt rooted, peaceful, at home. Ev sighed and rested her head on Joy's shoulder. Arms and fingers intertwined, the women, old and young, yielded to the time that passed silently over them. When the shadows started to lengthen across the vineyards Joy looked at her watch; helping each other up they walked back to town while having a long and extremely discursive discussion about what to make for dinner. Joy roasted some local trout that came right out of the tank at the market, and Ev did something with quinoa that was really, really good.

When Jake and Ev came downstairs the next morning, Elaine's ring was on Ev's finger.

35.

THE BALLROOM WAS awash in color and light. Joy was wearing a long blue dress slit halfway up her thigh, good for dancing, with a bit of décolletage and a rather dramatic cut-out back. Her hair was up. Hesitating at the door, she had a fleeting feeling that reminded her of a way she used to feel, long ago, when both her children were alive. She took the arm of her tuxedo-clad husband. You never knew what could happen. She might step on the hem of her dress, she might walk into the wrong ballroom, she might get maudlin in the face of her son's happiness, she might find so much grief pouring out of her that she would break the wedding. But Danny put his other hand on hers. She forgave herself and they glided into the room when the music played, right on time.

Jake and Ev were already at the head table. Jake was perfect but Evelyn was breathtaking, in strapless white satin that barely contained her. They were surrounded by old friends. Joy saw Max, and Bobby. Amanda was there with her husband, and Sarah with her wife Janice. That had been hard for Joey, at first, but now Sarah was six months pregnant and Joey was happy as a clam. *This is as it should be,* Joy thought, as Danny guided her to their table. Joey and Leah and Elaine were there with Lizzie and George, and Carly with her husband Jackson, married twelve years already. *Thank God Carly's not alone anymore,* Joy thought.

She felt Hiram's laugh in her chest and his spirit was in her heart.

Daddy, you would have loved this party. But now you're with Jenny and we're the old ones; old, but still alive.

Jake stood and raised his glass. The room quieted.

"It's impossible to have the joy of this day without acknowledging the person who should be here, who would have been sitting right here, next to me. Maybe her daughter would have carried the rings. Only a few of the people in this room actually knew Jenny, but I hope that you all think of her as a part of our family. My parents suffered greatly in those years, especially Mom, and I know that suffering still is with them, every single day."

He choked up. Evelyn put a hand on his arm. She stood up, right next to him, as close as she could get, arm around his waist, shoulder to shoulder, just the way he had learned from his parents. They turned toward Joy.

"Mom, you are my hero. I am so grateful to you for keeping Jenny real for me."

Joy grabbed at Danny's arm like she was caught in an avalanche, forcing his muscles to contract against the pressure. She had the honor of her son's love. Every moment of every day of every year of loss and fear and anger and guilt and compassion and love and humility flooded her body. Tears poured from her eyes. She weakly held up a hand to Jake as he led the assembly in lifting their glasses to her. Cheers and applause echoed through the room. Jake put the mike down, walked over to his mother, and extended his hand. The DJ played a foxtrot. They danced. Danny danced with his new daughter-in-law. Then they each danced with her parents and together and eventually with everyone else in the room.

The party was super fun and went on for a long, long time. First was swing dancing. Then they did Jewish folk dances. Eight men lifted the bride and groom in chairs and danced around with them while Ev and Jake were holding two ends of a handkerchief. Joy was relieved that went well. Then they ate a big meal and many heartfelt toasts were raised.

After dinner, Evelyn threw the bouquet, and then everyone danced nonstop through two straight sets of high-powered rock and roll. Lots of champagne was consumed. Much later, after Jake had carried Ev out the door to raucous catcalls from their friends, and all had said their goodbyes, Joy sat in Danny's lap in the nearly empty room. They watched the DJ pack up. The hotel staff were clearing tables and stacking chairs.

"I wish she could have seen this," Joy said.

"I know. She would have had a really good time."

"I liked what Jake said about her daughter having the rings."

"That's a nice thing to imagine," Danny agreed. "Maybe she's watching."

"We should have had the wedding outdoors."

"I think she found her way on her own, if she came."

"We should have invited her."

"Oy," Danny said. "We're still talking about the same things, aren't we?"

Joy pulled out a clip and shook her head. Long silver hair fell to cover her shoulders.

"Every damn day," she said.

"Yeah," he said. "We didn't get to pick that."

"Still," she said, "it would have been nice if she had lived to see this day."

"God yes," Danny said, and his face got that look and she worried that maybe she had pushed it too far, but he just said, "I'm glad our family did, Joy. Things were touch and go for a while."

She felt a subtle echo of Dead Jenny's voice. "I never would have left Jake, Danny."

"You didn't. Besides," he said, "Stockton was getting really boring. I would have come to my senses."

She punched him in the shoulder, but then leaned into him. He wrapped her up, and she felt a hand far inside her dress that pulled her to the sweet radiance of a kiss filled with all their years.

And Jenny.

Acknowledgments

Although this novel truly began with the death of my daughter Eva in 1997, it started to appear on the page in 2011 during a single twenty-minute exercise during a course at San Francisco's Writing Salon taught by Chris deLorenzo. Then it didn't stop coming. The writers Sherrill Jaffe Lew and Catherine Brady encouraged me to have faith in what I was writing. Early readers, notably Barbara Melson, Mady Schutzman, Steven Kahn, Marty Ollstein, Teresa Burns Gunther, Sarah Kahn and Marsha Douma offered gentle but pointed comments. The generosity of thought given in workshop by my fellow University of San Francisco MFA students cannot be overstated. Writers and teachers Lewis Buzbee, Elizabeth Rosner, Nina Schuyler and Catherine Brady engaged deeply with the manuscript, honing both my intent and my craft. John Koehler, Joe Coccaro, Marshall McClure, Carol Gaskin, and Shari Stauch helped bring this work to the public. The young women of the Eva Gunther Foundation—Alissa Bernstein and Della Leapman—carry Eva's love forward, and Emma Mayerson has made her legacy real at Alliance for Girls. My parents Richard and Lois Gunther survived the trying years of my youth; I'm grateful their long lives have allowed them to see this text. My daughter Sophie Gunther constantly teaches me that being alive is enough; her patience in dealing with her broken parent has been remarkable. Finally, for over forty-five years Anne Krantz has been my guide and follower, my mentor and student, my lover and friend. I would be a sallow man indeed without her in my life.

And to Eva Leah Gunther, our oldest: long gone, sadly missed. Your short time here showed me the meaning of love.

CPSIA information can be obtained
at www.ICGtesting.com
Printed in the USA
FSHW04n2234050418
46399FS